A HEART TO HEAL

BOOK 2 OF THE CALDWELL SERIES

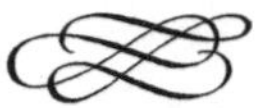

LAUREL WENSON

*This book is lovingly dedicated to
my sister Cheryl—
my dearest friend through life
and my number one fan.
May Concord forever live in our hearts.*

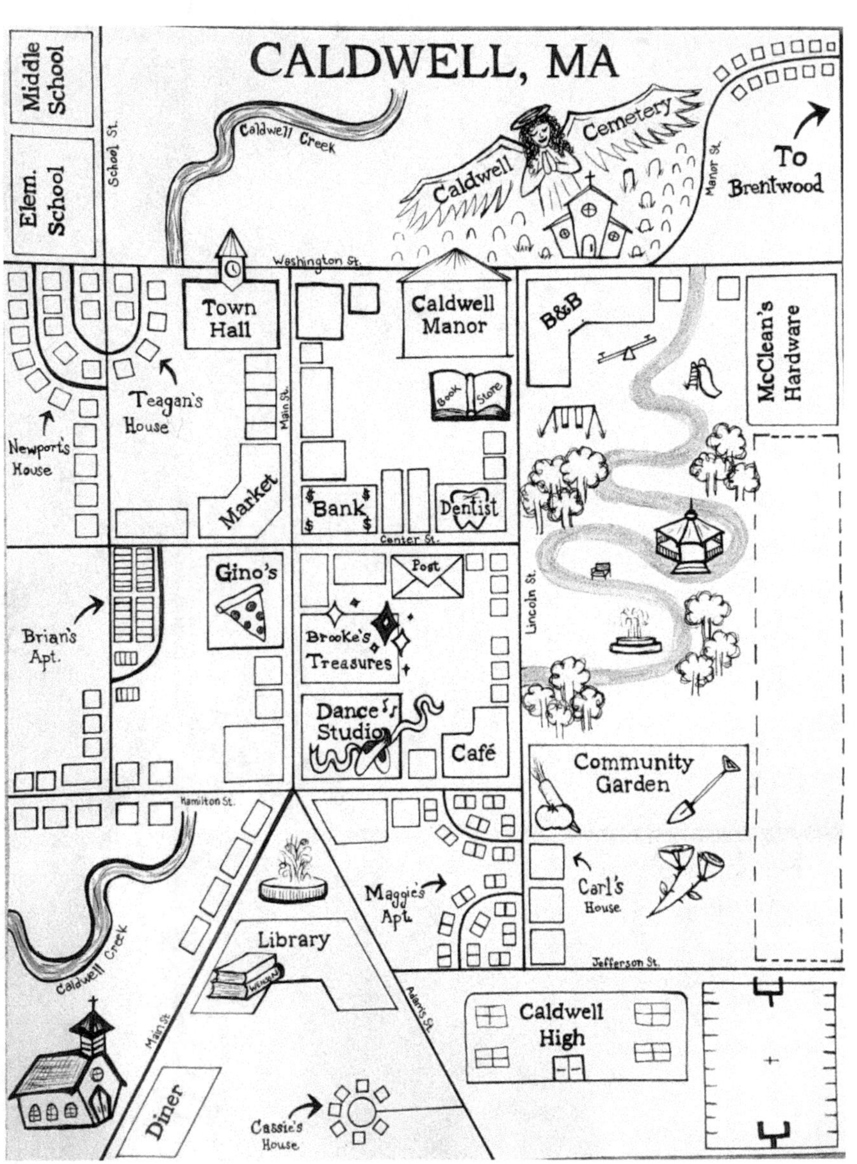
CALDWELL, MA
Middle School
Elem. School
School St.
Caldwell Creek
Caldwell Cemetery
Manor St.
To Brentwood
Washington St.
Town Hall
Caldwell Manor
B&B
McClean's Hardware
Teagan's House
Main St.
Book Store
Newport's House
Market
Bank
Dentist
Center St.
Brian's Apt.
Gino's
Post
Lincoln St.
Brooke's Treasures
Dance's Studio
Café
Community Garden
Hamilton St.
Maggie's Apt.
Carl's House
Caldwell Creek
Main St.
Library
Adams St.
Jefferson St.
Caldwell High
Diner
Cassie's House

CHAPTER 1

$\mathcal{M}$aggie Richmond loved having her hands in the dirt, which made it easy to get up early and walk the ¼ mile to the community garden. She grabbed her gardening basket which held gloves, tools, and a water bottle, and then took a leash off the hook by the door for her beagle Tramp, who was already waiting with tail wagging.

"Let's go, boy," she whispered as she clipped the leash to his collar. His tail whacked the side of her leg and he barked once. "Shh, let's not wake Lucy. It's still early for her."

She locked the townhouse door behind them and they headed toward the end of her little road. As they turned the corner they approached the home of Carl Pritchard, lovingly referred to as the "old curmudgeon" by most folks in town. Right on schedule, Carl was heading down the driveway to pick up his newspaper as Maggie and Tramp approached. While most 23 year olds would have passed by without ever interacting with the old man, Maggie always stopped.

"Morning, Mr. Pritchard," Maggie said with a smile.

As expected, he reached down to grab his paper with a scowl. "What's so good about it? It's gonna rain this afternoon, and the world's going to hell – as usual." He looked over the top of his newspaper at Tramp, who was sniffing along the front of his lawn. "And keep the damn dog away from my flowers."

Tramp looked up and wagged his tail and Maggie smiled. "I always do, Mr. Pritchard. You know that. And the rain is good for your roses and my vegetables."

He shook his head and turned away, muttering to himself as he walked back up the driveway. Despite his past grouchy outbursts about the community gardens being so close to his property line, Maggie knew that he had come to appreciate the friendly banter with her and the other regulars. This was the second growing season and almost all the plots were now taken, which meant that Carl would get to complain about the occasional gifts of produce left on his porch later in the summer.

As she and Tramp headed into the park she could see several others already working. These ladies had become Maggie's good friends despite a wide range in ages. Colleen Peterson, who ran the dance studio in town, Brooke Martin, who owned a gift shop, and Barb Owens, who ran the Caldwell Bed & Breakfast at the other end of the park were the three founding members of the Caldwell Community Garden, and Maggie had jumped on board early to help the project succeed. They all greeted her as she tied Tramp to his post by the edge of her plot; he knew his spot and eagerly plopped down to watch them work.

Maggie looked down at her plot of various vegetables – mostly greens and peas this early in the season. "Man, the weeds just keep coming back, don't they?"

Barb laughed. "Goes with every garden I've ever owned – and I've owned plenty!" She was the oldest of the group, with more gray hair than brown curling around her sweatband. She got up from her knees slowly and stretched. "Oh, to have your young knees, Maggie. Mine are getting creakier every year."

Brooke Martin nodded. "Doesn't matter how old you are – we all feel it in the knees after weeding. So Barb, are you all filled up this week?"

Barb nodded as she took off her gardening gloves. "Yep – you can tell that tourist season is starting up. I think every weekend is full through most of the summer – and we just finished the renovations for the room over the garage and a guy has it rented for the next month."

"And you were afraid the long term option wouldn't fly."

Brooke chimed in. "He must have heard about your cooking – who wouldn't want to stay with you instead of booking a hotel room over in Brentwood?"

Barb chuckled. "Speaking of which, I gotta head back and get the breakfast dishes done. You sure you're okay with doing my watering today?"

Brooke nodded. "Just throw your weeds into my compost bucket and I'll water both plots."

"Thanks, and I'll return the favor. Have a great day, ladies. You, too, Tramp." She picked up her supplies and put them in cart with wheels and headed back through the park toward the Bed & Breakfast at the other end.

Brooke took her bucket of weeds and carried them to the back of the gardens where she dumped them into a composting container. As she headed back she dragged one of the hoses connected to the garden's water spigots. As Maggie watched her return, she spotted someone walking around the old building that sat beyond the park between the gardens and the B&B. "Hey, who do you suppose that is?" She asked, gesturing toward the man.

Brooke put her hand up to block the morning sun as she peered across the lawn. "Hmm, looks like someone is checking out the old hardware store building. Wonder if someone's finally gonna fix it up?"

Colleen nodded as she stood up. "Yeah, it's become a real eyesore. There's a truck there, so maybe the McCleans are finally selling." She passed by Brooke and Maggie with her weeds and headed for the compost container.

Maggie took another look at the old building behind the park. "That's been just sitting there for most of my life, hasn't it?"

Brooke smiled at Maggie as she began watering her plot. "Longer

– I bet it's been 30 years. The original owner was Henry. He was good friends with the old man Pritchard here. Henry's son Sean went to school with my older brother and Carl's daughter Sharon. He was always in trouble – and hated working at the store. He took off as soon as he graduated."

"So why did the store close?" Maggie asked.

"Big fallout years later. Henry wanted Sean to take it over after college, and he told him there was no way he was living in Caldwell. To make it worse, he introduced the old curmudgeon's daughter to a friend of his, and after the wedding she took off as well. Carl hasn't seen his daughter in years, and he blames Sean McClean for all of it. From what I hear, he's still a jerk."

"Well, then let's hope he stays far away from Caldwell," Colleen said as she returned to her plot. "Once a jerk, always a jerk. Another day of weeding done. Spinach and lettuce are almost ready; makes the weeding a little easier to take, doesn't it?"

"That it does." Brooke passed the hose on to her as she walked over toward Maggie's plot. "You working today?"

Maggie nodded. "Yeah, I'm on 10-4. Then I'm heading over to Brentwood to see Cassie." Cassie Durand was a high school student who had entered an inpatient facility for eating disorders, and Maggie was a recovering anorexic who had promised to give whatever support she could toward her recovery.

"How is she doing?" Colleen asked. "I've missed having her at the studio, but I'm so glad she's getting the help she needs. I was getting really worried about her."

Maggie stood up and stretched. "She's doing okay. The first few weeks were tough, but it's been a month now and she's settled in. She said it's become a safe place for her. I'm going to be speaking to all the residents and some of the families today about my own story."

"I bet that's a little scary talking to a group of strangers," Colleen said.

"I remember the first time I spoke a year ago; I was definitely nervous that day. But it gets easier each time."

Brooke took a swig from her water bottle. "I imagine it helps the patients to hear another anorexic talk about recovery."

"Not just the patients. It helps my own recovery, too. It also helps family members and friends who are there to listen. Teagan's actually coming with me today. I think she's been over to visit Cassie at least once a week."

"I'm glad that Teagan saw the signs and said something," Colleen replied as she passed the hose to Maggie. "I know Teagan took it really hard when her friend Joanne died years back, so to see her be the one to reach out and get through to Cassie was pretty amazing. It seems like the show at the high school might have helped them to become friends."

Brooke nodded. "God, it was the best show in years! The two of them were unbelievable on stage. I never cared much for Shakespeare, but watching them in 'Kiss me, Kate' made me actually go over and order *The Taming of the Shrew* at the bookstore."

Maggie grinned. "They really were amazing. Between the show and Teagan's job at the Manor with Cassie's grandmother they were bound to finally connect. Speaking of which, I'd best head home and get ready for work." As she returned the hose to the water spigot and threw her weeds in the compost container she glanced over at the abandoned hardware store one more time. "Looks like whoever's over there is all done. The truck is heading out."

Brooke gathered her gloves and gardening tools. "It'd be nice if someone finally did something with that old place. It's a wonder our little town hasn't come down on the McCleans for letting it go that way."

Colleen laughed. "If one of the McCleans still owns it, I doubt very much they'd get anywhere. The sooner someone else buys it the better the whole town will be. Time will tell. So will I see any of you at the studio Saturday morning for yoga?"

"Wouldn't miss it, girlfriend. How about you, Maggie?"

"I'll be there. It's my favorite exercise now. Helps to keep me grounded, but doesn't trigger the exercise obsession like running did. Have a great day, ladies. See you tomorrow."

* * *

AN HOUR later Maggie arrived at Caldwell Manor where she worked as a social worker. She'd gotten the job right after graduating college and loved being back in her hometown. She had grown up in Caldwell, moving with her family to the bigger town of Brentwood during her high school years. The move had triggered her own anorexia as she tried to manage the changes of moving to a new school. Luckily her older sister Lucy had noticed the behavior changes and confronted her about the eating disorder.

With Lucy and two supportive parents behind her, she agreed to inpatient treatment at a new facility called The Phoenix Center, and over the years she slowly learned to deal with her eating disorder. Now she was living back in Caldwell with her sister Lucy, who worked as a secretary at Caldwell's Town Hall. She still drove over to Brentwood once a week for counseling at the Phoenix, and it was her input that helped Cassie Durand finally agree to go for her own anorexia a month earlier.

Melvin, one of the male residents, was sitting just inside the door as she walked in. "Morning, Miss Maggie!" he beamed. He loved serving as the official greeter to employees and visitors throughout the day.

"Hey, Melvin, how are you this morning?" she asked with a smile. He was one of the residents who had no family nearby, which was why he was so social with the staff.

"Doin' good. Waiting for Miss Teagan to get here. She doesn't have school today so she's working early."

"Another couple of weeks and she'll be able to work more during the day."

"That'll be nice. We're gonna play 'Name that Tune' right after lunch."

Teagan O'Sullivan was an activity aide who had started working at the Manor about the same time Maggie did. Now she was finishing up junior year at Caldwell High School, and she was a favorite among both staff and residents at the Manor. Maggie remembered back to when Teagan had started working, and how sad and angry was. Over time Maggie had learned about Teagan's best friend dying from anorexia in 8th grade, and she watched Teagan work through her grief with the help of the residents who loved her so much.

"I'll have to keep my ears open then," Maggie replied to Melvin. "I bet I'll hear you singing every song." Melvin smiled as he looked toward the door again. Maggie headed past the office as the head nurse Charlotte Hurd walked into the hall.

"I see that Melvin's at his post – at least until Teagan arrives." They both laughed, knowing that once Teagan arrived Melvin would follow her everywhere. "How are you, Maggie? Over at the gardens this morning?"

Maggie nodded. "Almost every day – it's the only way to keep the weeds under control. At least the greens are just about ready for picking. Anything important today?"

"We have the regular staff meeting at 11:00," Charlotte replied, "but there's something I want to run by you. What times are you free today?"

"I have a little time before the meeting; after that my day is pretty full. Do you want to talk now?"

Charlotte nodded. "Give me five minutes and I'll meet you in your office."

"Sounds good."

As she headed around the corner she heard Melvin greeting Teagan, so she stopped to say hello as well. "You still coming with me today to see Cassie?"

"Absolutely. Thanks so much for the ride – my mom said that she can come over to pick me up. I'll meet you back here in the lobby at four, if that's okay. Makes it easier than having to come and find me."

Maggie laughed. "Teagan, when you're in the building, I just have to follow the sounds of the music and the laughing and I can find you anywhere. God, these residents love you!"

"I love them, too – so much. And I better get my butt down there or Melvin here will be yelling at me. Are you ready to sing, my Casanova?"

He smiled and offered an arm. "Let's go, Miss Teagan!"

Maggie watched them walk down the hall, her heart filled with the joy of working in a field that she loved dearly. She headed for her office and took a look at her schedule before Charlotte arrived and sat down.

"Did I do something wrong?" Maggie asked hesitantly.

Charlotte laughed. "On the contrary; you do most things wonderfully. Which is why I'm here. I got a phone call yesterday from a friend who's a social worker over in Brentwood. Jane Simmons—do you know her?"

Maggie shook her head. "I recognize the name, but we've never met. I think she spoke at the college once just before I started attending."

"Well, she's involved in planning for this year's social work symposium, which I think you're registered for."

"Yeah, it's in a couple of weeks. Why?"

"One of her panel presenters has backed out, and she needs someone to jump in last minute. Someone suggested your name, and she called me to see if I'd recommend you, which I obviously did. I think you'll be hearing from her later on, so I wanted to give you a heads up."

"I don't know, Charlotte. Most of the people that speak there are experts in the field."

"This is a panel on the role of building relationships with nursing home residents. I think that's something that you excel at."

Maggie sat quietly for a moment. "I still think there would be someone else with more experience that could do a better job."

"Or maybe you're feeling a little self doubt. Hey, you don't have to accept when she calls – but I think you'd offer a fresh perspective. You're a younger social worker and the residents adore you. That's because you've taken the time to really get to know each of them."

"I'll think about it," Maggie said tentatively. "And thanks for the advanced warning."

Charlotte stood up to leave. "I really hope you'll consider it. I wouldn't have recommended you if I didn't think you could handle it.

Sometimes it's smarter to listen to someone who knows you well instead of those voices inside your head."

"I hate it when you quote my therapist," Maggie said with a smirk. She watched Charlotte chuckle and head out the door, and immediately turned to her computer to look up the symposium and check out the panel presentation she was being considered for.

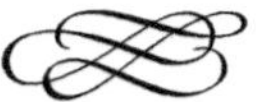

CHAPTER 2

At 4:00 Maggie and Teagan left Caldwell Manor and drove to The Phoenix Center in the neighboring town of Brentwood, a much bigger and more developed community. As they drove past the mall, movie theater, bowling alley, and various fast food restaurants Maggie realized how grateful she was to be living back in Caldwell. "Much as I appreciate all that Brentwood has to offer, I am *so* glad that I don't live here anymore."

"It's like night and day from Caldwell, isn't it?"

"You're not kidding. I remember when I first moved here in high school and I thought it might be nice to have all this stuff so close, but I hated it. No one at school knew me or really even tried to get to know me, and my friends back here drifted off once we didn't see each other every day."

"That's when your own anorexia kicked in?"

"Yeah. I mean, I was already judging myself for not being as beautiful or thin as my friends, but I still had people that accepted me and loved me, and a routine that was familiar. Once I moved here I felt like I was living in a big void where nothing made sense."

"Sounds a lot like what Cassie was feeling when she moved here.

No wonder she's been so receptive to your support. You really do understand – probably more than even I can."

"Don't sell yourself short, Teagan. Cassie's told me that she might be way worse off if you hadn't made the effort to reach out."

"Oh, I know that now, but as a fat teen who's comfortable with my size, I used to think that my being around her might have fueled her disease. She was so judgmental when she looked at me at the beginning of the school year."

"Yeah, she told me about the time that you let her have it after auditions."

"God, did I regret that day. I blasted her about me being more comfortable in my plus sizes than she was in her skinny jeans. When I saw that hurt look on her face I knew I had hit a nerve. I think that was the first time I realized how much she struggled with her body image."

"I'm glad you both ended up in the musical together."

"Me, too. I never would have had the connection otherwise. Well, maybe through Ida, but I don't think I would have gotten to know her enough to see any signs of the anorexia."

As they pulled into the parking lot of the Phoenix Center, Maggie replied. "To think that Ida is your favorite resident at the Manor and yet you had no idea that her granddaughter was your on stage sister. That's some major divine intervention."

Teagan nodded as they got out of the car. The Phoenix Center was as an old Victorian house which maintained the character and charm of the era while adding on a big addition that included some of the same décor. Side porches carried the gingerbread trim around the house, and a huge gazebo shaped porch at the back matched the one in the front. The entire building was painted a pastel blue with white trim, and peaceful wind chimes could be heard from various spots as they climbed the front steps. The front door window had a beautiful stained glass phoenix rising from the fire towards a blue sky.

"I still love this place," Maggie said as they stopped for a minute to admire the art work and peaceful surroundings. "I honestly don't know if I'd be where I am today if I hadn't started my recovery here."

"Let's hope Cassie's having the same experience. Thanks so being so involved. You've helped me so much in knowing the best way to interact with her. I never got the chance with Joanne – she just kept pushing me away until it was too late to help her."

"I think Cassie has a good shot at a great life – *and* a great friend to share it with. Now you're okay that I can't drive you home, right? I have a home visit to make after I finish speaking here."

"Not a problem. My mom's picking me up and we'll stop and grab something for dinner on the way home."

They had made their way into the building and stopped at the reception area to sign in and get visitor badges. The woman at the desk greeted both of them and spoke as she handed Teagan her badge. "I think Cassie is finishing up in the art room if you want to go and meet her there. Usually we have our residents come to greet their visitors, but Maggie knows her way around well enough. Will you be staying for Maggie's presentation?"

Teagan nodded, and Maggie led her through a set of doors and down a hall into the addition. Half way down they stopped at the door of the art room to look in and make sure that there was nothing formal still in session. Instead they saw about half dozen residents in various stages of cleaning up. There were numerous easels scattered around the room and each contained a unique painting in progress.

Cassie was just drying off her brushes when she spotted Maggie and Teagan, and her eyes lit up as she approached them. "Hey! It's so good to see you guys!" She hugged Maggie first and then Teagan. "Thanks for coming today to hear Maggie's speech."

Teagan smiled. "Wouldn't miss it. I wish I could get here more often. But with school and work and your therapy schedule it's tough getting here once or twice a week. By the way, your Gram sends her love."

"I miss her. Heck, I even miss Philip, and that says something. Never thought I'd miss my little brother. Now let's get out of here and go find someplace to chat for a few minutes."

Maggie looked around the room. "Not until we see which one of these is yours. That is, it you're willing to share."

Cassie shrugged a bit, but then smiled. "I guess. It's right over here."

She led them over to a spot by the window where an easel showed a small cemetery. The focal point was a simple gravestone with a heart etched on it and small cement bench beside it. Behind it there were other gravestones off in the distance, and a tree in blossom was sketched lightly in pencil but not painted yet.

"Oh, my God, Cassie, that's gorgeous!" Maggie exclaimed.

"Not just gorgeous – that's Caldwell, isn't it?" Teagan asked.

Cassie nodded. "I did my share of jogging there. We were asked to think of a place that we really liked, but that might not have been super healthy for us. The idea is that hopefully it won't be a toxic spot when we go back."

Maggie looked around the room. "Well that explains some of the *other* paintings – I see a refrigerator, and text books, and clothing racks. But this is gorgeous. And if I'm not mistaken, that's Mrs. Pritchard's grave you've painted."

Teagan looked closer. "You're right – that's where the old curmudgeon sits every Sunday."

Cassie looked at her quizzically. "The what?"

"That's his nickname in town. Mr. Pritchard. Grumpy old man, always complaining. Likes to wear flannel shirts and a tattered scarf in the winter?"

Cassie just shrugged. "Can't say I noticed. But I haven't exactly been too observant with anything outside my head this past year."

"I didn't realize how talented an artist you were. How long have you been painting?"

Cassie straightened up a few items in front of her easel. "I don't know. Since I was eight or nine, maybe? And I'm not *that* good. The first one I tried I painted a huge black 'x' over it 'cause it sucked." She paused for a moment, and then added, "At least that's what I thought."

Maggie nodded with understanding. "Sounds like you're starting to accept the fact that we're not the best judge of ourselves? Hey, where would like to go to chat? Your room?"

Cassie shook her head. "No, I think my roommate is in there right now. Maybe the back gazebo if no one is there. I really like the wind chimes."

"I love them, too. Spent lots of time out there journaling when I was here."

They continued to chat as they walked out to the back porch where only one other girl was sitting with a book.

"Hey, Ellie," Cassie said as the girl waved. "Will it bother you if we're out here talking?"

"Nope. I'll be heading back in soon anyway." They found a cluster of wicker chairs at the opposite corner and all sat down.

Maggie was the first to ask questions. "So, Cassie, how's it going? You seem more relaxed and centered lately."

Cassie nodded. "I can't believe I've been here over a month already. The first few weeks were the hardest – God, I hated it. I felt like I was in prison. It was even worse than that month of waiting before I finally got here."

Teagan smiled. "I remember how many times you said you'd changed your mind and didn't need to come. I know it wasn't easy for you keeping it together the month after the show."

Cassie took in a deep breath and exhaled slowly. "Seems like forever ago since that day I fainted. I think that was the first time I admitted I had a problem."

"And how many times after that did you deny it?" Teagan said with a grin.

"I don't know – maybe a million. Some days I still do. But at least now I'm learning that it's my eating disorder talking and not me."

Maggie nodded. "Seems like your routine has lightened up a bit here since those first few weeks?"

"Some – I mean, they let me go to the bathroom by myself now, so that's progress. That was honestly the worst part. It was so humiliating to have someone standing there when I had to take a shower."

"Or worse yet, a shit," Maggie replied. "Nothing like being stripped bare – I think that's why some just give up and leave after a few days."

"Yeah, I've seen a couple go right after getting here. Hell, I wanted to leave the first week I was here. It was so hard."

"But look at you now," said Teagan with a smile. "I can see the difference. It's like you're not fighting anymore. And you're not afraid to look me in the eyes now. I remember that with Joanne. During that last month before she went into the hospital she wouldn't look me in the eye anymore."

"Probably because she was scared of you. I remember those times when our eyes would connect during the show rehearsals and I'd freak out inside. I knew you saw it, and it scared me like hell. I think that's why I hated you so much at the beginning."

"Well, I didn't exactly help with my own attitude, did I? I'm glad we got past all that." Teagan looked at Cassie with tears in her eyes. "I wish Joanne could have come here. Maybe she'd still be alive today."

Cassie reached out and grabbed her hand. "I know. I wish I could have met her. I'm just glad that I got to come – and especially that I chose to stay through those first few weeks. I'm really beginning to feel that I have a chance with this thing."

Maggie smiled. "I think you definitely do. You're working really hard, and it shows. And one of the things I've learned fighting my own battle is that the more you put into your recovery the stronger you get. You're doing great, Cassie. You should be proud of yourself."

The back door opened and one of the Phoenix staff stuck her head out. "Hey, I heard you guys were here. Maggie, we'll be ready for you in about thirty minutes. Right inside the door here in the lounge."

"Thanks. We'll be in shortly." She took a notebook out of her purse and opened it. "You two can keep chatting. I want to look over my notes."

Cassie nodded and turned toward Teagan. "So how's Brian?"

"He's fine – baking up a storm as usual."

"Is he still seeing Lou?"

Teagan smiled. "Yup, they seem to be really hitting it off. I don't see Brian quite as much now, but we'll be working more during the summer anyway."

"Hey, he's always gonna be your bestie. You guys were like glue this past year."

"He's the one that kept me from totally losing it after Joanne died.

And after growing up with the two of them he's more of a brother. She was my bestie."

"I'm sorry. I didn't mean to make you sad."

"It's okay. It's getting easier every year – and finally keeping that promise I made to her to get back on stage was a huge step. It was a really good year for me."

"I wish I could have known her," said Cassie wistfully.

"You're so much like her – and not just the anorexia. I know she's really happy that we finally connected. I am, too."

Cassie smiled. "Me, too. I'm excited about having a friend for my senior year. I wonder what show they'll pick."

"No idea – although I'm sure that Mr. C. has some ideas already. God, I hope we don't have to fight each other for a role again."

"As long as there are two strong female leads I say we take out any other competition."

Teagan laughed. "I love it when a plan comes together."

"For now, the plan is to finish up our junior year."

"How are you doing with that? Is it weird doing all your classes online?"

"It's not too bad. I usually get the work done faster and it helps to fill my time between therapy sessions. Sometimes I miss chatting with Chelsea and Barb during class. Aside from that, I kinda like the online stuff – at least for classes."

"And how about the outside stuff?" asked Teagan tentatively.

Cassie sighed. "I miss dance like crazy. Got a card from the studio class, and Kyleigh and Julia both sent letters, but not being able to dance has been the hardest part of being here. I miss theater, too."

"At least school's almost done, and in the fall dance and theater will be waiting for you."

"I guess – for now it's just day to day. So, changing the subject, how's my Gram?"

"She asks about you every day I'm there, and I know she'll be expecting a full report tomorrow."

"I wish I had been in a better place when I visited this year – I treated her like crap when I first moved back here."

"Cassie, that was the anorexia kicking in. Ida knows it wasn't personal – and she's just so grateful that you got help. And you *know* she'll be wanting some time when you get home."

Maggie had closed her notebook at the sound of Ida's name and was now listening.

"How is she?" Cassie asked. " I mean, is she okay living there? Sometimes I feel like we moved back and took over her house and forgot about her. I know my mom doesn't even get in to see her all that much, and it makes me feel guilty that we might have screwed her over."

Maggie spoke before Teagan could reply. "Cassie, I have never seen a resident adjust so well to moving in. She looks at the Manor as a safe place to live while giving her the most independence she could have. And she's become a real leader with the other residents."

"How do you mean?"

"We've had two other residents move in since she arrived, and both were really depressed and angry. She helped them to see the positives about living in a place where there were people around to keep them healthy and involved instead sitting in an empty house with old memories."

"Sounds like Gram. She was always so self-sufficient. I always admired her so much – at least until I got sick."

"You'll have lots of time to spend with her," Teagan said. "Hey, why can't she come to visit?"

Cassie shrugged. "I don't see my mom being comfortable bringing her. She'd be afraid she'd fall or something getting in and out of a wheelchair."

Maggie smiled. "What if Teagan and I brought her? We do wheel-chair transfers when we have to, and Ida's wheelchair isn't the big, bulky kind."

Cassie thought a moment. "I mean, I'd *love* to see her, but I don't know if she'd be up for it. And then there's the timing – visitors are only allowed at certain times."

"I'm sure we can work it out. I mean, Ida still has the ability to walk a little when she has to. I can at check on it when I go in tomorrow. But right now I think we better head inside. It's almost time for me to start."

The three of them headed back inside and Cassie and Teagan grabbed two seats near the portable podium as Maggie surveyed the room. There were several staff members standing in the back, including her own counselor Natalie Bader. About a dozen other women were seated around the room, and more than half had either a family member or friend beside them. Maggie was always amazed looking around the room at how eating disorders were non-discriminatory; the age range on the faces that awaited her were from early teens up through middle age. Some suffered from anorexia, while others were diagnosed with bulimia. Some were first timers and some were struggling with relapse.

Maggie could almost always tell those who had newly arrived at the Phoenix Center. They often sat a little apart from the others with arms folded across their chests, wearing a more obstinate expression. She never wanted to forget those early days in her own recovery – and she hoped to touch the hearts of at least a few that waited for her to speak.

After being introduced, she began. "Quick question: how many of you right now would much rather go out for a run in the beautiful sunshine than sit and listen to me right now? And it's okay to answer honestly—there's no therapy penalties attached." She saw about half of the women chuckle and raise their hands, while the others were a bit more hesitant, wondering if this was a trick question. She continued, "For those of you that answered 'yes', I'm right there with you. My name is Maggie Richmond, and I'm a recovering anorexic – and that's largely due to the fact that I started my recovery right here at the Phoenix, like all of you."

Immediately she had their attention. "Some of you have only been here a short time, and I remember feeling like this was a pretty scary place to be. No one wants to have their privacy taken away or to have someone watching them almost constantly. I remember that first week of not only having to eat a certain amount of food, but to do so in front of someone who made sure I actually ate it. It was terrible, but it's okay to feel like the world is crashing in around you."

She saw a few faces soften a bit, and continued. "While every voice inside of your head might be screaming that you don't need to be here, and that you can handle it on your own if only you could get out of here, I'm telling you right now – having the courage to stay is what saved my life. And it can save yours, too."

She looked around the room and her gaze fell on Cassie's face, which was smiling and nodding. "I know some of you have been here awhile now, and I ask you guys to raise your hand if you know what I'm talking about." Cassie's hand was one of the first to go up, and almost half of the others joined her.

"When I first got here I was down to 100 pounds after months of restricting my food and exercising whenever I could. It took me being here, in a safe environment, to finally face myself for the first time. To learn what voices were me inside, and what ones were my eating disorder talking to me. Let's face it, our eating disorders lie to us every chance they get. Am I right?"

Almost every person in the room nodded. "So let's go over a few of those lies. I think the one I heard most often in my head was that I wasn't *worthy* of any kind of love – or even *food.* I literally thought that I didn't *deserve* to eat."

One of the newer residents began to tear up as her mother patted her hand. Maggie spoke to her as tenderly as she could. "It's okay. I can tell that you get it. And I can promise you that it gets better." The girl nodded, and the mom thanked her with her eyes.

Maggie continued. "Do any of you have to listen to your head telling you that you're a complete failure if you eat – or worse yet, if the number on the scale goes up?" Every person in the room was totally focussed on Maggie at this point. "That lie is crap. And it's important for you to learn that as early as you can while you're here, because recovery is all about eating and gaining weight, right?"

She looked around at some of the family and friends, and her gaze rested on Teagan. "This is a question for the guests that are here. How many of you love food? I mean, really *love* food?" About half of those questioned raised their hands, and Maggie continued. "See? Even some of the folks here that don't have eating disorders couldn't raise their hand. That's partly because society bombards us with the idea that being thin is the ideal, and that food is bad. And if we eat too much or gain weight then we're bad, too. And that's *crap*. Food is food. It's fuel for our bodies to keep them healthy. Our eating disorders take all the pleasure of eating away from us, and it sucks – but it doesn't have to. If you commit yourself to working at recovery while you're here, I can promise you that you'll learn to someday appreciate the colors and tastes and textures of food again, no matter what kind of food plan you end up with. I chose to be a vegetarian as I added food back into my life, but many recovering from eating disorders learn to appreciate meat as well. More importantly than the food, you'll feel comfortable in your own skin. I still struggle with these lies years later – but the Phoenix has taught me the tools and strategies I need for recovery, and I implement them every day. The support staff here will always be available for me – and you. I promise."

She took a sip of water, and then transitioned into the next part of her talk. "I know that some of you are now talking to your counselors about leaving – not to escape recovery, but because you've embraced it. You're ready to transition from this warm and safe cocoon to the big, bad world out there." She saw a few chuckle, while others tensed up a bit. "I can assure you that while that's scary, it's also pretty amazing to emerge back into life and learn to live without your eating disorder taking control again."

"And now I invite any of you – residents or guests -- to ask me anything. I figure that way I'm giving each of you whatever you most need. So fire away." She fielded a few questions about her daily schedule while at the Phoenix, and how that compared to when she left.

Cassie was next to put her hand up. "I'm a dancer, and dance has been a part of my life since I was four. I think the hardest part of my stay here has been that I couldn't dance. I was wondering if you had an exercise or passion that you had to give up – and were you able to get right back to it once you left here?"

Maggie could see the tears in Cassie's eyes, and she knew that pain. "I wasn't a dancer, but I was a runner. There's nothing I loved more than running. I used to throw on my shoes and hit that pavement, and the whole world slipped away. And those endorphins? They were the best. So I think I know a little bit of how you're feeling. Now I go for daily walks and practice yoga. It's not the same, but it does give me that freedom to move my body without triggering my disease."

There were several others who were nodding, and Maggie knew that exercise and movement issues were equally as important as nutritional ones. "Many of you here have had to face the fact that exercise is part of your disorder. I know you've accepted that your body needs time to heal. If you're anything like me, your head is telling you that as soon as you're out the door things can go back to normal, and I hate to tell you, but that's not true."

She saw Cassie's shoulders slump a little bit, her face losing the sparkle she was starting to find. "I'm not saying that you'll never dance again – but the key is finding a balance. You need an exercise program that won't compromise your recovery, but instead will enrich your long term success."

"So will you ever run again?" someone asked.

Maggie shook her head. "I don't know. As of right now I know that yoga and walking are better for me – they keep me centered and don't trigger that desire to push myself. But I do know someone who was here with me that has been able to run again – in fact, she just did a 5K race last week, and she's learned how to integrate it back into her life in a healthy way. And Cassie, I also know someone else that was here with me that dances. She was able to go back to dance shortly after she left – but had to go slowly, and really work with her teacher and her counselors to keep it honest."

She looked around at all the faces, and another hand went up. "What was the one thing that made the biggest difference for you?"

"That's an easy one. Without a doubt, for me it's all about the honesty. When I got here I had lost the ability to honestly look at myself. Learning to face myself, and *accept* myself – and my body – was the foundation of my recovery. It's why honesty is one of the most important things in my life right now. Without it, there's nothing between me and my eating disorder. I suspect that anyone who's here because of a relapse would agree with me."

There were several that nodded in agreement. Maggie got a "five minute" signal from one of the staff, so she asked for one final question. "So what's the biggest battle in your own life right now?"

Maggie thought for a moment before answering. "I think it's just staying grounded. My biggest fear is whether I'll be able to start dating at some point. The idea of letting someone else in to see the real me, complete with all my flaws, is hard—especially when I'm still learning to love myself for who I am. At the same time, it's kind of exciting to think that someone might be able to love me like that, and that I feel worthy of that love. Time will tell, I guess."

As she ended her talk, many residents and family came up to thank her. Cassie and Teagan were the last to approach her as others headed off to get ready for dinner. Cassie gave her a long hug. "Thank you so much," she whispered. "No one knows the inside of my head better than you do. You can think of me as I go down to eat with someone watching my every bite."

She saw their expressions change and put her hands up. "It's okay, I'm getting used to it. It's really not as bad as it was. I'm getting more choices with my meals now, so I guess that's progress."

Maggie nodded. "You're doing great. And you're gonna beat this thing. Well, not *beat* it, but you're gonna learn to live with it. Don't ever lose sight of your progress." Maggie looked at her watch, and then continued, "Hey, we gotta go."

"I know. Thanks so much for coming. And Maggie, thanks for sharing your story. I know I still have some work to do before leaving. But God, I hope I can dance again when I get out of here."

"If you can't, there will be something else." Maggie said. "Just stay honest as you work through recovery. Now give me a hug and let us get out of here." Cassie gave her a quick hug and then turned to hug Teagan as well.

"Thanks for coming. And give Gram a hug from me."

"I will. And you know I'll be back soon – I promise."

CHAPTER 3

Maggie got to the garden earlier than usual the next morning and found herself alone. "Guess it's just you and me this morning," she said to Tramp as he plopped down, "and the weeds."

She loved watching her garden come to life. Each day the plants got higher, and it promised to be a good week with plenty of sun. As she pulled the weeds she marveled at their tenacity to keep coming back. *"It's kinda like my eating disorder – always trying to surface again, but manageable if I keep dealing with it on a regular basis."*

She heard her phone ding and took her gloves off to see who was texting. It was her mom checking in from Florida. *"Hope your talk was successful, honey. Dad and I are so proud of you."* Their love and support had continued from afar since they moved to Florida, and her mom's text made Maggie miss them a bit. *"Thanks so much, mom. It went really well – will call to chat later this week. Love you both!"*

She put her phone away and smiled as her hands turned over the earth, feeling the cool grounding energy it had to offer. She finished with the weeds and began the harvesting part. "Looks like some spinach and lettuce for dinner tonight, boy. And peas." Tramp looked up and thumped his tail, but then looked beyond Maggie and barked.

Maggie turned around to see a strange man approaching. Tramp growled softly and stood up. The stranger smiled and waved. "Good morning. I don't mean to bother you – I just wanted to check out this garden that I've been hearing so much about."

When he saw her confused look, he continued. "My name is Tim, and I'm staying over at the B & B. Barb served home grown greens and beets last night and we had a long chat about the garden. When she showed up with more in the kitchen this morning I thought I'd walk down and check it out."

Maggie got to her feet, brushed the dirt from her pants, and patted Tramp to reassure him of her safety. She removed a glove to extend a clean hand. "Hi, I'm Maggie – and this is Tramp, my body guard." By now the beagle was wagging his tail and looking toward the stranger expectantly for a head scratch.

Tim laughed. "Yeah, he looks pretty ferocious right now. Can I pat him?"

Maggie nodded as Tim reached down to scratch Tramp behind the ears. "And now you'll have a friend for life. Welcome to the Caldwell Community Garden; I'm sure Barb gave you a full history. It's one of her favorite things in the world aside from the B & B."

"Yeah, she gave me the basics. And promised me fresh produce for the length of my stay. Looks more extensive than I thought it would."

Maggie nodded appreciatively. "So, are you in town for business or pleasure?"

"Mostly business. I have a couple things going on in the area and I live over an hour away up on the north shore. It was easier to come down and stay than deal with the traffic every day. I'd heard that it was a really nice little town, and from everything I've seen, it seems to be."

"It's not for everyone – but if you like the quiet small town lifestyle then you won't find a better place. If you want variety you'll need to head over to Brentwood – but we have the best of the basics here."

"Well, I've already found the donut place and the sandwich shop, and Barb has told me that I have to eat at Gino's sometime – although her food is so good I'm not sure I need to."

Maggie laughed as she gathered her tools together. "Trust me, as good as Barb's cooking is, you really DO need to get to Gino's while you're here. Best Italian food in town. Even Barb would vouch for me."

"Well, then, I guess I'll have to put that on my list. Anything on the menu I should try first?" Tim's smile was warm and relaxed, and his brown eyes matched his wavy hair. Maggie took note and smiled. "Probably best to check with Barb on that one, unless you want the vegetarian options. I myself can highly recommend the pasta primavera. Or the veggie lover's pizza."

"Those both sound delicious even without the meat." Tim looked beyond Maggie at the old house next to the gardens. "What a beautiful farmhouse."

Maggie followed his gaze to the Pritchard property. "Been here forever. Could use a little sprucing up, but the old curmudgeon lives alone and it's tough to manage."

"I'm sorry, the old what?"

Maggie laughed at his perplexed face. "The old curmudgeon – it's a nickname that most folks in town use for the old coot. I think it was actually Gino that first used it, and it stuck. Some call him grumpy, but I think he's lonely."

She watched him as he continued to study the house and property with a pensive look on his face. "Gorgeous roses out back. He must love gardening."

"I'd advise keeping your distance – he's pretty protective of them. But yeah, they're beauties. Look, I hate to seem rude, but I have to get going. Gotta get this stuff and this guy back home before heading to work."

"Sorry to have kept you – it was nice meeting you, and maybe I'll see you around again."

"Probably. It's a small town, after all," Maggie said with a shy grin.

"That it is," Tim said. "And so far the people I've met have been super nice."

He flashed his wonderful smile, reached down to pat Tramp once more, and added, "and the dogs, too. See ya, Tramp. You too, Maggie."

Maggie watched him as he headed back down through the park toward the B&B. *"Okay, Maggie, girl. Calm down. He's mighty fine to look at, but you don't need that kind of complication in your life right now."*

She looked down at Tramp, who was also watching with his tail wagging. "Yeah, so what if he gave you a good head scratch? We don't need that right now. Let's head home, boy. I gotta get to work."

* * *

AN HOUR later Maggie was in her office reviewing the day's schedule. She had a meeting first thing, and at some point she wanted to find Ida and give her an update on her visit with Cassie. Before the meeting started she stopped by the office of Charlotte, the head nurse.

"Morning – got a minute?"

"I'll give you two," Charlotte said, "what's up?"

"I wanted to check in on whether it would be physically okay to take Ida out for a few hours some afternoon this week to visit her granddaughter over in Brentwood. I figured I'd better check on the medical end before talking to her about it."

"It would be great for her to get out. Her mobility's not that bad and she does her physical therapy exercises faithfully to keep muscle tone, but sometimes I think she uses her wheelchair more out of fear than necessity."

"I know that Teagan will come along as well, and the two of us can easily transfer her to the car and back. Any other issues we need to know of?"

"Just that she gets a little more nervous of falling when she's not in her chair. But seeing Cassie might be really good for her – I know she's missed her visits, short as they were. How is she doing, by the way?"

"She seems to be doing really well. I think she got help early enough to make a difference. I'm so glad that Teagan didn't ignore the signs. I don't think anyone else saw them."

"I agree. I think it's been good for her as well to see Cassie responding to treatment."

"I think the two of them are becoming real friends. And no one is happier about it than Ida."

"Well," Charlotte said looking up at the clock on the wall, "your two minutes are up, and we have a meeting to get to."

Later in the day Maggie headed off to find Ida. She had no trouble, as the sounds of laughter and noises led her to the activity room. Numerous residents were gathered around tables with bowls, wooden spoons, and an array of baking supplies. Teagan and a young man were laughing along with the residents over some story one of them was sharing from their youth. Ida was right in the middle of it all and enjoying herself tremendously.

"Looks like I'm in the right place if you guys are getting ready to bake," Maggie said cheerfully.

Kitty, one of the more vivacious residents, turned to her and beckoned for her to come closer. "We're making cake, Maggie – and this handsome hunk is our cooking teacher!" She winked at Teagan's friend. Her roommate Gladys, who was much quieter, just rolled her eyes. She was used to her roommate flirting with every man that came through the Manor.

Teagan laughed. "Maggie, I don't know if you've met my friend Brian yet. He's going to be coming in a couple times a month to do some baking with the gang."

Brian flashed a smile. "Hey, nice to meet you Maggie – Teags has told me all about you."

"I hope it was all good. Are you the one that made Ida's birthday treat this past spring? She's still raving about that."

Ida smiled and nodded. "It's him alright. And today's another recipe from Greece – an orange honey cake – he's spoiling me!"

"He's spoiling *all* of us, Ida," Kitty corrected. "And *next* time we're gonna make *my* favorite treat--blueberry muffins!"

"Well, I'll leave you to it, then," Maggie replied. "And Ida, I'll catch you later on to fill you in on my visit with Cassie yesterday – that is, if Teagan hasn't beat me to it. Besides, I might manage a small piece of that cake if I time it right."

* * *

AFTER WORK MAGGIE stopped by *Brooke's Treasures*, Brooke Martin's gift shop in town. Brooke had opened her shop years before, and it had been a great success from the beginning. She supplied a perfect mix of homemade gift items along with craft supplies, candles, wind chimes, and books by local authors. Her craft items included both country and Victorian style gifts which offered something for everyone.

Maggie was greeted with the peaceful sounds of a water fountain and quiet music playing. The potpourri smells were subtle but not overpowering, as were Brooke's homemade candles. She spotted Brooke helping a customer at the back of the store, so she waved and headed over to the crafting section. She wanted to pick out a few items to bring to Cassie that might help her creative outlets.

"God, that smells so good." A familiar voice spoke nearby, and she turned around to find Tim, the gentleman from the garden, slowly sniffing one of Brooke's candles. He caught sight of her and smiled. "What? No guard dog? It's Maggie, right?"

She chuckled. "He's probably home waiting very impatiently for me right about now. And you're Tim, if I remember correctly. I see you found another of Caldwell's little treasures."

"This town is amazing – like, right out of a Norman Rockwell painting," Tim exclaimed.

"I told you it was a small town. So which scent won you over?" gesturing toward the candle.

Tim lifted the lid and extended it toward Maggie to smell. "Apple pie – and it smells good enough to eat."

Maggie took a whiff and was transported back to times when the smell would make her queasy. Now it smelled wonderful and reminded her of home. "Brooke makes all the candles herself – and none of them have that overpowering fake scent. I don't know how she does it."

"How I do what?" Brooke had just finished with her customer and approached them. She extended her hand out to Tim. "Brooke Martin.

Nice to have you stop in – and you've made a great selection. That one is my top seller."

"Tim Collins. I'm staying over at the B&B and checking out a few of the places in town."

They headed toward the counter as Brooke replied. "I'm sure that Barb has given you a list. And it looks like you had already run into Maggie."

"Found her with her knees in the dirt with a handful of spinach this morning." He winked at Maggie and she felt unfamiliar flutterings in her stomach.

"Ah, I must have missed you then. Usually I'm out there with Maggie in the morning. What did you think of our garden?"

"Quite impressive," Tim said. "And so far I've gotten to taste some of the harvest with Barb's cooking. Woah, is that penny candy?" His eyes widened as he spotted the display.

Reminiscent of days gone by, a small penny candy counter greeted customers as they checked out. Kids of all ages still came in to choose from candy necklaces, flying saucers, licorice, gummi bears, Swedish fish, caramels, and non-parels. Brooke also had homemade fudge and local candies made by a few Caldwell residents.

"I haven't seen a real penny candy counter since I was a kid. Can you throw in a few Swedish Fish – and maybe a couple pieces of fudge – into my bag?" He turned to Maggie and continued. "It really *is* like a Norman Rockwell painting."

Brooke smiled. "Thanks, Tim. I take that as a high compliment. And I hope to see you again while you're in town."

Tim took his bag and grinned, showing off that dazzling smile that Maggie had noted earlier. "You can count on it. And Maggie, it was nice to bump into you again. Tell Tramp I said hello."

As he headed out of the store, Brooke caught Maggie's expression and raised an eyebrow as she watched him leave. "He's pretty easy on the eyes, isn't he? Maybe we should have Barb do some detective work to see if he's single."

"Oh, cut it out. I don't time for a relationship right now – even if he *is* really attractive." As she headed out to her car, she found herself thinking of how that smile revealed a small dimple in his left cheek. *"Easy on the eyes. Indeed he was."*

* * *

WHEN MAGGIE GOT HOME she was greeted not just by Tramp, but by a German Shepherd named Watson. Liz Wilson, her sister's girlfriend, was over, and her dog and Tramp got along like brothers. Both dogs wagged their tails furiously as she tucked her bag from Brooke's treasures into the hall closet.

"Hey, Watson! How are you boy? Did you come to play with my guy?" She reached down to give Tramp a two handed head scratch, and the turned to scratch Watson's back right near his tail. "You like that, don't ya, big boy? Hey, Liz, how are ya?"

Liz was curled up on the couch with her laptop, typing madly away. She looked up and smiled, gave a quick wave, and then turned right back to her homework. Liz was studying for a degree in Greenhouse Management and certification as a Master Gardener, and she was taking summer classes at Brentwood College.

Maggie left her to her work and walked around into the kitchen where Lucy wore an apron and was chopping broccoli and the fresh spinach from the garden.

"Hey, Maggie, I'm making a stir fry for dinner, so hope you'll join us. I'll keep the shrimp separate. We took the dogs out for a walk earlier so you wouldn't have to."

"Thanks sis, you're the best! It's smells delicious! Let me go and change and I'll come help you." Within minutes she was in capris and a tee shirt and headed back to the kitchen.

Lucy gestured toward the seats at the counter that separated the kitchen from the living room area. "Just sit and keep me company – I'm almost done."

Maggie walked around the corner and grabbed a piece of broccoli before sitting down. "My stomach's growling, so this will be my appetizer." She took a bite and crunched on the vegetable as she admired the bright green color. "Hmmm.....I'm so glad that recovery has allowed me to appreciate food again."

"That makes two of us, sis. How was your day?"

"Not bad. Got permission to take Ida over to see Cassie and she agreed that she'd love to go. Teagan's gonna come along, too. Hey, whatever you just added to the stir-fry smells *so* good."

"It's the garlic, I'm sure. Can hardly wait to have this fresh spinach from the garden."

"Soon enough we'll have tomatoes, peppers, and zucchini as well. Did you find the peas? They could go in, too," suggested Maggie.

Lucy nodded as she lifted a lid from another pot. More garlic aromas filled the air. "I'm so glad Liz taught me how to add the fresh garlic and mushrooms right to the rice when cooking it – makes it so much better." She poured a little oil into a pan and soon the sizzles of onion, pepper, broccoli, and spinach filled the kitchen.

Liz had opted to leave her homework and join them. "God that makes me so hungry. Can I get the plates out?"

"Yeah, leave them on the counter. Maybe we can fill plates and then eat in the other room where it's comfortable."

As they settled down with their dinner in the living room, Maggie turned to Liz. "So how's your class going?"

"Pretty good, actually. The teacher is decent and has really good communication skills. Finishing up a paper tonight, and once I turn it in early I'll have a day or two off. You might find me and Watson camped out here for most of it." She grinned at Maggie and gave a wink to Lucy.

Maggie smiled. "Hey, Tramp *loves* when Watson comes to visit. And I think Lucy is pretty happy, too, I might add." She turned to her sister. "And how was *your* day?"

"We had quite the visitor at the town hall today. This absolute jerk was in to talk about a business proposal and he got into it with one of the zoning committee. After he left the whole office was talking about him."

"He's obviously not from Caldwell if he was acting like that," Liz said.

"Actually, he lived in Caldwell years ago. His dad owned the old hardware store behind the park, and he's decided to renovate it into a golf shop and driving range."

"A driving range? In Caldwell? What the hell do we need a driving range for?" asked Maggie.

"Yeah, that was the general consensus."

"You're talking about that Sean McClean guy, right?" Maggie asked. The ladies in the garden were talking about him and there was a truck over there checking the place out yesterday."

"Yup, that's him," Lucy replied. "I've never met such a rude ass. He kept calling me 'girlie' and wanted me to drop everything to give him a paper clip or get him some tape. I wanted to throw my water at him."

Liz chuckled as she loaded her fork with rice. "I would have liked to have seen that. So how did it turn out?"

"Well, the zoning guy was trying to explain some of the procedures to him and he got obnoxious and argumentative over every point. Going off on how it was *his* property and he should be able to do whatever he wanted with it."

"I bet that went over well," Maggie said.

Her sister nodded. "He finally agreed to have a public meeting – only because he had to. After he left everyone was talking about him. A couple of the older folks remembered him and said he was a trouble maker all through school. He thought Caldwell was a dump and couldn't wait to leave."

"According to Brooke, that's exactly what he did when he graduated," Maggie said. "His poor dad thought he was going to take over the family business."

Liz frowned as she put her plate on the coffee table. "That must have been hard for him."

"Oh, it gets better," Maggie continued. "He also went to school with Carl Pritchard's daughter Sharon, and eventually introduced her to one of his friends, who she married."

"I bet the old guy loved that."

"I don't know, but at some point there was a huge fight between him and Sharon, and she left town, too. They haven't spoken in decades."

"Wow," Lucy replied. "That's really sad."

Maggie nodded. "He blames it all on Sean for some reason."

"But why would he come back now?" Liz asked. Caldwell hasn't changed at all – and does he really think a golf place will fit in here?"

Lucy shook her head. "With his personality I doubt any business he runs will succeed."

Liz nodded. "Sounds like a real piece of work."

"Well, if nothing else, it'll give the town a little excitement this summer. Remember how some fought the community garden a couple years back? We need another good town meeting for folks to complain at."

"Oh, my God," Maggie interjected. "Can you imagine the old curmudgeon this time? He was so against the gardens being right next to his property. He'll blow a gasket when he finds out a driving range might be going in behind his house—especially considering his history with Sean."

Liz took a sip of water and smirked. "Might be a fun summer in Caldwell after all."

aggie and Tramp passed by the old curmudgeon's house on schedule the next morning, and Carl was already standing there with his paper in hand. *"He must have seen me coming on his way out and waited to chat,"* Maggie thought to herself. *"I love this grumpy guy."*

"Morning, Mr. Pritchard. Anything in the headlines I should know about?"

Carl rolled up his paper and looked over his thick rimmed glasses at her. "Don't even know why I bother any more. There's never anything good in the paper."

"It does seem to focus on all the negative stuff, doesn't it? At least the weather's gonna be nice today. That's something."

"Pfft. Just means more heat and humidity. I hate the summer," he grumbled.

"Well your roses are looking beautiful. We can see them from the garden and the colors are so vibrant this year."

"Just more work in the hot sun. And you," he said pointing toward Tramp--

"He stays far away from your roses," Maggie interjected. "You know that. I keep him tied right at the edge of my plot."

"Well yesterday there were kids running around, and they were over to cause a ruckus."

"That must have been the Sanderson kids. I'm sure they just wanted to come over and smell them. And last year they gave you a bunch of free zucchini if I remember."

She saw a slight smile cross his face before his scowl returned. "Well, they still shouldn't be running onto my property."

"If I see them I'll mention it. In the meantime, can you use some fresh lettuce or spinach? I can drop some off on my way home."

"Don't eat salad. That's rabbit food. But you can leave those extra tomatoes like you did – they make good sandwiches."

"It'll be another week or so, Mr. Pritchard, but you'll get the first one off the vine, I promise."

She saw his smile come back as he turned toward his car. "I gotta get to the market before it gets too hot."

"Have a great day, Mr. Pritchard!" He didn't look back, but gave a backward wave.

Maggie and Tramp continued on to the park and met up with Brooke and Colleen who were already there. They greeted her as she tied Tramp to his usual post.

Maggie looked down at Colleen's basket. "Wow, your lettuce is still coming in fast and furious."

Colleen nodded as she threw in another few leaves. "I think it's the last hurrah for the greens. I had four different types of lettuce this spring and they all did great. I'll have to plant more once these are done so we'll have it for when the tomatoes are ripe."

Brooke looked past them. "Looks like Barb is bringing a friend. A mighty fine looking one, I might add." She winked at Maggie as they watched Barb and Tim make their way through the park.

Colleen saw the wink and leaned back on her legs. "Okay, spill, you guys. Who's the guy? And hurry, before he's within earshot."

Brooke laughed and answered. "Met him at the store yesterday, and Maggie evidently made an impression on him in the garden yesterday. All I know is that he's staying at the B&B on business. And I *think* he's single."

Maggie rolled her eyes. "I told you, I'm not ready for dating yet. Besides, we don't *know* that he's single." As she spoke she studied his build and noticed the way he rolled up the sleeves of his oxford shirt. *"Casual, but professional"* she noted.

Barb and Tim approached as Barb chatted away. As they got to the gardens he laughed at something she said, and Maggie loved the way his whole face lit up – especially that dimple.

"Morning, ladies," he said with a smile. "And Tramp, of course." The beagle had gotten up and started wagging his tail as Tim spoke. He leaned down and gave his head a scratch. "I guess you remember me, don't you, boy?" He turned toward Maggie and flashed a smile, and that dimple made her heart beat a bit faster. "Morning, Maggie. Nice to run into you again."

Maggie smiled, her face feeling flushed. "This is usually where you'll find me every morning."

Tim stood back up and looked at the other ladies, extending his hand to Colleen. "Haven't had the pleasure yet. Tim Collins. And Brooke," he continued, "that fudge was to die for. I'll be stopping back this week to get more."

"Good to hear," Brooke said with a smile. "I see Barb dragged you down to do her weeding, huh?"

"I certainly did not," Barb replied as she threw her gardening glove at her friend. "He said he was coming this way and thought we could chat en route."

Tim nodded. "Decided to walk over to the library and do a little research, and then walk up through town to see what else I can discover. It's such a great little place. I'll leave you ladies to your gardening."

He turned to go, and then turned back and gestured with his head. "Maggie, you got a sec?"

She looked at the others who were all smiling mischievously, and stood up. "Sure." She took a few steps out of the garden plot to where he was standing and looked into his face.

"So, everyone is telling me I have to try out Gino's, and I'm gonna head over tonight for dinner. Was wondering if you might be free to join me? Ya know, so I don't have to eat all by myself."

Maggie paused for a second, lost in those brown eyes before nodding. "It would have to be after 6:30; I get out of work at 4 and then have to zip over to Brentwood for a while, but I'm usually back by then."

"How about seven? That gives a little extra time so you're not in a rush. I could either meet you there or pick you up – whatever's easier."

"Let's meet there. And thanks for the extra half hour to get home."

Tim smiled. "No problem. I look forward to it. You have a great day, Maggie Richmond."

Maggie watched him walk away and sighed. *"I think I already did,"* she thought as she admired his backside. *"God, he's handsome."*

When she turned back to the garden her three friends were all sitting there staring at her with huge smiles on their faces.

"What? It's just a dinner. Jeez." But she was smiling as she knelt back down to work, and she knew the others were chuckling.

Colleen bent down to pick up her bucket of weeds for the compost container. As she started down toward the back of the garden she gazed across the lawn and paused. "Looks like the truck is back over there. Wonder what's up?"

As the others looked on, two men got out and began carrying surveying equipment toward Carl's property.

Maggie watched them. "It's a good thing Mr. Pritchard isn't home. I'm sure he'd be out yelling at them to keep their distance."

Brooke squinted in the bright sun as she watched the men setting up. "Looks like they're going to measure the property lines. I wonder if one of them is Sean McClean."

Barb followed her gaze. "No, they're both too young. Sean would be in his fifties now."

"I actually got some info from Lucy last night on that," Maggie replied. "Sean caused a little scene at town hall yesterday."

The ladies turned their focus to Maggie as they resumed their gardening.

"Spill, Maggie," Colleen said urgently. "What's the big town news?"

Maggie laughed. "Seems like Sean is planning to renovate the place."

Brooke scowled. "Why? Doesn't he know there's another hardware store in town now?" She noticed Maggie's smirk. "Okay, what?"

"He's not doing a hardware store. He wants to open a golf shop and a driving range."

"Are you kidding?" Colleen asked. "In Caldwell?"

They all laughed at the idea as they each settled in to finish their gardening chores.

Awhile later Barb was the first to pack up her stuff. "Well, those two look like they've made progress over there. Oh, jeez, look how close they are to Carl's roses."

Just as they all turned to look, Carl Pritchard slammed his car door and charged toward the back yard.

"You!" he called. "What are you two doing?! Get away from those roses!"

"Oh, God, he's home," Maggie said. "We better get over to intervene."

One guy stopped and took a step toward Carl as he approached. "It's okay, sir, we're not bothering anything. Just doing our job. We won't be long."

Carl's voice was already getting louder as he got closer. "You're darn tootin' ya won't be long, 'cause you're leavin' *now*, ya hear me?!"

As Maggie arrived, the surveyor looked toward her for backup. "Look, we just need a couple more minutes and we'll be done."

"Everything okay, Mr. Pritchard?" Maggie asked.

The old man turned toward her, his face flushed and his expression a grimace. "What do *you* think? I'm telling these two clowns to get off my property. And take your damn stuff with you."

"Mr. Pritchard, it's okay," Maggie said, turning her attention to the surveyor. "Are you the owner? And did you give Mr. Pritchard any warning that you'd be here today as a common courtesy?"

"Notices went out two weeks ago. I don't know if they specified a date. But we were hired to get this surveying done and we really need to finish. We won't bother anything, sir."

Carl was pacing back and forth watching the other surveyor at work. "What are you doing back there? You need to go back to your own lot!"

"Just watch the roses," Maggie whispered to the surveyor. "They're his pride and joy."

The guy nodded, and cautiously turned his back to the old man, trusting that Maggie would keep him from attacking physically.

"Mr. Pritchard," Maggie began calmly. "I promise they won't touch your roses. They're only doing their job so they can turn in accurate measurements. You know how important that is – you created blue-prints for years."

Barb and the other ladies nodded as they joined them.

"There's probably still some left in your old garage office," Colleen pointed out.

"Carl," Brooke said gently, "can you tell me what types of roses you have? There must be four or five different varieties here with all the colors." She definitely knew how to distract Carl, as his body relaxed a bit to answer her.

"There's four – each one a different color. The red are *Mr. Lincoln*, the pink are *Sweet Mademoiselle*, and the yellow are *Romantica*."

"How about the pink and white ones? Those are my favorites," Barb chirped in.

"Those are *Rainbow Niagara*," Carl answered, looking back to keep an eye on the surveyors. "Hey, hey, hey! Not too close! You don't need to be on this side of the bushes – this is *my* property."

Maggie gestured for them to keep working. "Mr. Pritchard, they're just getting their measurements – and they've been really careful. I'm sure they're almost done."

Almost on cue, the surveyor nearest to them closed his notebook. "She's right, sir. We'll finish up further away now. And we appreciate your patience. We just wanted it to be accurate."

"Well, now you can get your stuff and move on. Don't know why you're so damn interested in my property line. What the hell are they doing with the place, anyhow?"

"I think the plan is for a golf shop – oh, and a driving range. Have a good day, sir."

Maggie watched Carl's face turn bright red and looked toward the other ladies. The expected response came.

"A driving range? A *driving* range? With balls flying around and hitting roses and breaking my windows?" Carl started after them arms flailing. "Oh, like hell you are!"

"Not us, sir," the guy said as they backed away quickly.

"Who then?" shouted the old man. "Who the hell put you up to this? It better not be that McClean kid." His fists were clenched tight and Maggie wondered if he'd go after them.

"Carl," she said, trying to appease him, "I'm sure—"

"I'm sure he'll be in touch, sir," answered the worker as they turned and carried their equipment away as fast as they could.

"That damn kid," Carl muttered. "It *is* him that's back."

Brooke took step and tried to touch his arm. He waved her off and yelled across the lawn. "You tell that no good boss of yours that I'll fight him! He ain't puttin' no damn driving range next to my property, ya hear?!" As he turned back and saw the women all watching with concerned faces, he shook his head as he stormed back into the house. "That McClean kid is good for nothing. Always has been and always will be. Damn him!"

The ladies all exhaled as he rushed back into his house and slammed the door.

"Well," Barb said, "something tells me that this fight is gonna make the community garden protest look like a walk in the park." They all nodded in agreement as they headed back to gather their harvest and head home.

CHAPTER 5

When Maggie arrived at work she had a message from Jane Simmons on her desk. Despite her self doubt, she called her back and agreed to participate on the panel.

"I'm so glad!" Jane responded. "I've heard nothing but great things about you. Give me your email and I'll send you a packet of information and then we can chat after you look through it. Does that work?"

"Sounds fine," Maggie replied, feeling the nervous flutters in her stomach as she shared her email. "Thank you for your confidence in me, Jane. I'll do my best." She hung up the phone and reflected on what she'd said, realizing that recovery had given her the ability to feel self worth again. *Maybe I can offer something to the discussion,* she thought as she reached for a resident's file.

* * *

All day Maggie had three men on her mind. She wondered about the mysterious Sean

McClean and Carl's violent reaction to him. It seemed to be much more personal than the protectiveness of his roses. And, of course, she was even more intrigued by the arrival of one Tim Collins, and a certain dinner scheduled later that day. *"What the hell have you gotten yourself into?"* she thought as she finished up with a file and threw it on her desk.

Charlotte Hurd was walking by her door and saw her expression. "Is it safe to come in? You don't look your usual cheerful self."

Maggie sighed and waved her in. "I'm fine. Just distracted, that's all."

"Anything here at work?"

Maggie shook her head. "Men."

Charlotte laughed as she sat down. "Maggie Richmond, distracted by *men?* As in plural?

So what men are we talking about?"

"It was a weird morning. I don't know if you heard that the old hardware store is being renovated, but there were surveyors there today, and man, did Carl go off on them. I've never seen him so worked up."

"Wow. I hadn't heard. But I imagine that drudged up a lot of history—that is, if it's still the McClean family involved."

"Yeah, it's Sean – Lucy got to meet him at town hall this week, and he wasn't exactly charming. Seems he's putting in a golf shop and driving range."

"Well good luck to him getting *that* past zoning."

"I was thinking more good luck getting it past Mr. Pritchard."

Charlotte chuckled. "Oh, my Lord. Does he know that's the plan yet?"

Maggie nodded. "This morning. I honestly thought he might go after the surveyors. They were scared to death of him."

"Man, I feel sorry for Carl. This is gonna really get to him."

"Yeah, Barb talked a bit about some kind of family feud."

"That it was. He lost his daughter over it. I'll have to pull out his wife's file from the archives. When she was here we got a fair amount of what was going on, and it might be good for you to know since you deal with him a lot."

"But that was so long ago – didn't she die like fifteen years ago?"

Charlotte nodded. "Yup. A few years after I started here. He came every day, and back then even his daughter came on occasion to visit. But things were so bad between them by then that she stopped coming all together. I don't think he's seen her since Ruth's funeral."

"His own daughter? What the hell happened?"

"Well, Carl didn't talk about it much, but we pieced together the information we had. It seems that he and Henry – the older McClean – were decent friends for a long time. I guess the wives were really close. And then their daughter Sharon was a school mate of Sean – the younger McClean."

"You mean the obnoxious one."

Charlotte agreed. "Yeah, from what I heard he was a handful growing up. Got into drinking and drugs and spent most of his time with older kids over in Brentwood. But he and Sharon worked together at the hardware store and even dated a few times."

"I'm sure Carl wasn't too keen on that. Is that what caused the feud?"

"No – that came later. Henry had always assumed that Sean would take over the family business. But when Sean finished college and told his dad he wanted nothing to do with the store – or Caldwell, for that matter – things started falling apart."

Maggie looked at her pensively. "Did he and Sharon still date after high school?"

"No, that didn't last long. But Sean introduced her to a friend of his, and that's who she ended up marrying. And then the boys ended up starting their own business. Engineering or architecture – or maybe both?"

"But that's what Carl did – you'd think he'd be happy about that."

"I think he was initially, but Sean had some shady clients and they got involved in some bad investments. Carl kept telling Sharon that she and Steve should quit and come to work with him, but Steve declined. No one knew that he had started drinking heavily. I guess the alcohol is what really destroyed the family in the end."

Maggie sighed. "As it so often does. So what happened?"

"All I know is that when Carl's wife moved in here there was no relationship with their daughter at that point. I think she might have come to see her mom a couple of times, but always when Carl wasn't here, and she never stayed long. And she came alone to the funeral, and from what I heard hardly spoke to her father. I don't think she's been back since."

"That must be so hard on him," Maggie responded. "It's hard enough to lose your wife, but to lose your daughter as well?"

Charlotte nodded. "And he's blamed Sean for all of it."

"Sounds like he deserves every bit of it. I can understand why he was so upset this morning. Heck, if I had known maybe *I* would have gone after the surveyors."

"This will be tough on him – no question about that." Charlotte looked at her watch. "And I have an interview in ten minutes, so I better let you get back to work. By the way, did you ever hear from Jane?"

Maggie rolled her eyes. "You knew I'd say yes, didn't you?"

"I was pretty sure. And I'm so proud of you for pushing yourself. You'll be great."

She got up to leave and then turned back. "Hey, you said *men* when I popped in – so who's the other?"

Maggie smiled. "Just a guy in town. He's staying at the B&B . And I'm meeting him at Gino's tonight for dinner."

"*A date?* Lady, you better put me down on your calendar for first thing tomorrow morning. I wanna hear all about it!" She turned the corner and Maggie could hear her cheering.

* * *

At the end of the day she headed over to Brentwood for her own counseling session with Natalie, stopping by to drop off the art supplies she'd bought for Cassie beforehand. She checked in and found Cassie on the back porch with a book in hand. The latter smiled when Maggie came out the door.

"Hey! I didn't know you were coming today."

"Just for a minute or two. I have my own counseling appointment, but I wanted to drop some art supplies off for you. I left them at the front desk. You know the rules."

Cassie nodded. "It's still weird knowing that they have to check every little thing that comes through the door. What kind of art stuff? I can hardly wait."

Maggie sat down on the chair beside her. "A sketch book and some pastels. I wasn't sure if brushes or pencils would get through inspection. Heck, I'm not totally sure about the pastels!"

"Worst case scenario, they might keep them and let me use them during supervised sessions. But I think I saw another girl with stuff the other day, so hopefully I'll get them." Cassie smiled genuinely. "Thanks so much for thinking of me."

"When I saw that painting you were working on I couldn't resist. How have you been?"

"Doing okay. I have it just about finished, so I'll show it to you next time. I'll also have to show you my new mask, too."

"Is that the one for roleplaying? I know I still have all three of mine at home."

Cassie nodded, bringing her legs up onto the chair and hugging them tightly. "I think out of all the therapy I've done so far that's what's impacted me most," she said nervously. "Having to create a mask that symbolizes my anorexia and then have to actually wear it and talk like it's my disease talking – it's pretty intense."

"I bet you noticed a difference already with the second mask, though, didn't you?"

"Not until it was done and they were side by side. The first one was black and covered with all this dark stuff – I actually had black sandpaper over one of the eyes. But this week's mask had more color, and I even painted a little butterfly on it. It felt good to see the difference."

"Well, you'll do one more the week before you leave. Any news of when yet?"

Cassie shook her head. "Nothing definite, but maybe a few more weeks? It's a little scary thinking about going home."

Maggie smiled. "But also a little exciting to get back to your own space again?" As Cassie nodded she continued. "It's an adjustment, believe me. I remember how hard it was to go from having the staff here monitor your meals to having your mom or sibling sit across the table to watch you eat."

Cassie frowned. "That's going to be really hard."

Maggie reached over and patted her hand. "Give it time and you'll adjust. Besides, you'll still be here a lot for outpatient therapy, and I'll be around if you need to talk. Which reminds me, it's time for my own appointment with Natalie."

"She's so nice. I love talking to her. But she hates it when you're even a minute late, so get going. Hope to see you soon."

"Actually, Teagan and I are planning to come later this week—with a special visitor."

"Wait, Gram's coming?" Cassie asked excitedly as Maggie nodded. "I've missed her. It'll be so good to see her again."

"She's really looking forward to it, too. Until then, keep hanging in there. You're doing great, Cassie. Really."

Cassie smiled. "Thanks. It feels good most of the time now. I'm so glad I came when I did. I feel like I have real shot to beat this thing."

"You will, Cassie. I know you will."

CHAPTER 6

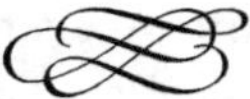

An hour later, Maggie headed back to Caldwell for her dinner date with Tim. She wasn't sure she'd have enough time to head home to change and take Tramp out, so she called her sister who agreed to walk Tramp. She hated not seeing him for the whole day, but knew he was in good hands. Living with Lucy had been one of the smartest decisions she'd ever made. Her parents had announced that they were moving to Florida right after she got her job at the Manor, and for a couple of days she came close to relapsing at the thought of having to move again. When Lucy suggested moving back to Caldwell to help with the rent in her townhouse, she was thrilled. She could walk to work some of the time, and she loved being with her sister. While most of her childhood friends had moved away after school, she'd become friends with those at work and in the garden. It seemed that Caldwell truly was a place for those that loved small towns. She hoped it always stayed that way.

She thought of parking at home and walking over to Gino's, but the humidity hadn't dropped that much during the day and she opted for keeping her hair a little less frizzy. As she pulled into the lot beside the restaurant she felt butterflies in her stomach. This was her first date in years, and she was nervous.

"Just be yourself," she thought. *"That's what Natalie said."* She'd been working with Natalie since her high school years at the Phoenix Center, and still loved her sessions almost seven years later. She approached the door to head inside and took a deep breath. *"Here goes nothing."*

As soon as she entered Gino's the smells of garlic and cheese hit her nose, and she felt at home. Garlic was one of her favorite foods and she loved eating it on almost everything she cooked. *"Maybe I shouldn't eat garlic tonight – what it Tim might kiss me? Would the taste of garlic turn him off?"* Gino smiled at her from behind the counter, his hands busy twirling a piece of dough that would become a delectable pizza from the oven. Maggie relaxed and smiled back. *"Then again, no guy is going to keep me from eating Gino's food. I've come way too far in my healing to let anyone judge me for what I eat – especially garlic."*

"Buena serra, Maggie! Are you here for takeout?" Gino knew almost every long term resident of Caldwell by name, including her, which was another reason the place was one of her favorites.

"Not tonight, Gino," she answered with a smile. "I'm, ah, actually meeting someone."

Gino's face lit up like the old romantic he was as a familiar voice came from behind.

"I think that might be me." Maggie turned to find Tim standing off to the side with a genuine smile on his face. He was wearing a casual pair of trousers and a light blue oxford shirt, again with the sleeves rolled up. If he'd had a tie on earlier it was off now, and the undone button at the top caught Maggie's attention. *"God, he looks nice,"* she thought.

"Hi, Tim. I hope you weren't waiting long."

"Just got here a minute or two before you. Gino said he'd have a table ready as soon as my guest arrived. Looks like he knows you – and everyone else that walks in the door."

Gino had wiped his hands and grabbed a couple of menus as he nodded. "Caldwell is my *familia*.. I know almost everyone by appearance, but the regulars I know by name. And I've been serving this one pasta since she was in pigtails. Come, let's get you a nice spot."

He led them to a quiet table by the back window.

"And I'm Gino," he said as he handed Tim his menu. "I don't think we've had the pleasure of meeting yet." He reached out and gave him a warm handshake.

"Tim. Nice to meet you at long last. I've never felt so welcomed. Everyone in town has raved about you since I got here, and I'm beginning to see why."

Gino laughed. "You eat first, and then you'll know why." He glanced over at Maggie as he gave her a menu, and then added in a stage whisper, "And you treat this one nice. She's a first class lady." He winked as he headed back to seat another group that had arrived. Tim smiled at her and once again flashed that dimple that made her insides flutter.

"I'm a little nervous, now. Will he kick me out if I say something you don't like?"

Maggie laughed. "Don't worry about him. He's just a hopeless romantic. But yeah, if I asked him to, he'd probably kick your ass to the curb. Not exactly first class language, huh?"

"Thank God. I'm not sure I could handle someone all prim and proper. Besides, the first time we met you had your hands in the dirt. I figured you were pretty down to earth."

Maggie nodded. "Now that you mention it, I think most of us that garden tend to be that way. I don't think I've ever met a 'prim and proper' gardener before. At least not in Caldwell."

"So," Tim said as he opened his menu, "what do you suggest I try as a first timer at Gino's?"

"Pick anything – literally. I don't think I have ever eaten a bad meal here. And I've eaten here since I was a kid."

"Not even a little help? This is a huge menu."

"Oh, all right. Keep in mind I haven't eaten meat in years, but I haven't heard any complaints on stuff I used to enjoy. I'd recommend either veal or chicken parmigiana, or the chicken marsala – unless you're in the mood for pizza, which will never be a bad choice."

"What are you having?"

"I think I'm in mood for pasta, so I'm going with the pasta primavera."

"Well then, I think I'll try the chicken parm. I could use a little pasta myself."

"You won't be disappointed – the cheese alone makes it awesome."

A waitress arrived with water and a basket of fresh bread, took their orders, and promised to return shortly with their salads. Tim picked up the basket and held it out toward Maggie. "Bread?"

"Does the sun rise in the east?" She pulled a warm piece from the basket and waited for him to do the same. He offered the butter dish to her and she shook her head. "I don't need it, thanks. I don't eat a ton of dairy, and my pasta will have plenty of oil. Besides, this bread doesn't need anything to make it taste like heaven."

She took a bite and savored the flavor of the warm bread. "Hmmm," she said, not realizing how hungry she actually was.

Tim had finished buttering his slice and joined her as he took a bite. "Man, that's good."

She smiled at him as they each finished their slice in silence, and then he reached for a second. "Something tells me I might be taking home a doggie bag tonight – I might fill up on bread."

"I think everyone I know takes home a doggie bag from this place. Wait till you see how much food is on your plate."

"So, you've been coming here since you had pigtails – a lifelong resident?"

"Almost. We moved over to Brentwood when I was in high school – end of my freshman year. Probably about the worst time ever to have to move. It's a year too late to make friends with all the other incoming freshmen. I really hated it."

"From what I've heard the school in Brentwood is bigger?"

"About three times the size. Don't get me wrong – every kid in Caldwell is thrilled to have Brentwood next store. There's way more to do. I think my folks meant well, thinking it'd be good for me to have more kids around. My sister had left for college and they thought I'd have a better shot at making some new friends in a bigger school. Too bad they were wrong."

"What about your friends here? It doesn't seem that far away."

A waitress interrupted with salads and Maggie held up her finger as she took a big forkful. "Sorry, I'm very hungry and I love their salads. I could eat this every day."

Tim took a bite of his and nodded. "That's nice. It's a bold vinaigrette," he said, pausing to analyze the flavors in his mouth. "I'd guess red wine vinegar, dijon mustard, and maybe some red pepper flakes for that extra kick. I approve."

Maggie stopped with fork mid-air. "Woah. I didn't expect that out of your mouth just now."

Tim smiled. "I consider myself an amateur chef, with a palate for flavor. Something about taking a whole bunch of random items and putting them together to create something that tastes phenomenal is mind blowing. I love coming up with new combinations of food, and seeing people enjoying my cooking is the best part."

"Maybe I should send you back to the kitchen – Gino might have a great spot for you."

Tim took another bite, and then said, "Not until I hear the rest of the story about your childhood friends."

Maggie sighed. "It's not really the classic Caldwell happily-ever-after storyline. Once I moved away, the connections started to fade. I mean, we meant well, but they were all involved with stuff here, and I was over there feeling totally out of place – they tried to stay in touch, but I started to push them away because I didn't want to hear what I was missing. And then things just got bad for a while..." She hesitated on saying more, not sure how real she should get on a first date. Time was wonderful so far and she didn't want to scare him away with her honesty. *"But if Natalie has taught me anything,"* she thought, *"it's admitting and accepting the truth about my anorexia to myself and others."*

Their meals arrived before she could say more and Tim's eyes grew wide when he saw the platter the waitress placed in front of him. "Man, you weren't kidding! That's a ton of food." He grabbed his knife and cut a small piece of chicken, twirling it with some cheese that stretched from the plate as he brought it to his mouth. He closed his eyes and Maggie could tell that he was savoring the first bite. "That's the best mozzarella I've had in a long time."

She chuckled as she chewed her own primavera. "Told ya."

"Thanks for the recommendation – this is superb."

They ate in silence for a few minutes, both devouring their meals too much for conversation. Maggie found it comforting that she could eat normally in front of him without feeling self-conscious. Tim finally put his fork down. "I think I better pace myself before I inhale it all and feel sick. So what did you mean about things getting bad? Although don't feel pressured to talk if you don't want to. God knows I have my own issues to deal with."

"It's okay," Maggie replied. "It's much easier to talk about now. By the time Christmas rolled around during my sophomore year I had developed an eating disorder – anorexia, to be exact. My sister was off at school and both parents were working. I had no support at all, and no one at school knew me. Kind of a perfect storm for eating disorders to just take over. By the time the year ended I was in pretty bad shape, and started having fainting spells. I played all kinds of games to hide it from my folks. I think they knew something was wrong, but didn't know enough about the disease to really see it. It wasn't a good time."

Tim was sitting still, listening intently. "That must have been really lonely."

She nodded. "It wasn't until Lucy came home for the summer that things changed. She'd seen various eating disorders on the college campus and knew right away what was wrong – and she knows me well enough that I couldn't play the game with her. She called me right out. I never thought you could love someone and hate them so much at the same time, but I did then."

"So what happened?"

"I ended up at the Phoenix Center over in Brentwood. It's a great facility that deals with eating disorders of all types, and it was relatively new at the time. I lived there for about three months – and I have no doubt that it saved my life."

Tim chose his words carefully. "But, that's not something that goes away, does it?"

Maggie laughed. "Oh, I wish. No, I'll deal with it for most of my life, I suspect. But after an inpatient stay I went several times a week for outpatient therapy, and even now I head back once a week to see Natalie Bader– she's the best therapist in the world."

"I don't mean to sound tactless – and tell me to shut up if I am – but are you okay eating out? Like, I hope I didn't cause any inner turmoil inviting you to dinner."

Maggie smiled and was touched by his concern. "It's not a stupid question. I appreciate you asking, though. Two years ago I probably wouldn't have been able to be here. But I've learned to deal with it, and I recognize it for what it is. I know I'll always have to work at not slipping back into making excuses or believing the lies that my head tries to tell me, but I'd rather do that than be dead."

Tim was sitting quietly. "Thanks for trusting me enough to share that. I think you're incredibly brave, and it's refreshing to hear such honesty—especially on a first date."

"I'm honestly a little surprised that I did." She sat up straighter and grinned. "I mean, I've gotten up and spoken in front of groups about my anorexia, and my current friends know about it, but I never thought I'd be sitting out on a first date telling a guy all about it."

Tim raised his glass. "To you, then – and I'm really glad to be that guy." Maggie felt herself blush.

She knew that she was getting full, and from the way Tim had slowed down his own eating, she thought he might be as well. "I think I'm gonna have to ask for a box for the rest of this. I told you the servings were huge."

Tim gestured for the waitress as she passed by. "Can we have two boxes please?" He turned to Maggie. "Should we get coffee? Or dessert?"

Maggie shook her head. "I'm really full. Just coffee for me. But you might consider asking her to slip a couple of cannoli in your bag for later. I promise you won't be disappointed."

He nodded, and within minutes hot coffee was in front of them and their dinners waited in bags on the table. "I'm really glad you came tonight, Maggie. I wasn't sure if you'd be interested in going out, but Barb kinda gave me a nudge."

Maggie laughed. "Now that doesn't surprise me one bit. I think she, Brooke, and Colleen have been on a mission to get me into the dating world. They must have had you marked the minute you hit the B&B."

"Hey, to be clear. I didn't need the nudging in terms of wanting to ask you out – I was just nervous that you might say no." He flashed that dimpled smile across the table and Maggie felt the now familiar butterflies in her stomach.

"I'm kind of surprised I said yes. I haven't really thought about dating. I've been really focused on myself and getting better. But I'm comfortable with you – and maybe a little bit nervous, too." She sipped her coffee and met Tim's gaze.

"I feel the same. Like you, I haven't really thought about dating in quite awhile."

"So what's your story, then? I feel like I've talked through this whole meal. What about you?" She was curious to know more about him.

Tim grinned. "Maybe it's a genius plan to get you to go out with me again. You know, next time will be my story?"

"I'd like that, if you're asking."

"See, what did I tell ya? Pure genius. But to pique your interest, I'll answer any three questions right now."

Maggie laughed. "I could sit here until closing trying to come up with the most unique questions ever asked on a first date, but I'll go easy on you."

"Fire when ready," Tim said as he gazed into her eyes.

Maggie's mind raced, trying to think of all the questions she wanted answered.

"How old are you?" she blurted out.

Tim laughed. "I don't know, that's kind of personal, don't ya think? I'm kidding. I'm 28, and I'll throw in that I'm a Taurus for a bonus tidbit."

"Taurus, huh?" Maggie thought to herself. *"Definitely compatible for a Virgo."*

"As long as I'm being a little boring with my questions, what do you do? You said that you're an amateur chef, so I suspect something else pays the bills."

He nodded. "I work at an architectural firm up in Danvers. Most of our work is up on the north shore, either building apartments on the waterfront or finding other options to keep them away."

Maggie's perplexed look invited a longer answer.

"It's all about balance," Tim continued. "Some towns can really benefit from new housing and the money it brings in, while other places are better off restoring the waterfront as it is. I've worked on both."

She looked at him thoughtfully. "So it's not all about development and making money."

He laughed. "Trust me, there's plenty of that mentality in the field, and I've had to work with a few folks that I really didn't like very much." He paused for a moment and Maggie thought he might add more, but instead he stopped and said, "You have one more question for tonight."

"Okay," she replied. "I know you like cooking, but do you have any other hobbies?"

Tim finished his coffee before answering. "Reading, walking outdoors, and…this might be a deal breaker for another date, but I love museums. History, art, science. You name it, and I'd go. I guess I'm a bit of a nerd."

Maggie laughed. "Actually, that answer probably guaranteed you another date. Well done, Mr. Collins."

He flashed her a smile as they got up to leave, and after saying goodbye to Gino he held the door for her as they left. His arm brushed hers as she passed by, and she felt a tingle all over.

She thought about his smile all the way home, wondering where their next date would be. And she smiled as she anticipated hearing all about his story.

CHAPTER 7

The next morning when Maggie got to the community plot her three garden buddies were already there, and once she had Tramp secured she turned to see three expectant faces staring at her.

"What?" she asked, knowing full well that Barb must have heard something from Tim.

"You know darn well what," Colleen said with a smile. "Come on, spill it."

"We went to Gino's and had dinner. It was nice. Okay?"

Brooke laughed. "You think after months of trying to find someone to hook you up with we're gonna be satisfied with *that* answer? So what did you have? And what did you talk about?"

"Jeez, you guys are worse than my sister last night. Okay, I had pasta primavera, he had chicken parm. He loved the bread and he loves to cook. And he was super impressed with Gino's and seems to really like Caldwell. Is that better?" She smirked at them, knowing that she'd reveal a little more, but she was having a little fun with them.

"And….?" Colleen prodded.

"Okay. He's 28 and he's a Taurus. He works at an architecture firm up in Danvers that focusses mostly along the north shore, and he loves museums. Is that better?"

Barb shook her head. "Don't rely on her, girls; if you want the real dirt I can give you the guy's version."

Maggie felt the butterflies immediately and blushed. "And what exactly did he say?"

"He came in for breakfast in a great mood – I think I heard him whistling as he crossed the driveway. And since I knew he hadn't been there for dinner last night I just casually asked him if he enjoyed his dinner at Ginos. Man, the smile on his face told it all." She looked at Maggie knowingly and smiled. "Girl, he is *smitten*."

"Yes!" chirped Brooke victoriously as she high fived Colleen. "Our little Maggie has a real admirer!"

While Maggie couldn't deny that the butterflies felt really good, she was also a realist and didn't want to get their hopes up. "Might I remind you guys, that he's staying at the B&B, which means he's only in town for a short period. So yes, he's really nice, but for all I know he's got a girlfriend – or a wife, for that matter – back from wherever he came from. I'm not jumping into anything until I know a whole lot more about one Tim Collins."

Barb walked over and hugged her, then looked back at the others. "That's what I love about our girl here. Only 23, and she's got my sensibility. Of course, I might have heard a few interesting tidbits over coffee this morning..."

Much as Maggie tried to appear neutral, they all knew that she was dying to know everything she could about Barb's latest guest. "Well?" she asked eagerly.

"Relax, honey. He's not married, and he hasn't been seeing anyone for a long time. He said work's been crazy and he's been putting in lots of extra time. He also told me that he owns a townhouse up in Gloucester, but after being here he's thinking that he might really prefer a small town instead..."

"Is that it?" Maggie asked, almost holding her breath from that piece of news.

"He really likes you. He told me all about your dinner and how much he admired your recovery. I have a feeling that even after he leaves town you might still be seeing him – that is, if you're interested."

Brooke laughed. "Just look at her cheeks and you don't have to ask. Admit it, Maggie. You're as interested as he is."

Maggie could feel the flush in her cheeks getting a little hotter. "Okay, I like him. But I'm also scared to death. I haven't been in a relationship before, and I don't know how it will affect my recovery – and that has to be my priority, no matter what."

"But Maggie," Barb said, "there have been lots of women who have managed both. Especially if the guy is supportive and sensitive – and my gut tells me that Tim is one of those guys. So you enjoy those feelings flying around inside. We've got your back, and Lord knows you'll be as cautious as you can before giving your heart away. And now," she continued as she got back on her knees, "I say we all turn our attention to the real reason we're gathered this morning." The others laughed as she cut a handful of lettuce off its stalk.

As Maggie knelt down her phone chirped, so she pulled it out and opened the text.

"*I had a wonderful time last night. Thank you for a lovely evening, and I hope to see you soon. Have a great day.*"

Her heart raced as she typed a quick reply. "*Me, too. I enjoyed every moment, and look forward to talking again. Hope you have a good day as well.*" She debated on whether to include a heart emoji, but settled for a smile instead. She looked back up to see her three friends beaming before they turned back to work.

"Smitten," she heard Barb say, and she smiled at the possibilities that might lie ahead.

* * *

A COUPLE of hours later Maggie pulled into the lot at Caldwell Manor, and she couldn't help but look across the street to the B&B. "*Is he over there working right now? And how soon will I see him again?*"

She was still staring when Teagan came riding up on her bicycle.

"You're here early – done with school?

Teagan shook her head. "Two half day finals later this week and I'm free!" She glanced across the street to where Maggie's gaze had been. "Anything interesting over there?" she asked with a smile.

"Is it that obvious?"

"Sure looks like someone who's got a crush going on. Then again, I'm not exactly an expert in that department. I can recognize the signs, but I don't have clue as to what's going on inside."

Maggie smiled at her warmly. She knew that Teagan was aromantic and asexual, and she admired her honesty about it with those that didn't understand it. "Is it ever weird for you? I mean, not feeling anything like that?"

Teagan laughed. "Of course it is. At least I know *why* I don't feel attracted to others, and that makes it okay. I feel bad for those that don't know yet that they're ace or aro. They must feel like there's something wrong with them, when they're totally normal. That sucks."

As they headed inside Melvin greeted them at the door, and Maggie knew that he'd choose to follow Teagan down the hall. She watched them and the other residents come out of their rooms and join the "parade" down toward the activity room. *God, Teagan's like the Pied Piper when it comes to our residents.*

"And how was *dinner* last night?"

Maggie turned to find Charlotte just standing there tapping her file folder with her pencil.

"It was lovely, thank you. I'm surprised you weren't at the garden this morning to join the inquisition."

Charlotte laughed. "I'll have to stop by Brooke's or make it to yoga with Colleen on Saturday. They can give me the full run down. Unfortunately I have a meeting this morning, so you're off the hook with me." As she headed toward her office she added, "But I'm glad you had a good time."

"Thanks, Charlotte," Maggie replied. "If I don't see you during the day I'll stop in before we take Ida over to Brentwood."

She decided to stop in to see if Ida was still in her room, and found her sitting in her wheelchair holding a photo of her with Cassie and Teagan, taken right after the closing performance of 'Kiss Me Kate' earlier in the year.

"Morning, Ida," Maggie said with a smile. "I guess I don't have to ask if you remember where we're heading today."

Ida returned the smile as she carefully place the photo back on her bookshelf. "How I loved watching the two of them perform that night. I'm so grateful that their friendship has continued to grow. I'd be ready to go right now, if we could."

Maggie chuckled. "They wouldn't even let you in the door at this time of day. But I'll come back to fetch you at 3:30 so we can get over there by 4:00 when visiting hours begin, okay?"

"Will Teagan be riding with us?"

"Absolutely. She knows how to keep you in line better than I do. You better get yourself down there soon or she'll come looking for ya – or worse yet, they'll send Melvin."

"I'm on my way."

"I'll give you a push if you want – then you'll have all your energy later when you need to get in and out of my car."

"That would be appreciated, my dear. I can't thank you enough for lining up our visit today. I'm looking forward to seeing my grand-daughter again."

Maggie grabbed the handles of the wheelchair and guided her down the hall. "Well, Ida, I stopped in briefly yesterday, and she's just as excited to see you again."

"Is she doing okay? I do worry about her."

"She's really committed herself to getting better. I think you'll notice a difference today when we see her."

"I'm so grateful that Teagan recognized the problem-- hard as that was for her."

"We all are. And look at them now! I think that's a friendship that will last. They have this certain old lady in common who they both adore and talk about all the time."

"Who are you calling old?" Ida joked as they entered the activity room. Maggie waved at Teagan who kept right on singing, and then watched as residents greeted Ida and made room for her in the circle. She remembered when Ida first came and how she always stayed on the perimeter, and now she was a well-loved member of the Caldwell family.

"I guess it's all about being brave enough to take risks," she thought as she headed to her office. She wondered if she'd ever be as brave as Ida had been when she decided to open her heart to new friendships— heck, a whole new life really-- this past year. She had managed it gracefully and Maggie was inspired by her.

Later that day, with Ida in the front seat and Teagan in the back, they headed to Brentwood. Ida was excited to be out and it showed. "Much as I love being at the Manor, I do miss getting out and seeing the sights."

Teagan leaned forward so she could talk easier to the two in front. "Ida, why haven't you ever gone on one of the van trips with Karen? She usually takes out a crew every couple of weeks to take a ride and sometimes stop for a treat somewhere. I would think you'd love that."

"Oh, I probably would. But I wouldn't want to be a bother and hold up the others with the wheelchair. I could never climb into the van. My legs aren't that strong anymore."

"That's what the wheelchair lift is for, Ida," Maggie said, "so you could stay in your chair if that was easier."

"I thought it would be more enjoyable for the others if they didn't have a wheelchair to deal with."

"Ida Vasilikas," Teagan said, "Are you saying that others would judge you for being in a wheelchair? Or is this maybe a little of vanity talking?"

Ida glanced back at the face peering from the back seat. "You really are one direct young woman, you know that? You know exactly what button to press."

Teagan laughed and reached up to give Ida's shoulder a squeeze. "You know it's only because I love you, lady. But either reason for not going out with the others is hogwash. I'm gonna call you out on it if I don't see your name on the list in the near future."

Maggie smirked and looked at Ida. "You know she will, too."

They passed the Brentwood Theater and Teagan pointed it out. "Remember when we realized that you had taken Cassie there to see Fiddler on the Roof the same night I was there with Joanne and Brian all those years back? Maybe we can look at what's coming soon and Cassie and I can take you together. How about that?"

Ida smiled at the memory. "That would be delightful. As long as it's a show that I know. I'm not sure about some of the new ones out today."

"You mean you don't want to fight Brian for his ticket to Hamilton next month? Not that you'd have a chance in hell to get it. Hamilton is one of the most popular new broadway shows in the past five years and I can't wait to see it."

Maggie looked in her rearview mirror. "Wait, you got tickets to Hamilton? How did I not know about this yet?"

"My folks got them for me for Christmas when the tour had just been announced. They're finally coming to Boston next month, and I can hardly WAIT."

"What an awesome gift. So, Ida, you don't think you'd wanna go and hear a lyrical rap musical depicting the birth of our country? Look around, look around at how lucky we are to be alive right now," she sang, and Teagan joined in.

Ida shook her head. "No, I don't think that's one I'd put on my list. I like the old classics, thank you very much."

Teagan laughed. "Don't worry, Ida, we'll find one that you can sing along to. But mark my words, you and Cassie and I have a *date* in Brentwood at some point!"

At that point Maggie pointed to a building up on the right. "That's the Phoenix Center, Ida. Isn't it a beautiful place?"

Ida studied the Victorian style and nodded as they pulled into the driveway and around the circle to the front door.

Maggie kept the car running as she opened the door. "I'll get your wheelchair and Teagan can take you in to sign in when I park the car, okay? I'll find you once I'm in there."

Teagan chuckled. "Yeah, Maggie knows her way around this place really well."

Ida's legs were weak, but she was able to take a few slow steps to get in and out of her wheelchair. Teagan smiled as she unlocked the chair. "Look at you, lady. You can still get around perfectly. Must be all the time you spend with that young physical therapist."

"His name is Jason, and he's a very nice young man. I often wondered if he wouldn't be a good match for Maggie."

Teagan laughed. "I thought that as well, but she didn't seem interested. But now I hear there's a nice looking guy staying over at the B&B." She leaned down to whisper in Ida's ear as she added, "Maggie actually went out on a date with him."

"Is that so," Ida replied with a twinkle in her eye. "I'll have to tell Jason he better move fast if he doesn't want to lose his chance." As they headed inside, Ida put her hand up for Teagan to stop a second to look at the stained glass phoenix. "That's simply stunning," she said, "and what a perfect image to greet anyone coming in or out."

The receptionist greeted Teagan and smiled kindly at Ida. "You must be Cassie's grandmother. She's told us that you were coming today. I even have a name tag all ready for you. Is Maggie with you today?"

"She's parking the car. Said she'd meet up with us," answered Teagan.

"Cassie is down in the lounge by the back door. She thought she might show Ida around a little bit at first and then head outside to visit. I think you remember the way?"

"Absolutely – and tell Maggie we'll wait there for her."

Teagan pushed Ida down the hall, and the older woman was thrilled to finally see her granddaughter curled up on a couch with her new sketch book and pastels. As soon as Cassie saw them walking in she put down her work and jumped up. "Gram! I'm so glad you finally got to come! I've missed you so much!"

After giving Ida a hug, she gave one to Teagan as well. "No Maggie?"

"She's on her way – just parking the car. I told them we'd wait here for her."

Cassie nodded, and then sat down on the couch as Teagan

arranged Ida's chair right next to it. "So how's my favorite family member?"

Ida reached over and patted her hand. "I'm so happy to see how much healthier you look. It's in your eyes. You have that sparkle back that was gone for a while."

Cassie nodded. "You're right, Gram. This place has given me a second chance. I've gained some weight back since being here and I feel okay about it. I know I still have a *long* road ahead of me, but I'm finally feeling like I can make it."

"It's nice to see you making eye contact again. I missed that so much. When your mom first told me that you were moving back from Houston I was so eager to spend time with you. And then, when you got back—" Ida's voice trailed off, as she didn't want to guilt trip Cassie when she was making such good progress.

"I wasn't a very good visitor, was I, Gram?" Cassie said, reaching out to take her grandmother's hand. "I'm really sorry if I disappointed you."

Ida squeezed Cassie's hand warmly. "Never mind that. The point is that's behind us now, and you're not alone in this battle."

Cassie nodded as she looked at Teagan, who had grabbed a chair and sat across from her. "I have this one to thank for that – even if I hated her at first."

Teagan winked at her friend. "Seems like forever ago, doesn't it?"

"Yeah, it does. Hard to believe it's only been a few months. God, I'm glad that you ended up in that show with me. I shudder to think where I might be right now if you hadn't seen what was going on."

She looked up to see Maggie walking down the hall, and turned to Ida.

"Now that Maggie's here, how about I give you the grand tour of this place?"

Ida squeezed her hand again. "I would love that—truly. I'm forever grateful that a place like this exists. I can see that it's brought my Cassandra back."

Cassie smiled. "It's a long road, Gram. But I'm definitely on my way."

CHAPTER 8

Friday morning when Maggie and Tramp headed around the corner from their apartment she was surprised to see Mr. Pritchard already dressed and heading down his walkway. What's more, the paper had already been picked up and put inside.

"Morning, Mr. Pritchard! You're up bright and early today!"

Tramp tried to approach him, wagging his tail, but stopped when the old man put his hand up. "I don't need dog hair on my clothes! Bad enough that you dig in my roses."

"Mr. Pritchard, Tramp has never dug in your roses. I watch him whenever we're in the garden. You must know that."

"Well, *something* was digging there when I was out yesterday. Can still see the holes, and I know beagles like to dig."

"Well, I can guarantee you that is wasn't him. We were only there for a little while in the morning, and then I was at work all day. Besides, Tramp has never been much of a digger. Where are you off to so early?"

Carl scowled and pulled a piece of paper out of his pocket. "Did you see this?"

Maggie recognized the article in the local paper about the proposed driving range and the scheduled town meeting.

"I haven't read it yet, but my sister was reading it this morning and gave me a summary."

"Well, I'm heading up to town hall to find out more about all this nonsense! Why the heck are they even giving him the time of day on such hogwash!"

Maggie remembered how he had fought the community gardens, and knew this would be a far more personal battle.

"Well, I think they *have* to have a public meeting – like we did for the gardens. That's where you'll have your chance to share your concerns about—"

"You think I'm waiting for a meeting? Those are just a bunch of people spouting off their mouths over nothin'. I'm heading up there right now to give them a piece of my mind!"

"But this meeting might be different, Mr. Pritchard. After all, we'll be on the same side supporting you this time. I think most of Caldwell will agree with you on this one."

"Well I'm still gonna be the first one to file an official complaint! That McClean kid is doing this on purpose, and he's not going to get away with it!"

As he stormed past them and crossed the street, Maggie called after him. "Have a nice day!" She looked down at Tramp and added, "Poor Lucy. Should I call her to warn her that Hurricane Carl is on his way to town hall?" Tramp wagged his tail and looked up at her innocently. "C'mon, boy, let's go get some veggies."

As she turned back toward the park her heart skipped a beat. She could see Tim by the gardens, and it appeared that he was studying Carl's house again. *"I wonder if he saw the old curmudgeon heading off to do battle? Or if he's even had the pleasure of meeting him yet? Or maybe he's waiting for me?"* A thrill went through her at the idea but she quelled it.

When Tramp caught sight of Tim he barked and picked up his pace. He clearly liked this new person in Maggie's life, and Maggie noted that Tim started walking toward them when he heard Tramp bark.

"Morning, Tramp. How's my favorite dog this morning?" He squatted down to welcome the beagle's warm greeting before looking up and smiling. "Morning, Maggie. I hope you don't mind that I greet your dog first. It's proper manner, you see, to make sure he won't attack me."

"Actually, you get extra points for that. Besides, he's a pretty good judge of character, and he's obviously given you his approval. I saw you studying the old house again, or maybe

you saw me talking to the old curmudgeon – his voice gets a little heated when he's riled up."

"He looked like he was off in a hurry."

"I imagine he'll be yelling at my poor sister in the next few minutes."

"Huh?"

"My sister Lucy works at town hall, and that's where he's heading."

"Should you be worried? He seemed like he was really mad."

Maggie smiled and shook her head. "That's his manner."

"So your sister's safe, then?"

Maggie chuckled. "Lucy can hold her own, trust me. You should have seen him in action when the community garden was being planned."

"He was against the garden?"

"He's against anything that gets too close to his house. And now that," she said as she gestured with her arm toward the old hardware store, "is supposed to become a golf shop and driving range, and he's fit to be tied. At least on this one he'll have lots of folks behind him."

"How do you mean?"

Maggie stared off toward the abandoned building. "I don't see it. There are so many things that building could be converted into, but a driving range? The ones here that golf are used to heading over to Brentwood—they have a beautiful course over there. I don't see the town getting behind this plan, and I can guarantee the old man will be leading the fight."

Tim's gaze traveled from the old hardware store toward Carl's house. "Yeah, I guess his house is the closest."

"Oh, it goes way beyond the house on this one. Unfortunately, I really don't have the time to get into it. I came to check on my plants, pull a few weeds, and harvest some veggies. Need to be to work a little earlier today."

"How about I pull the weeds while you harvest? Seems only fair since I took all of your time."

Maggie smiled. "Can I trust you to know the weeds from the plants?"

Tim looked mockingly offended. "I'm a culinary genius and you doubt my ability to tell a weed from a plant," he scoffed, but Maggie saw a grin and she couldn't help but smile herself.

"I have yet to get to know you better, my amateur chef. You'll have to prove your culinary genius to me soon so I can trust you with my precious plants," she teased.

"Fair enough. If I'm not sure, I'll ask. How's that?"

She looked at the sun shining on his brown locks and nodded. "Sounds like a plan, chef."

As they worked she shared more about the gardens, and how the three ladies had spent a year talking to town residents and gathering support. It had passed the previous year, and was now in its second season with almost all the allotted plots taken.

Tim looked at all the vegetables growing everywhere. "I'm kind of surprised. Wouldn't most of the town have garden plots in their yards? It seems like everyone as the space for it here."

"That's what we were afraid of when we started, but across the street there are two blocks that have apartments and townhouses, and they don't allow gardens. We were thrilled that so many residents expressed interest in this concept and thought it was a convenient spot."

"Well, judging from what's growing I'd have to agree."

"Besides, it's a great place for folks to gather and work together. If there's one thing I'd say against Caldwell—"

"Woah! You have something against Caldwell?" He placed his hands on his chest and fanned himself melodramatically. "I thought it was the perfect small town."

She laughed. "It really is--but there's no main gathering place. I mean, different churches have various groups that meet in their buildings, and the school runs a summer camp out on the ballfields." Maggie paused a moment to swat a fly that had landed on her arm. "We also have the library, the park, and the garden, but that's about it for communal spaces."

"So what's missing? Like, a community center?"

"Maybe. Or an arts center?" suggested Maggie, thinking about Cassie and useful a place like that could be in Caldwell. "I don't know – I know we don't need anything like Brentwood has with their fancy pool and modern building, but it's the one thing I wish we did have." She looked down at her watch and was disappointed with how fast the time had gone. "I really have to get going – and once again I did all the talking. I'm so sorry!"

Tim smiled. "No, I enjoyed it. I love hearing you talk about this little town. It's like I get to see the heart of this place."

Maggie blushed. "I'd love to hear you talk more. I know so little about you, and I keep on gabbing."

Tim helped her to gather her tools and produce. "Are you by any chance free tomorrow or Sunday? I have an idea that will help us to get to know each other better."

"O-kay….are you gonna share it or do I have to guess?"

"I think I told you I live up on the north shore. I need to head up for the day to check on my place and pick up my mail. I wondered if you and Tramp might want to come along. We could take a walk on the beach and then grab something to eat. Or better yet, I could cook for us. I have a great kitchen up there."

"Spoken like a true amateur chef," Maggie said kiddingly.

"Look, as good as Barb's cooking is, I really miss my kitchen – I'd love to make you lunch, if you're interested. No meat, of course. Every chef enjoys a good challenge."

Maggie looked down at Tramp and how he was so intent listening to Tim as he spoke.

"Well, I guess anyone who asks my dog to tag along on a date is hard to say no to."

"So…it's a yes?" He smiled as she nodded. "Which day works better for you?"

"Let's do tomorrow," she replied. "I think it's supposed to rain on Sunday."

"Sounds great. I'm looking forward to spending the day with you, Maggie."

"I am, too," she said as she gave him her address. *"More than you know."*

CHAPTER 9

Maggie was up super early the next morning so she could have time to get ready. She found her sister in the kitchen, and Lucy poured coffee into Maggie's favorite mug and handed it to her immediately.

"You're the best sister in the whole world," Maggie said as she took her first sip of the day. "Oh, God, that's delicious. And what smells so good this early?"

Lucy smiled. "I have blueberry muffins in the oven – they should be out in about fifteen minutes, which gives you time to take a shower and get dressed."

"Sounds heavenly, but I think I'll take Tramp out for a quick walk first. It'll be a long car ride."

Lucy put her arm up to block Maggie from heading for the door. "You'll do no such thing. You're gonna get ready and I'm gonna take my favorite dog nephew out for a quick walk. Then we can sit and wait for your dream date to arrive. C'mon, Tramp. Let's go greet the day!"

By the time the muffins were ready she had gotten dressed in a pair of tan capris and a tee shirt with a phoenix design much like the one at the Phoenix Center. She had pulled her hair back into a pony tail, hoping it would keep the frizziness to a minimum in the salt air. She hadn't been to the beach in ages. When Lucy got back with Tramp there were muffins, plates, and butter out on the kitchen counter.

"I'm almost too nervous to eat," she said. "I mean, I really don't know anything about him. What if he's a serial killer and he's taking me up to slice me into pieces and throw me into the harbor?"

Lucy laughed. "That's why you're taking a big ferocious guard dog with you." She looked over at Tramp, who had already sprawled out on his favorite throw rug in the living room. "Seriously, though, it's okay to be nervous. This is a big step for you heading off for a whole day with a guy."

"Hell, it was a big step when I joined him at Gino's for a couple of hours for dinner. This seems *huge* in comparison. What will I say? What if I realize he's really a jerk half way up there – then what will I do?"

"You'll tell him to go all the way around the rotary at the end of the highway and head straight back home – but I don't think that's gonna happen. I think a romantic walk on the beach and maybe even a kiss is far more likely."

Maggie laughed and felt herself relax a little. "I'm taking my time with this one. Will you have your phone on all day in case I have to text?"

"You know I will, sis. I'll be waiting up to make sure he gets you home before your curfew, too."

"And what time might that be?"

"Depends on how good a time you're having," Lucy said with a wink.

Just then the doorbell rang, and Tramp gave a loud bark as he headed to the door.

Maggie took a deep breath. "Well, here goes nothing." Lucy gave her a thumbs up sign as she went to let Tim in.

She opened the door to find him leaning on the porch railing. "Morning. Nice little porch here. Bet it's a great place for morning coffee."

Maggie smiled. "It is – although this time of year it gets a little warm. I love it in the fall when the leaves are all turning on the maples across the street. Come on in while I get Tramp's stuff ready." She led him in and gestured toward Lucy. "This is my sister Lucy. Lucy, Tim." Lucy got off the kitchen stool and extended her hand. "Great to finally meet you."

Tim took a step forward to shake her hand. "Likewise. And how is this little guy today?" he said as he bent down to give Tramp a welcomed scratch.

Lucy gave her sister a quick glance and mouthed the word "wow." "So would you like a couple of muffins before you head out? They're fresh out of the oven and probably still warm."

Tim took a long whiff and nodded. "Blueberry? How could I refuse?"

Lucy grabbed a plate and passed the basket of muffins. "Help yourself – there's butter here as well. If you want coffee there's still some left. I could even make you a cup to go."

"Thanks, but I already have coffee in the car. But maybe a little water?" He took a bite and smiled. "Hmm, these sure didn't come out of any box mix. Is that a hint of cinnamon I detect? Who's the chef?"

Maggie smiled and pointed toward Lucy. "We both cook, but she's taught me most of what I know at this point."

"I tip my hat to you. This is a nice place, too," Tim said as he looked around the living room. "I recognize one of Brooke's candles over there. What scent?"

"Strawberries and cream. We probably have another half dozen assorted varieties around the apartment. I think you bought an apple pie scent, if I remember?"

He nodded. "I went back and got a peach one the next day. They smell heavenly. So, do you have everything you need? I think we might hit the tail end of traffic heading up for the early parking spots at the beaches."

Maggie nodded. "I put everything into a bag last night. I just have to grab Tramp's leash and then we're good to go." She gave Lucy a hug. "Have a good day. Tell Liz I said hi. And Watson."

"I will. We're taking Watson to the park later on – or maybe up through the cemetery. It's gonna be a gorgeous day with low humidity. You two have fun. Drive safe."

"Aye, aye," Tim said as they headed out the door. His silver sedan was waiting out front, but before opening the front door for Maggie he opened the back door for Tramp. "Here you go buddy. You can play chaperone." He had laid a nice blanket on the back seat, and Maggie noticed a small dish of water on the floor behind the driver's seat. *"That's so thoughtful,"* she mused as she unhooked Tramp's leash and put her bag on the floor behind her seat.

Once they were in the car with seatbelts fastened Tim pulled out. "Music?" he asked as he pointed to the stereo system. "I have some smooth jazz on right now, but feel free to pick whatever you'd like."

"Jazz works for me," she said. "I like just about any music – except for maybe opera. Please tell me you don't love opera."

"Oh, dang. Should I drive around the block and bring you back home? Don't worry, I'm kidding. Definitely not my genre of choice."

"Then we're good – drive on." Maggie took a deep breath and exhaled slowly as the music calmed her. "Hmm…..nice sax. I don't think I know the song – but I like it."

"Harlem Nocturne by Bobby Zee. It's probably my all-time favorite jazz piece. You say you like all music, but do you have a favorite?"

"Depends on my mood and what I'm doing. If I'm working on the computer I usually have classical in the background. If I'm doing yoga then it's usually new age or meditative. If I go for a walk or I'm out for a drive I sometimes blast classic rock. Oh, and I'm slowly learning to like the *really* old music that my residents listen to."

"Like how old is really old?"

"I'm talking Mitch Miller, gay 90s, and then all of the big band stuff from the 30s and 40s. Some days it's hard to concentrate on my work if they're doing a music group – man, those guys like to sing. Loudly, I might add."

Tim smiled. "Sounds like you really like working with the elderly. Did you think you'd end up there when you first started social work?"

Maggie shook her head. "Nope. I thought I'd end up working at some kind of treatment facility for eating disorders – like the Phoenix. But then an internship opportunity came up for my senior year at the Manor, and a full time job opened up right after I got my license. By then I loved it so much that I was thrilled when the position was offered to me."

"It's good that you found the right spot early on. Some of us are still working on that."

Maggie turned toward him a bit. "Is this where I finally get to hear your story? I thought that was the genius plan, after all."

Tim laughed, but then his expression got more serious. "I'm dealing with a lot of frustration right now. Like, I know the path I'd *like* to be on, but it seems so complicated and I don't know how to get there."

"Are we talking work, family, or personal life?"

"Is 'all of the above' allowed as an answer?"

Maggie's face grew somber. "Wow, that's a whole lot of complicated."

Tim saw her face and continued, "Let me start by clarifying that I'm not married, divorced, or in another relationship. I realized that I sounded like I could be juggling a wife, an ex, and a mistress."

Maggie laughed. "Well, that's a relief. I admit that I briefly wondered if you might be married. You know, that whole 'complicated' line is usually a red flag from what I hear." She chuckled and added, "But then, my own personal life doesn't exactly make me an expert on dating."

"Honestly, that's the one area I feel pretty good about -- at least for today." He gave that dimpled grin that Maggie had come to love. "I'm glad you came along."

"I am, too. Although I wondered several times last night if I wasn't crazy. I even told Lucy that for all I knew you might be a serial killer who was gonna slice me up and throw my pieces into the harbor."

Tim's laugh made her day. "Do you want me to pull over so you can inspect my trunk for weapons?"

"Ahh….but maybe that's when you were planning to push me into the trunk."

"Good point. You better stay here where Tramp can keep an eye on you." He looked the rear-view mirror and smiled. "Then again, he looks pretty content right now – you might be in trouble."

"Thanks for letting me bring him along. I know some days are so long and I hate him being home alone."

"Do you kennel him when you're gone?"

"Nope. He has free run of the apartment. Most of the day I think he just sleeps. Or watches the world go by – I don't know if you noticed the bay window in the living room, but it's just wide enough for him to stretch out on."

"I suspect he sees a lot of squirrels and birds during the day."

Maggie chuckled. "Probably more of them than people, although the center of Caldwell invites a lot of people to walk from one place to another. I think he gets as much reality television as he wants during the day."

"I imagine you get a warm welcome home, though."

"Every night. Talk about unconditional love – I think he's really the one who taught me to love selflessly. He's such a good boy. It's been great for my health to have a pet. I'm never alone and I have a genuine reason to stay healthy for him." She reached back to stroke his head and he licked her hand and looked up.

"Sorry, boy," Tim said, "we still got a little bit of a ride. Do you think he'll need a pit stop along the way?"

Maggie shook her head. "He should be fine. He's used to being home all day."

She looked out the window to get her bearings. "It's been so long since I was up on the north shore. I think it was a 9th grade field trip up to the Salem Witch Museum."

"That's a pretty cool place."

"Yeah, it was. I wished we could have gotten a little more free time to walk on the beach, but you know how planned field trips are – not much room for spontaneity."

"When was the last time you were on the beach?"

"I went down to the Cape with Lucy and Liz one weekend – right after I graduated with my Master's degree. I remember how much Tramp and Watson loved playing in the sand and surf."

"Watson?"

"Liz's German Shepherd. He and Tramp are like best buddies."

"I take it that Lucy and Liz are a couple?"

Maggie nodded. "Yeah, I imagine one of these days they'll get married. They've been together about five years now."

"Any other siblings?"

"Nope, just Lucy and me. We were lucky – we've actually gotten along all of our lives. She's been my best friend for a long time. But hey, here I am talking all about myself again. This is supposed to be the day for Tim's story, remember?"

He smiled. "Hey, I love listening to you talk, what can I say? Besides, we still have all day."

"That's true. Do you have any siblings?"

Tim shook his head. Only me. Unlike you, my childhood wasn't all that great. I don't have a whole lot of happy memories to share like you do."

"I'm sorry. That must have been hard. I can't imagine not having the support that Lucy and my folks gave me."

"Yeah, well, that unfortunately wasn't my life. I mean, I think I've worked through it as best as I could. I did some therapy and that helped to let go of the anger, but the hurt sticks around longer."

He got quiet and Maggie let him just drive in silence for a while as she studied him. She could tell there was something there under the layers and knew well enough not to push. Her anorexia had taught her plenty about lingering pain and the time needed to heal completely. She closed her eyes and listened to the jazz, letting the smooth saxophone melodies lull her back to a calm place.

"I'm sorry," Tim said softly. "Did I come across as shutting you out just now? It wasn't meant that way. I haven't had a lot of practice in opening up about my past."

Maggie opened her eyes and gave him a reassuring smile. "Trust me, I get it. It wasn't until I was in recovery that I realized how hard it was to trust someone. I sensed that you've carried around a lot of pain and didn't want to push that."

Tim sighed. "It amazes me how well you seem to read me. I don't think anyone has ever made me feel so comfortable being myself. Thank you for that."

Maggie heart filled with peace and longing for the man sitting beside her. "I feel that same connection, and it's kind of exciting and scary at the same time, you know?" He smiled and nodded as she continued. "Let's table the painful childhood discussion for another time. Can you tell me about your school years? Where did you go to college?"

"University of New Hampshire at Durham. It was a nice campus and a good location for me. My parents were up in Maine and it was far enough away to not have to deal with them much."

"Did you always want to be an architect?"

Tim relaxed and shook his head. "I actually started as a history major – told you I was a nerd."

She chuckled. "So what changed your mind?"

"My roommate was from Manchester, New Hampshire, and he had invited me to spend the first fall break with him back home. While I was there I stumbled across the Currier Museum of Art, and they happened to own and manage two homes that had been built by Frank Lloyd Wright. I took the tour of both of them, and was in awe of how he designed two entirely different style homes to complement the relationship between building and the environment. I went back to school the next week and promptly changed my major to architecture and design."

Maggie studied him with regard. "That's pretty amazing that one day could change the direction of your life. Any regrets?"

"Absolutely none. I've loved the entire process from conceptual design to the finished building right from the start. Besides, my love of history has continued, and now I can appreciate the architectural aspects of what different timeframes have to offer."

"Do you have a favorite project that you've worked on?"

Tim laughed. "There have been a few waterfront projects I've really enjoyed – especially those that involved restoration of some of the older buildings. But on a personal note, I guess I'd have to say my favorite is the townhouse I live in. I helped to design the complex."

Maggie sat up with interest. "Now I can hardly wait to see it."

Tim grinned. "We're actually not too far away at this point. The traffic wasn't as bad as I expected – it'll probably be worse when we head home."

"I imagine it's a popular spot with so many beaches."

"From now until mid-September the weekends are crazy. Some weeks I just hole up at home for the entire weekend rather than deal with the traffic."

"How close are you to the beach?"

"About a block away. Which is nice, don't get me wrong. I like it better off season when all the tourists go home."

Maggie chuckled. "So instead you decided to play tourist yourself and annoy all us Caldwell folks."

"I sure hope that's not the case."

"You know I'm kidding. I can't imagine anyone in Caldwell not liking you."

Tim's expression grew more serious. "I'm not so sure about that."

"What's not to like? So what job are you—"

"Hey, watch it!" Tim yelled as a driver cut him off. "Sorry, there's a lot of crazy drivers this time of year. Some folks think they own the road, and others are all lost and trying to figure out where they're going."

Tramp had gotten up and was sniffing the air eagerly.

Maggie gave him a pat. "Did that scare you? It's okay, boy – he's a good driver."

"I bet he smells the salt air. Roll down your window a bit and keep your eyes open on your side when we get around the corner."

She did as he suggested and had to breathe in deeply as the salt reached her nose. "I must admit I envy you a bit if you get to smell that every day." Tramp tried to climb in her lap to get closer to the window. "Stay back there – that's your spot."

Tim responded by cracking open the back windows a bit, and

Tramp was quite content to move to the window closest to him. Maggie knew he had his front paws up on the door to get his nose closer to the window. "Hey, get down."

"He's okay. He can't hurt anything. And I have the back door locked so you don't have to worry about him hitting anything. Look, through the trees there," said Tim, pointing toward a clump of evergreens.

Maggie looked and suddenly saw the sun shining on the harbor with endless blue that extended to the horizon. "God, it's beautiful."

"We're almost there. Another mile or so."

Maggie enjoyed the scenery as more of the harbor became visible. She stared out the window at little cottages with clapboard siding, all painted different pastels and decorated with various seaside themes. Some people were working in their gardens, others were suntanning, and a few carried beach towels as they walked along the side of the road toward the harbor.

"When you said you were close you weren't kidding. Must be nice to be able to walk to the beach."

Tim made a right turn into a small townhouse complex that sat on a slope that led down to the harbor. The view from the top of the hill looked out over the water. Off in the distance, there was a stone breakwater wall that jutted out from the opposite side of the harbor. On that point stood a lighthouse with a caretaker's cottage beside it. Both were painted bright white with a red roof.

As Tim pulled into one of the first units Maggie took it all in. "I don't know, Tim. With a view like this every day the drive might be worth staying home instead of staying at the B&B."

He grinned as he turned the car off. "It's nice, but I really like the view in Caldwell."

Maggie blushed a bit as he came around to her side of the car as she got Tramp's leash attached to his collar. He opened her door and extended his hand, and she felt electricity as she touched him. Tramp's barking interrupted the moment as he insisted on being let out of the car. He immediately went to some of the landscaped walkways along the edge of the property, sniffing and discovering this new place.

"Do you need a pit stop? If not, I thought we could take a walk to stretch our legs a bit after sitting so long."

"That'd be nice," she answered. "I can just leave my bag in the car if that's okay and I'll grab it on the way back."

Tim pointed down to the lower end of the road. "There's a set of stairs down there that leads right down to the beach, but I thought we might head up through the park to see the harbor from the middle."

"As long as you can promise me that I'll get to feel sand between my toes at some point today I'm good with whatever."

"I wouldn't dream of driving up here without hitting the beach later on. The walk to the harbor won't include the beach, but it's a beautiful walk. It's about ½ mile each way if that's okay."

"Lead on; you're the tour guide today."

They turned right onto the main road and walked past a couple of houses and a small market before Tim led her to the right. A narrow road was full of cars parked along one side. To the left was a neatly mowed lawn that eventually sloped up a hill, and to the right, the lawn was scattered with picnic tables before gently sloping down to the ocean. Every table was occupied by groups enjoying their picnics, and blankets and towels were spread out all around with people reading, tanning, and talking. The chatter was accompanied by the steady rhythmic sound of waves in the background.

"Wow. This place is beautiful," said Maggie with wide eyes.

"This is Stage Fort Park, and as you can see, it's a mob scene throughout the summer. There are two small beaches, a gazebo for entertaining, a ball field, and a visitor center up there on the hill. A little too crowded for my tastes right now, but it's peaceful when it gets colder."

Tramp trotted alongside of them, stopping to sniff the grass and trees and wagging his tail at anyone who passed them by.

As the road sloped upward, Tim pointed down to the right. "That's Cressey Beach down there."

Maggie's gazed quickly down to see the beach, but was distracted as she turned her eyes to the gigantic rock formation that was ahead to the right. "That thing is huge!"

Tim laughed. "Yup, it is. About sixty feet high. That's Tablet Rock."

"I bet the view is amazing for all those folks up on top."

"If you look closely you can see lots of little stone stairways leading up and down. There's lot of little grassy picnics groves all around it, with some great rocks to climb all the way down to the water."

At the top of the hill, across from Tablet Rock, a white gazebo and modern visitor center provided restrooms and water fountains. Across the road was a huge parking lot.

"I wondered where all these people parked. The spots along the road didn't seem to be enough."

Tim nodded. "Like I said, this place is full every weekend. Do you need to use the restrooms or get a drink? And how about Tramp?"

Maggie looked down at the beagle, who was still happily taking in the sights and smells.

"He seems okay. Maybe on the way back."

As they continued toward the other entrance ahead, Tim pointed again to the right. "There's another little beach called Half Moon Beach down that hill, and then the point to the left has the actual remnants of the old fort."

"I kind of wondered why it was called Stage *Fort* Park. Any cannons left?"

Tim laughed at her excitement. "There are, actually – along with some of the old walls. I imagine it was a great defensive spot being right out on the harbor."

As they exited the park, the main road continued right alongside a huge stone wall that ran the length of the harbor with a rocky beach below. On the opposite side of the street, houses, shops, and vacation rentals faced the open harbor with only the main road between them.

"They must get some amazing sunrises," Maggie said, admiring the homes.

"Yeah, this is the highest rent district. I looked at a couple of town-houses up ahead, but decided the view wasn't worth the extra money."

They finally stopped when they reached a bronze statue of a fisherman looking out toward the harbor as he grasped the captain's wheel in his hands. Maggie read the caption etched on the base: "They that go down to the sea in ships…" Smaller plaques bearing names and dates lined the walkway.

"Gloucester's a major fishing town, and it's not an easy life. All those names are in honor of the locals who have lost their lives at sea."

Maggie stopped to lean her arms on the railing as she looked out over the harbor. "It's a nice memorial. And what a beautiful spot. I really like Gloucester – thanks for giving me a tour."

Tim leaned on the railing beside her. "It's been a nice spot to live, but I can't say that I've really connected to the community at all. I love the history, and the seafood is the best I've ever eaten, but I don't see myself staying here long-term."

"Is he really thinking of moving to Caldwell?" she thought cautiously. Pressing the issue, she answered, "So where would you go?"

He turned sideways toward her and grinned. "Right now I'm thinking I might like to try small town life. You happen to know any nice small towns to check out?"

Maggie laughed, loving the dimple that lit up his face. "I might have a lead for you on that."

"This is usually where I turn back. Are you up for the walk now, or would you like to sit awhile?"

Maggie looked at the benches along the walkway, and shook her head. "Nope, I think Tramp and I still good. It's hard to complain about walking when the view is so gorgeous."

As they started back, Tim took a long slow whiff. "Hmmm…..you can smell the seafood across the street. I must admit that I'm getting hungry."

"Yeah, I think Lucy's muffins are wearing off a bit."

"Too bad you don't eat seafood. The fried clams are awesome here."

"Hey, I'm fine with French fries if you want to get yourself some clams."

"Not today, lady. Remember, I told you I wanted to cook for you. I miss my kitchen."

"I will never say no to something home cooked – if you're sure."

He flashed her that dimpled smile that she was getting so used to. "Hey, I have a small cooler in the trunk of my car with groceries that I picked up last night. I think I would have been disappointed if you chose the French fries."

* * *

TWENTY MINUTES later they were back to Tim's car and Maggie grabbed her bag while Tim grabbed the cooler. He led them up a short walkway to a light gray clapboard style townhouse. As they entered, Maggie's eyes were drawn immediately to the opposite side which had a huge window overlooking the harbor. "Wow – that's a view I could get used to." She looked around the room and admired the clean lines and open space. "So you designed this place? It's so full of light – I love it."

"Glad you like it. I think most of the residents like it as well; not many have moved away since we first sold them."

Tim placed his bag of groceries on the table and unlocked a sliding door that led to a small patio with a table, two chairs, and an umbrella. Off to one side was a two-seated glider. "I'm thinking we could eat out here – the humidity's really low today, and if it gets too hot we can put the umbrella up."

Maggie put her hands on the smooth wooden railing and took a deep breath of salt air. "Why would you leave all this to stay down in Caldwell? This is magnificent." Tramp looked out the slats of the railings and yawned.

"Well someone's less impressed," he said with a smirk as Tramp plopped himself down. Tim surveyed the harbor. "It is pretty awesome." He placed his hands on the railing as well, touching her hand with one of his in the process. Maggie loved every touch but was nervous about reacting too quickly. Tim continued, "Great as it is, it's still missing something."

"Really?" she asked.

"It's still just a place. I mean, it's gorgeous, but aside from a couple of neighbors and some clients, I don't know anybody. It doesn't have that small town feeling that Caldwell has."

Maggie glanced at him sideways. "It sounds like you really want a place that feels like home. I'm sorry you haven't had that all these years."

"That's exactly what it is. I want a place that feels like home – like I belong there. Don't get me wrong; I love this townhouse. I pictured it in my head and it was amazing to watch it come to life. When the place was ready to start selling units, I was lucky enough to be able to afford one. At the time I thought it might satisfy that yearning, but I've realized lately that it's more about the people than the building." He paused for a moment, and Maggie wondered if he'd share more, but instead he stood up straight and gave her a smile. "You hungry?"

She nodded and followed him back inside where he started unpacking the food he'd brought along. They left the door open as Tramp was heading off to sleep. He gestured for her to sit at the bar. "Can I get you anything to drink? Water? Juice? Coffee?"

"Iced water would be wonderful. Can I help?"

"Nope, this is my kitchen and I'm thrilled to be back in it. All I need is for you to keep me company while I work. Besides, I've been looking forward to cooking for *you*."

"Well," she said teasingly, "when you put it *that* way I guess I can settle for being a spectator."

She watched him as he opened cabinets and pulled out a cutting board, a wok, and a bag of rice. "When did you learn how to cook?"

"Pretty early in life, actually. My mom worked so I was home by myself most afternoons. She wasn't super happy as the marriage wasn't a good one, so she had no motivation to cook those typical family dinners. I learned how to fend for myself by junior high. When I started reading cookbooks I realized that I could take a bunch of fresh ingredients and put them together in different ways to make great food – better than anything you'd find in a microwave dinner. In high school I started to walk to the local farmers' market and found the best price on the freshest produce. That's why I got so excited when Barb starting talking about the community garden in Caldwell."

Maggie watched him get the rice and water into an instapot and then pull a fancy knife out of a knife block on the counter.

"So what are you making today, my amateur chef? These ingredients look wonderful; the colors are so vibrant."

He gathered the fresh produce and washed it all in the sink before answering her. He had brought fresh broccoli, red pepper, yellow squash, carrots, onion, mushrooms, and fresh ginger. He removed a small plate from his cupboard and then sliced up a little pepper and julienned a carrot before placing them on the plate between them. He took a piece of red pepper in his fingers and gently reached over to feed it to her. "Try this. It's actually one of Barb's."

Maggie felt an odd excitement as his fingers touched her lips, and she could feel herself blushing as her eyes met Tim's. She bit into the pepper and gave a "thumbs up" approval. "That's good—and thanks for the appetizer plate. I have to say for a second it was a little weird having someone feed me."

Tim stopped short, his face concerned. "Oh, God, I didn't trigger anything, did I? It never even occurred to me that it might not be healthy for you."

She smiled reassuringly. "Again, there was a time when that might have caused a reflex action, but after having someone watch my every bite for many months, I finally learned to make peace with the food and recognize it as being something I could love."

"Thank God. I'd hate to think that my touch made you react negatively."

She paused for a moment before replying. "Quite the contrary – it was a pretty positive reaction." Nervous at being so open, she grabbed a piece of carrot and started munching to avoid a follow up question.

Instead, Tim just grinned and reached into the cooler, pulling out a small package of tofu. "To answer your earlier question, I thought I'd do a stir fry with tofu and a teriyaki sauce. You *do* eat tofu?"

"Almost weekly….and that sounds incredibly delicious."

Maggie loved to watch him work. He really was a master in the kitchen. She watched his hands as his knife skillfully cut through all the vegetables, and then admired how his body gracefully moved around his kitchen as he grabbed soy sauce and spices to make the sauce. He had no recipe, but moved like he had performed this "dance" enough times to memorize each movement. *"I bet he's an amazing dancer,"* thought Maggie, *"and I wonder what it would be like to be in his arms."*

As the sauce sizzled and the savory aroma wafted across the kitchen, Maggie admired his butt and how well his jeans fit. *"God, woman, get ahold of yourself! You can't rush this. Not until you know it's absolutely the right thing."*

The instapot gave a ding to signal that the rice was ready just as the stir fry was finished. Tim had perfect timing in the kitchen, and Maggie watched him plate the food to highlight the colors and textures perfectly. "I am so hungry looking at that beautiful creation," she said.

"Then let's eat. If you can carry the plates I'll get the utensils, napkins and drinks."

Maggie stepped outside and looked down at Tramp, still sound asleep in the sun.

"He doesn't look ready to eat yet," Tim said as he stepped out behind her.

"I think the long walk did him in for a while." She took a bite and smiled. "This is wonderful. A perfect mix of sweet and savory. And I love the colors. By the way, thanks for the tofu. That was really thoughtful of you."

"I admit, I did ask Barb if she knew what some of your favorite protein sources might be. I didn't want to serve something that you couldn't eat."

"Well, a stir fry is always a good choice. And I appreciate you accommodating my dietary needs. I was a little nervous about having someone cook for me."

"So what would you have done if I had forgotten the vegetarian part?"

Maggie laughed. "Let's just say that Tramp's bag doesn't just have food for him in it. I've gotten used to carrying a few staples that I know are safe to eat. I always have to plan, or I might find myself in a place where I can't eat something – and that might trigger me getting back into skipping a meal. I don't wanna go there."

Tim sipped his water. "There's still a lot about eating disorders that I don't know. Promise that you'll always be straight with me if there's an issue on anything I'm making."

"Does that mean I get to enjoy your cooking again someday soon?"

Tim flashed her that dimpled smile. "I sure hope so--but next time you have to help. This meal was your only freebie. I have to admit that I haven't felt a connection like this in a really long time."

Maggie felt the butterflies and returned Tim's gaze. "I feel the same. I'm not gonna lie – it's a little bit scary…but kind of wonderful, too."

Tim reached out and took her hand. "For me, too. I think I'd like to see where this relationship takes us."

She felt her hand in his, and how warm his touch was as his thumb caressed the back of her hand. "As long as you're okay with taking it slow. I don't know if I'm ready to jump into something really fast – this is the first relationship I think I've ever really had."

He leaned in and brought the back of her hand to his lips and kissed it lightly. Those butterflies turned into fireworks at the touch of his lips on her skin.

"We can take it as slow as you need to. I'm not exactly a pro at serious relationships myself."

Maggie sat back, her hand still in his. "I can't believe there hasn't been someone along the way. That dimple is enough to drive any woman wild."

Tim smiled. "There was one – right out of college. It became clear early on that she wasn't the one. Or maybe I wasn't ready for a relationship at that point. Heck, I can't promise that I'm ready for one now – but you make me hope that I might be."

Maggie smiled shyly. "I hope we both are. More than I can say."

Tim looked deep into her eyes, and then let out a sigh. He spoke quietly in a husky tone. "I think I better take these dishes inside before I decide to do something that might scare you off. You are so beautiful, Maggie Richmond."

He got up and took both plates, smiling at her before turning toward the door. She watched him go for a moment and took a deep breath. *"He thinks I'm beautiful,"* she thought. She followed him inside and gave thanks for the ability to feel worthy of someone's affection after years of hating herself.

Tramp stretched and followed them both inside, and Maggie pulled out his travel bowl and the food she'd brought for him. When she turned to put it down for him, Tim reached for the bowl. "Allow me?" He gently placed the dish on the floor as Tramp wagged his tail and began munching. "You're a good boy, Tramp dog." He stood back up and walked over to get the dishes, but Maggie scooted in around him and picked up the sponge by the sink. Tim tried to protest, but she held up her hand. "Hey, you cooked for me. It's a fair trade that I get the dishes clean."

"I do have a dishwasher, you know."

"But when you will you be back again? Isn't it easier to wash them now and put them away?"

"Okay, you have a point – but I'll dry then."

He grabbed a towel hanging on a hook by the window and they chatted more about cooking as the task was completed.

"Favorite meal to cook?"

"For myself? Probably a good steak – or some kind of fish. How about you?"

"I tend to keep things simple as I still haven't mastered some of the vegetarian sauces, but my macaroni and cheese is supposedly the 'bomb' according to Liz."

"Well that settles it. You'll make that for *me* when it's your turn to cook."

Maggie dried her hands on the towel he handed her. "I'd like that."

"Would you like to walk down and put your toes in the ocean before we have to head back? I'd like to get back before dark."

"I would have fought you if you'd try to leave beforehand."

He laughed. "How about we get our stuff now. I'll stop for my mail on the way out, and then we can jump in the car when we get back."

"Sounds good." She looked down at Tramp who was sitting and

looking out toward the patio, still licking his lips from his meal. "C'mon, Tramp. Time for some more exercise!"

They walked down the steps at the end of the road and Tramp immediately wanted to run.

"I think he's remembering how fun the beach was," Maggie said, holding his leash. "Wait a sec, boy. Let me take my shoes off. Gotta have bare feet for the beach."

Tim joined her, rolling up his trousers to just under his knees. He reached out for her hand, and she shyly accepted it as they crossed the small beach to the shoreline. There were very few people along this private stretch of beach and Maggie understood Tim's preference for quiet beaches.

"Just a warning," Tim said. "The water's gonna still be pretty cold this time of year. It's not as warm at the beaches on the Cape."

Maggie let out a little yelp and jumped backwards a bit as a wave hit her foot. "Yikes! You're not kidding! That's cold!"

He grinned. "Yup – but you get used to it." He splashed through the water like it was nothing.

They took a brisk walk along the shore line to the jetty at the end of the property and then walked back to the steps to retrieve their shoes. Rather than put them on, they both just carried them back to the car.

"I have a towel in the trunk – we can wipe our feet off a bit."

"Smart man. I can't promise I'll get all the sand off of Tramp, though."

"That's what the blanket on the back seat is for, so don't worry."

As they got settled in the car for the ride home, Maggie sighed, feeling content. "Thanks for bringing me along today. I had a blast."

Tim started the car and smiled. "As did I. I didn't realize how much I needed to get away and have a little salt air therapy."

"So what's going on that you needed an escape?"

"It's one of those complicated things on the list," he said as he drove. "Every now and then I find myself on a job that I don't enjoy and I don't agree with. But walking away or passing it on to someone else isn't always an option. I just feel stuck. And you know what?

Talking about work is just gonna bring me down. This day's going too well to mess up."

"I agree with that last point. But I can tell you after all my therapy that at some point you're gonna have to make a decision, and feeling stuck really means that you *do* have a choice but you're maybe afraid to make it. In the end our choices are all we really have control over."

"When did you get to be so wise at such a young age?"

She smiled back at him. "Do you *know* how much therapy I've had over the years? A little bit of sense is bound to rub off."

They got to the highway and Tim put the music back on. "Mind if we just drive for a bit? Music is good for me when my brain starts trying to talk too loud."

Maggie laughed. "Listen pal, I'm probably the queen of the talking brain syndrome. So if music helps, by all means play on."

The slow jazz coupled with the salt air lulled Maggie to doze for awhile. She woke back up to find that they were over halfway home.

"Hey, sleepy head," Tim said with a smile.

"Oh, my gosh, I fell asleep?"

"Hm-mm. So did Tramp. I think the salt air did you both in."

Maggie yawned as she tried to wake up. "I guess. I don't usually sleep in the car. I'm sorry about that. I'm a little embarrassed."

"Don't be. It was good for me – I was thinking about what you said about choices, and realized I need to look at that more. I guess I'll have something to do tomorrow. How about you? What's on your agenda?"

Maggie sighed nervously. "Actually, the next few days will be a little crazy for me. Tomorrow will be a major planning day."

"Planning? For what?"

"I was asked at the last minute to step in for someone who had to back out of panel presentations Monday and Tuesday at a social work symposium. I'm feeling totally out of my league, but I made the commitment to do my best. I guess I *do* understand that feeling of being stuck."

"Sounds like quite an honor. I'm sure you'll be awesome."

"Thanks for that. I know I'll spend all day tomorrow putting together my notes."

"Where's the symposium?"

"It's in Boston this year. I'll take the train in early Monday morning and get back Tuesday night. I keep telling myself that I wouldn't have been asked if I couldn't handle it, but I still get nervous. And being in a banquet situation where I don't have control over my food always puts me a little on edge."

"Well, your emergency bag is still packed," Tim joked. "Seriously, though, I'm sure you'll do an amazing job. I'll miss you, though."

Maggie smiled. "I'll miss you, too. Heck, I won't have much contact with the outside world at all once I get in there – but I think I'll miss you more than anyone else."

Tramp got up and began to look out the window again. "Someone knows we're getting close to home."

"See? That's what I'm missing in Gloucester. Caldwell isn't a place you live in– it's *home.* That's something I've never really felt, and I want that. I want a place where I feel like I belong. Being in Caldwell has made me think that places like that exist in the world."

"Well....there's nothing stopping you from making Caldwell a permanent home," suggested Maggie, grateful that he wasn't looking her as she blushed.

They had pulled up in front of Maggie's apartment, and Tramp was eager to get out.

"Don't think it hasn't crossed my mind," Tim said as they headed up to the porch. Maggie unlocked the door as Tramp was eager to go inside. "But even that's kinda complicated."

Maggie smiled. "Do you wanna come in for a bit?"

Tim shook his head. "As much as I'd love to, I have a few things I have to get done for work. But thanks for the nicest day I've had in a long time."

"Me, too."

Tim reached out and took her hand again. "Would I be moving too fast if I told you how much I want to kiss you right now?"

"I don't think so," she whispered.

He gently cupped her face with his hands and leaned down to kiss her softly on the mouth. His lips were like velvet on hers, and when he pulled back he held her face as he looked into her eyes. Maggie could feel his breath warm on her cheek and thought her heart would explode with emotion. He gently wrapped his strong arms around her and pulled her close, and she rested her hands on his chest as her face nestled into his neck. *"He smells so good,"* she thought, content to stand there in his arms feeling safe.

"Thanks for coming today," he whispered into her hair.

"I'm so glad you invited me. I hate to see it end."

"We'll do it again soon – I promise." He pulled away slightly, kissing her lightly on the forehead before letting her go. "This was the best day I've had in a long time. But I guess reality awaits."

Maggie leaned against the door frame and waved as he got back into his car. *"Soon. God, I hope you mean that."* She smiled as he pulled away, and headed inside to where her sister was no doubt waiting to hear all about her first real kiss.

CHAPTER 10

Maggie woke up Sunday morning and immediately smiled. She lay in bed thinking about her day in Gloucester – the comfortable conversation, the romantic walk on the beach, and the kiss on her front porch. Especially the kiss. *"Oh, God, what have I gotten myself into? And am I ready for this?"* Accepting that she had no absolute answers at that point, she got up, got dressed, and headed for the kitchen. A quick breakfast, followed by some time in the garden, would be the best therapy around.

Lucy had left a note on the counter saying that she'd be out with Liz for the day. "Guess it's just you and me today, boy." Tramp wagged his tail and walked toward the door, looking at her expectantly. "Let me grab a muffin and a swallow of coffee and we'll head out, okay?"

He sat down where he was and watched, his tail still wagging slightly. She was sure that he could understand her some days.

Lucy had made coffee and put it in the carafe, so it was still warm. Maggie enjoyed that first sip of the day and gave a long stretch toward the ceiling before taking that a bite of muffin. The sweetness of blueberries with a hint of cornmeal swirled in her mouth. "Hmm. I am so glad that I can enjoy the simple flavors of a home made muffin."

Tramp looked up at her listening to her every word. "Okay, boy – he kissed me. And it was really nice. So what do I do now?"

Tramp stood up, knowing she was still talking to him, and looked up at his leash.

"Yeah, I know. You like him. You think I should go for it." Tramp barked softly. "You're probably not the most objective therapist, ya know? I know, I know you need to go out. We can continue therapy later, okay?" She took another long sip of coffee, grabbed a water bottle, and then went to grab her gardening basket before reaching for Tramp's leash. She gave his head a good scratch after attaching his leash. "I think you're more ready for this than I am. You might have to help me, okay?" Tramp answered by helping to open the door with his paw and heading out the door quickly when she opened it.

Mr. Pritchard was just getting out of his car when she and Tramp headed by.

"Morning, Mr. Pritchard! You're up bright and early again!"

He scowled. "Needed milk for my eggs. Slept lousy."

"I'm sorry – hope it's nothing major."

"Nothing major? What would you call that atrocity they're gonna build behind my house? I'd say that's pretty major, wouldn't you?"

"It's not a done deal yet, Mr. Pritchard. There's still the zoning committee – they might not give him permission."

"Like he cares about that! That kid's been ignoring the rules all his life, and I bet he'll go ahead anyway. Those dang golf balls will destroy my roses – and your garden, too!"

"Well that's why we're gonna both be there at the meeting this week – to share our concerns."

"Won't matter. Town's gonna end up like Brentwood, you wait and see. And it's all because of that dang McClean!"

"Mr. Pritchard, why don't you concentrate on going in and making some delicious eggs for breakfast. We'll face that Sean McClean together on Wednesday, okay?"

He walked past her and up the steps grumbling as she called after him. "And this time I'm glad we're on the same side."

She could see the slight smile when he went in and closed the door.

The ladies were already in the garden, and from their expressions she knew that Barb must have heard a little from Tim about their trip.

"I hear that someone had quite a lovely time up on the north shore," Colleen said with a grin.

"The question that remains," Brooke replied, "is just *how* lovely!"

Barb laughed. "Well, judging from the smile on my guest's face this morning I'd say that it was quite lovely indeed."

Maggie chuckled, shaking her head. "You guys are like having three mothers, ya know that?" After she tethered Tramp, she turned back and added. "We had a really nice time. His place is gorgeous, the beach was wonderful, he's an amazing cook, and he's really easy to talk to."

"You gonna see him again?" Colleen asked.

Maggie nodded. "Sure seems that way." She could feel her face blushing and the other could evidently see it.

"Awww, look at her," Barb said. "We might have a real romance budding here, ladies."

"Can we focus on these buds for a while?" Maggie asked, hoping to redirect them.

Brooke laughed. "All right, Maggie--but only 'cause it's Sunday. Expect us to resume in the morning!"

For the next thirty minutes they chatted as they worked – mostly about the garden and the various vegetables that were starting to come in. Other community residents showed up while they were working as Sunday was always the busiest day at the garden. There was considerable talk about the upcoming meeting at town hall, and several residents planned to attend.

"Sounds like Sean McClean might not have a warm reception," Colleen surmised.

Barb laughed. "I'm not sure he deserves one. But it sure doesn't sound like many folks are behind his idea."

Brooke nodded in agreement as she stood up and stretched. "I can't imagine being here on a Sunday having golf balls flying that close by. I can understand the concern of parents with younger kids that are here at the park, too."

Colleen looked at Brooke and nodded in agreement. "You going to the meeting?"

"I'm not entirely sure. I hope to, but work is starting to get a little hectic now that the summer tourist season has started. I know it's still another couple of weeks before it gets busy, but I might need the time to get things ready ahead of the rush."

"Are you hiring extra help this year?" Barb asked.

"I'm thinking I might need to," Brooke replied. "It's hard finding the right person. They need to be okay to help in the store with customers when extra busy, but it would also be nice to have someone with some real artistic talent that could help prepare things to sell and tag the stuff that's ready."

"Maybe you should call the high school and check with the art teacher," Barb suggested.

"Good idea," Brooke replied. "Biggest problem is that most kids want full-time jobs, or at least twenty hours a week. I'm probably only looking for someone for ten to twelve hours at the most."

Maggie had an idea. "Brooke, how soon do you have to have a person hired? I might know a really good candidate, but it would be another couple of weeks until she could start."

They all looked at her quizzically. "Would you consider hiring Cassie if she was interested? She's incredibly talented, but I know she'd only be able to handle a job with fewer hours since she'll still be doing outpatient therapy. She's supposed to be coming home in the next few weeks."

"That might just work. Tell you what. I'll hold off advertising another week so you can talk to her about it. If you think she might work out then I'd definitely consider her first."

"I'm heading over there later this, so I'll talk to her then— and maybe her therapist as well."

"Is that allowed?"

"She can't talk about anything from actual therapy sessions, but because of my background – and how involved I've been with Cassie – she can at least offer general clinical observations."

"You've been a great support for her," Colleen said. "Maybe even more so than Teagan has been."

Maggie shook her head. "I'm not sure about that. I know that Cassie trusts me because she knows I've gone through it. But Teagan? She's become the friend that Cassie needed."

Colleen smiled. "I'd say that works both ways. Cassie's become just as important to Teagan. I'm so glad that their senior year is still ahead of them. I'd love to see them both back at the studio at some point."

"You might see Teagan, but Cassie still has a way to go yet before she can start getting back into any kind of intensive exercise. Maybe by fall she'll be okay to start slow."

Barb stood up and brushed the dirt off of her knees. "That must be hard for a dancer not to be able to dance."

"Every person is different. Some people need to stop exercising for a while to give their bodies time to heal. Anorexia effects more than weight – and part of putting the weight back on is tied into the distorted body image. It takes a lot of work to get better."

Colleen nodded. "I have to deal with students who have to stop because of injuries, so I can understand the time it takes for healing. I've seen a few come back before they should – must be even tougher when it's not just physical healing that's needed."

"Well, Cassie's been working hard. I know there have been good days and bad, but she's making really good progress. And now, ladies, I have to get going. I need to spend the afternoon getting ready for the symposium tomorrow."

"That's right," Brooke said. "You're heading into Boston in the morning, aren't you?"

Maggie nodded. "Yup. I don't know if told all of you, but I got asked to fill in for one of the panel speakers who had to back out at the last minute. I sure hope that I wasn't crazy to say yes."

Colleen looked at her approvingly. "That's awesome! What are you going to be talking about?"

"I'm on a panel that's discussing the need for building relationships with residents to optimize their care. I have some notes written down, but I need to organize them this afternoon."

"You'll be great at that," Barb said. "You've been such an asset to Caldwell Manor. The symposium will be lucky to have you."

Maggie laughed. "I don't know about that. I still have days when those old tapes start playing in my head, believe me. But so far a whole lot of therapy – and some great people – have helped me stay on track."

Brooke bent down to grab her stuff. "And now there might be someone new to add to that list of great people."

The others all chuckled as they gathered their daily harvest. Maggie unhooked Tramp's leash and faced the others. "That may be, but I'm still nervous as hell about how he might mess with my head."

Barb gave her shoulders a little hug. "Hey, romance can mess with anyone's head, sweetie. We've got your back, don't you worry—and we'll take care of your plot the next couple of days. Enjoy the ride – it's great to see you blush, girl." The others all nodded in agreement as they said their goodbyes and headed home for the day.

* * *

THAT AFTERNOON MAGGIE talked to her mom and filled her in on everything going on with Tim and the symposium. Her mom was excited to hear that she was "ready for romance", as she'd put it, and Maggie knew she'd have the support of both parents for whatever happened in her life. After hanging up she curled up on the couch with her notes on one side and Tramp on the other. She had packed most of what she needed for the next two days and now was glad to have the quiet time to prepare for her talk at the social work symposium.

While she was nervous about speaking at such a big event, she also reflected on how much her recovery had helped her regain a sense of worth and a willingness to take risks. She turned her attention to her notes, and within a few hours she had put together an organized outline of points to cover. She and the other panelists would each

99

have twenty minutes to speak individually followed by questions from those attending.

"That should work," she told her dozing beagle, who quickly woke up when he realized she was done. She got up and stretched, as did Tramp, and he followed her into the kitchen where she refilled her water bottle. She opened the refrigerator and glanced at the leftovers: some Asian veggies and rice, a container of roasted potatoes, and some salad fixings. She closed the door and looked down at Tramp. "I'm kinda in the mood for pizza – wanna go for a walk and we can go pick one up from Gino's?"

Tramp immediately spun around and headed for the door. He knew the word "walk" and was clearly in support of the idea. "Wait a sec, boy. Let me leave a quick note for Lucy in case she gets home, and then I can call in the order." Once the order was placed, she grabbed Tramp's leash and her keys and they headed out the door. They started in the direction of the park, but then turned left to head toward Main Street. It was only a few blocks to walk and it would be a perfect break from sitting all afternoon.

As they walked passed the dance studio on the right Maggie gave thanks that Colleen offered yoga classes weekly. Walking and some yoga had replaced running for her, and she was glad to have exercise options that didn't trigger her old obsessions. Past the studio on the corner was an attorney's office, and then she turned right onto Main Street to pass by Brooke's Treasures on the next block. Gino's was on the opposite corner at the next intersection of Main and Center Streets. As always, the parking lot was almost full as she crossed the street.

As the little bell signaled her arrival, Gino looked over from behind the corner and smiled. "You brought my favorite beagle!" he said with a smile. "I have your order ready."

He went to grab her pizza as a familiar voice spoke behind her. "My favorite beagle, too."

Tramp immediately turned around and started wagging his tail vigorously as he trotted over to Tim. Maggie stood at the door almost stuck to her spot. "Hi! I never expected to run into you here."

Tim smiled as he gave Tramp a good back scratch. "I guess great minds must think alike. I had actually considered calling to see if you wanted to join me--but didn't want to seem like I was pushing too hard."

"I can't say that I would have turned you down."

Gino brought her pizza and another bag to the counter. "Now how come you two order separately when here you are together? You could have eaten at the same table."

"It was a surprise to both of us, Gino. And I have Tramp with me, so we can't stay." As she gave Gino her money and waited for her change, Tim looked a little disappointed.

"Maybe I should have called," he said, handing Gino his credit card. "I would have enjoyed this calzone a whole lot more with your company."

Maggie smiled. "I suppose you could bring it over to my place and we could eat there…if you want."

The dimple in his cheek was there in an instant with his smile. "I would *love* that! And Gino, the next time I promise we'll come back together."

The old man smiled as he turned back to his pizza dough. "Buena serra! Enjoy that meal!"

Tim picked up both items from the counter. "I figure you have Tramp, the least I can do is carry your pizza."

"Do you have your car or did you walk?"

"I walked. I figured if I was gonna gorge myself with calzone I better walk over to get it. I'm assuming you're on foot as well since Tramp's along."

She nodded as they crossed the street and headed back past Brooke's Treasures. "I spent the afternoon getting my notes ready for this symposium tomorrow, so I figured I deserved some pizza as a reward. I figure I can take a couple of leftover slices along with me for my hotel room fridge."

"Good choice for emergency food," he said with a chuckle. "So are you ready?"

She rolled her eyes. "As ready as I can be, I guess. I didn't have much time to prepare, but maybe that was a good thing since I didn't have as much time to doubt myself."

"That makes sense. I'm sure you'll do an awesome job. I suspect that you bring a lot of joy to the old folks that you work with every day."

"I love going to work every day, and those guys touch my heart in countless ways."

"I imagine you touch a lot of hearts as well, Maggie Richmond."

She felt herself blush wondering if there was a hidden meaning in what he said. "Enough about me. How did you spend your day?"

He grinned at her. "It started with a lot of thinking about the great day I had yesterday." As Maggie smiled at him, he continued. "I let my history nerd out for awhile. Brooke had a pamphlet on her counter with some of the local landmarks from the Revolutionary War period and I drove around to see a few. I can see why Caldwell would attract some history buffs during the summer. I wish you could have come along."

"I would have loved that," she said warmly. "I remember touring them as a kid during class field trips, and I thought they were pretty boring. But then I went back through them in the past couple of years and had a new perspective. I think school field trips are more pleasing to the chaperones in terms of history."

"The kids probably just like getting out of school for a while."

Maggie chuckled as they turned onto Hamilton Court. "So this is our little townhouse development. There are eight buildings, each with two townhouses. Pretty basic, but I love being right here in town."

"Is it okay with your sister that I'm barging in tonight?"

"Well, you're hardly barging in if I suggested it, but she may not be home yet. She had left early this morning to spend the day with Liz. I imagine she'll pop in at some point if she's not already home. Otherwise you might have to help me with this pizza."

Tim grinned. "From everything I've heard about Gino's pizza, I don't think that will be a problem."

Within minutes they had gotten back to Maggie's place, unhooked Tramp's leash, and taken plates and silverware out of the cabinets.

"Can I offer you something to drink?" Maggie said as she grabbed a couple of glasses.

"Iced water would be great."

She smiled, loving that he shared her appreciation of good old water.

"Why don't we get our plates ready here and sit in the living room to eat," she said.

"Since you expect help with the pizza, I'm cutting this calzone into quarters so you can return the favor. It's just spinach and cheese."

"How can I refuse? I love almost anything with spinach and cheese together."

Maggie grabbed her notes off the end of the couch and put them on the counter. They both sat down, and she watched him take his first bite of pizza.

"Oh, God, Gino alone is reason to live in Caldwell. How can something be that good?"

Maggie smiled, taking a bite as well. She gestured toward the calzone. "You'll love that, too – guaranteed."

They ate in silence for a few minutes, enjoying the flavors as much as the company. Maggie finally spoke first. "So, what's the next installment of the Tim Collins story? I've still only heard bits and pieces."

Tim slowed his chewing as if in thought. "Last night I was thinking about what you said regarding choices yesterday, and how that's all we have. I realized that there are a few really important choices that I need to make—and *want* to make--and then," he stopped is as though trying to find the words, "there's that part about choices having consequences. It makes it a whole lot scarier."

Maggie put her pizza on the table and turned to Tim. "Look, I don't have any idea what it is you're trying to say or avoid saying. But I do know that sometimes you just gotta take that step and let the chips fall. I like to think that I could handle whatever it is you had to tell me – I mean, you *did* assure me that you're not married or a serial killer."

Tim put his plate down and gently reached for Maggie's hand. "There's something I really need to tell you – it's related to all the reasons I'm in Caldwell right now. And I really hope you can—"

The door flew open with a bang and Lucy came in. Tramp barked and ran to greet her, and Lucy stopped short when she saw Tim and Maggie on the couch holding hands.

"Ah, jeez, I'm sorry. I didn't mean to barge in. I can come back later if you want."

Maggie pulled her hand away from Tim and stood up to hug her sister. "That's silly, sis. It's your house. I think you remember Tim."

Tim stood up as well and extended his hand. "Nice to see you again, Lucy. And you didn't interrupt. We can always pick it up later on."

"Grab a plate, sis, and join us. There's pizza and calzone."

Lucy grabbed a plate and did just that, leaving Maggie wondering what Tim was going to tell her.

CHAPTER 11

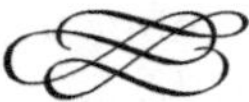

*M*onday morning Lucy dropped Maggie off at the train station and she settled into her seat for the forty minute ride into Boston. The rhythmic clickety-clack of the train helped to calm her nerves about speaking later that day, and she looked out at the window and thought back to Tim the night before. He had seemed reluctant to leave when they all finished dinner, as though he really wanted to continue their conversation before Lucy arrived home. *"I hated cutting the night short,"* she thought, *"but I knew I had to practice self care to get enough sleep for today."*

She sent him a quick text. *"Morning. On the train and wanted to say I was thinking about you. Have a good day."* This time she only hesitated a moment before adding the heart emoji. Within minutes her phone vibrated and she smiled when she saw his name pop up. *"You, too, Maggie. I know you'll be wonderful today--good luck. Miss you already."* He had also added the heart emoji, and Maggie took a deep breath and let it out as she enjoyed the feeling of new romance. The man beside her was focussed on his newspaper, so she pulled out her notes to look them over one more time. During the trip she got other texts of support from her mom in Florida, Brooke and the garden ladies, and her therapist Natalie, who kept her message short: *"You've got this. Go show them what you've got."*

* * *

THE DAY FLEW by and Maggie's presentation was well received. Her fellow panelists told her she had done a fabulous job, and Jane Simmons stopped her during dinner to thank her for jumping in last minute. "I caught the first half of your panel discussion and you were amazing," Jane said. "I can't thank you enough for joining us on such short notice.

"Thank you so much," Maggie responded. "I enjoyed being a part of it."

"I hope you'll consider being a speaker again next year—everyone I've spoken to agreed that you offered so much insight on the different ways our seniors can thrive and grow in their later years with us."

Maggie was taken aback, but smiled with composure. "I'd...be delighted to. Thank you so much for the opportunity." By the end of the day, she was both exhausted and grateful for how much she'd been able to experience. *"Another amazing day of recovery,"* she thought as she headed up to her room.

She was getting ready for bed when her phone vibrated. *"I hope all went well today. I wish you were home – I really wanted to finish our talk from last night."*

Maggie smiled at his thoughtful text and considered calling him, but she knew she had to consider her recovery first. She had another full day coming up and knew she needed to sleep. *"It went well – thanks for your kind words. I wish my schedule wasn't so crazy. Heading to bed now, but I'll call you tomorrow when I get back. Sleep well."*

* * *

TUESDAY FLEW by as quickly as Monday did, and Maggie was tired when Lucy greeted her at the train station. "How'd it go?"

"Really well," Maggie said wearily, "but I'm beat. I want dinner and pjs, not necessarily in that order."

Lucy chuckled. "Get your pjs on first. I have dinner in the crockpot all ready."

Maggie closed her eyes and smiled. "I have the best sister in the entire world."

"Don't you ever forget it, either," Lucy teased.

The drive from the train station was only a mile long, so in no time at all Maggie was in her pjs on the couch with Tramp beside her and a bowl of vegetarian chili in her hands. She savored every bite of the warm and spicy bean dish and licked her spoon when done. She turned to her sister after placing her bowl on the coffee table. "That was perfect. Thanks so much for having it ready."

"Not a problem. I figured you'd be wiped. And you can tell me about it tomorrow, or even Thursday. Don't forget we have the town meeting tomorrow night."

"Couldn't if I tried," Maggie replied. "And much as I'd love to talk, I think I'll take you up on putting it off. What I really *should* do is call Tim. He texted last night and I get the feeling that he really did want to tell me something the other night. I told him I'd call tonight, and I think that's all the energy I'm gonna have for conversation.

Lucy nodded as Maggie took out her phone and texted. *"Hey, I'm home. If you still wanted to chat I can call now if you'd like. Looking forward to seeing you again."*

The response wasn't what she expected. *"Would love to talk, but work got insane today. Will be working late again. Time to look for a new job. Thinking of you."* At least he had added a heart emoji. She turned to Lucy as she put her phone down. "Turns out tonight is his turn to be busy. I guess that means I can go to bed early. Night, Lucy. It's good to be home." With that, she brought her bowl to the sink and headed off to to her room with Tramp right behind her.

* * *

WEDNESDAY MORNING MAGGIE and Tramp passed by the old curmudgeon's house right on schedule. "Morning, Mr. Pritchard. How are you today?"

The usual scowl greeted her as he got his paper. "Ask me that tomorrow, after that no good McClean kid shows up for the council meeting."

"I'm glad you'll be there to help us fight this one, Mr. Pritchard. I think there's a whole lot of town folk on our side on this debate."

"Yeah, well we'll see. Sean McClean has a way of wreaking havoc everywhere he goes."

"Do you need a ride tonight? I'd be happy to swing by to pick you up."

"Gonna walk. I can practice my speech on the way." He turned to head back up the driveway.

"Well, maybe a ride home, then," Maggie called out after him. He did his backhanded wave as he went up the steps.

"C'mon, Tramp. Let's go get some fresh veggies. Maybe we can leave some on his porch tomorrow."

The ladies were all in their adjoining plots and eager to hear about Maggie's symposium. After catching them up on her presentation, conversation turned to the upcoming council meeting. "So Mr. Pritchard is ready to go on the warpath tonight. I'm glad we're not on the opposite side tonight," Maggie said.

Brooke laughed. "He didn't like us very much when this garden got approved. I can't imagine what he'll be like if the driving range gets the okay."

"God help the poor soul who accidentally hits those rosebushes with a golf ball," Colleen added. "I swear those roses are the most important thing in his life right now. So Brooke, are you gonna get there tonight, or do you need to work?"

"I'll be there. I can spend some extra time over the weekend in the store. I remember how good it felt to have so many behind us for the gardens. I wanna give that support back to the opposition tonight. Maggie, I'm assuming you'll be there – unless you have another date."

Maggie smiled. "Wouldn't miss it. I haven't seen Tim since Sunday – but I've been pretty busy."

"So has he," Barb chimed in. "He's left the B&B right after breakfast the past two days and gotten back well after dinner. I've seen his light on late in the apartment as well."

"Maybe he's sitting up thinking about a certain young lady in town," Brooke joked.

"Nope, he's definitely working – super stressed, I might add. Last night he texted that it was time for a new job, so it must be bad."

"Hmm, I wonder…." Maggie said quietly to herself, then noticed the others looking at her. "It's just that he started to tell me something the other night – it seemed really serious – and then Lucy got home and we never got back to it. It might have been the job stress."

"So he was at your place Sunday?" Colleen asked with a smirk.

"It wasn't planned. We ran into each other Gino's picking up our food, so we ended up taking it back to my place to eat together." She paused a moment, and then added, "It was kinda nice, not gonna lie."

Brooke got up and started gathering weeds and scraps for compost. "I suspect there's gonna be a lot of travel between here and Gloucester once Tim leaves the B&B. That's my prediction, anyway."

"I hope you're right," Maggie said with a blush.

"Oh, I second that prediction," Barb said. "I think there's definitely a budding romance going on in our little town of Caldwell."

Colleen got up to stretch. "May it thrive and bloom as long as Mr. Pritchard's rosebushes." They all laughed as they finished up their watering and headed in different directions.

A couple of hours later Maggie dropped in to the activity room at Caldwell Manor as the smell of something wonderful mingled with laughter from various residents. Teagan and Ida both waved as she walked in, and Teagan's friend Brian was helping Kitty to spoon batter into muffin tins.

"Must be those blueberry muffins you talked about last time," Maggie said. Kitty nodded, smiling warmly at the young man who was holding her hand to steady it as she worked.

"She'll be flirting with men until the day she dies," thought Maggie. Teagan came over to chat as Brian continued and echoed the senti-

ment. "She sure knows how to flirt to get her way with the men—even the gay ones."

Maggie laughed. "Doesn't look like Brian's having a terrible time."

Teagan looked back at her friend and agreed. "He loves coming here, and the residents adore him – especially the ladies! Hey, how was your conference?"

"Jam-packed, but I learned a ton and met some nice contacts. I even made it through my panel discussion with flying colors."

"I'm not surprised at all by that," Teagan said, peeking back at the others to see if she was needed yet.

"Have you seen Cassie the last couple of days? I missed getting over there yesterday."

Teagan nodded. "I went over Monday for visiting hours and chatted with her and her roommate for awhile. Molly hasn't been there as long, but she seems to be progressing."

"She's got a good role model with her. Did Cassie mention any discharge date yet?"

"Not yet, but she talked about it. She's a little nervous about what she's gonna do for the rest of the summer."

"Actually, I have an idea on that."

Kitty interrupted them from across the room. "Miss Teagan! Brian said there are ready for the oven! Can I help him?"

Teagan nodded. "Be careful and use that potholder. I'll be over in a minute to help with clean up." She turned back to Maggie. "I guess I better get back to work. I'll bring you a muffin when they're done."

"That would be awesome – I'll share my idea with you soon to see what you think."

She stopped in to Charlotte's office next. "Morning. I was checking in to see if you had all the medical info ready for Alice Kennedy's transfer today."

The nurse handed her a file. "She's all set to go. The family's picking her up later today, and I have her meds organized and packaged for when they leave. Did you work out her physical therapy issue with Jason?"

Maggie nodded. "Works out perfectly. Because he's an outside contractor with us, he can add her to the clients he works with on his other days. I have to clear it with insurance and he'll be set to start with her at home for another month."

"That will make her happy. She loves Jason."

"Don't we all?"

"So how was the symposium?"

"It was really informative. I owe you for recommending me to Jane – the panel discussion was a big hit and I met some great contacts. She even asked if I'd commit to going back next year as a speaker."

Charlotte beamed. "Look at you, lady! You've come so far in the past few years. I'm proud of you." She smiled a bit, and then added, "I guess you'll be looking forward to seeing someone now that you're back?"

"Not tonight, Charlotte. I'll be spending this evening with a much older man." She waited for the questioning expression. "It's the public meeting tonight, and I told the Mr. Pritchard that I'd give him a ride home. Tim will just have to wait."

Charlotte laughed. "I guess Tim's learning early on that part of your heart will always be with the old folks in your life. Somehow I don't think he'll mind sharing."

"Time will tell," Maggie surmised. "For now, it's time to go and battle with the insurance company." She headed to her office and got a few productive hours in before her phone dinged. She smiled when she saw Tim's name come up. *"Work is insane. I really need to talk to you tonight. I know you have that meeting—promise me that we can talk when it's over. Missing you so much."*

"This must be what he was trying to tell me Sunday; it sounds so important," she thought. *"I wonder if he's actually going to quit his job and move to Caldwell?"* She smiled at the prospect before replying. *"Sorry work is so terrible right now. I'll call you when I'm home from the meeting. Maybe we can go to the diner afterwards – it's open late. Miss you, too."*

CHAPTER 12

That night town hall was filled to capacity to finally hear the proposal from Sean McClean. Maggie arrived and walked through the two sets of thick wooden doors that had been installed years earlier as a sound barrier for outside noises. She stood by the back row and looked toward the front until she spotted the three ladies from the garden; Barb gestured that they had a seat for her. At the same time, she noticed Mr. Pritchard sitting in the back row with a free spot next to him. He sat there alone among the crowd, his arms folded tightly across his chest as he waited for the meeting to start. Maggie gestured back to Barb that she was going to sit where he was.

"Hey, Mr. Pritchard – is this seat taken?"

"Don't see anyone sitting there," he said with his usual scowl, but he scooted over with a slight smile on his face. "Glad you're on my side this time."

She smiled back and winked at him. "Me, too."

Carl's eyes narrowed as his gaze went past her to the front of the room. "There he is, the arrogant bastard."

Maggie followed his gaze to a middle aged man in his fifties wearing a wrinkled suit that looked like it had been purchased when Sean was twenty pounds lighter. He sat alone at a table, looking at his watch and the empty chair beside him, then sat back shaking his head as he wrung his hands together. *"He sure doesn't seem too confident,"* Maggie thought to herself.

She spotted her sister Lucy at the end of the front table, as she made a little extra money taking notes for many of the public town hall meetings. There were five on the zoning committee, headed by Teagan's dad, Rich O'Sullivan. He called the meeting to order with his gavel and addressed the room.

"Tonight we're hearing a proposal from Mr. Sean McClean for the site where the former McClean's Hardware Store is located. Mr. McClean will have time to make his proposal, and then we'll open up the meeting to residents for comments and questions. Please remember to stand and raise your hand if you wish to speak, and wait to be acknowledged. You'll be asked to give your name and your address. Only town residents are allowed to speak. Any questions on procedure?" When no one answered he added, "Refrain from any comments outside the procedure I outlined, or you may be asked to leave the meeting."

Maggie was sure that the speaker was looking directly at the man seated next to her, as Carl quietly muttered to himself. She could see the tension in his left hand as he squeezed his right elbow, arms still tightly crossed in front of him.

Rich O'Sullivan addressed Sean directly. "Do you have any visuals on a flash drive? If so, you can hand them to Lucy and she'll have the clerk set it up."

Sean shook his head. "I don't really do any of that modern computer stuff – just the papers."

A couple of the committee members looked at Sean questionably as Rich once again addressed the meeting. "Sean will have the microphone at this time. Mr. McClean, the floor is yours." *"Here goes nothing,"* Maggie thought as Sean stood up to speak. He tapped the microphone hard with his finger, causing loud thumps to come through the sound system. He chuckled as he turned to face the crowd. "Hey, it works," he said, oblivious that no one had laughed along with him.

"Yeah, so I'm obviously here to talk about the property that was once my dad's hardware store. I know it's been sitting for a long time, but I decided it was time to bring a good business into town that will spruce the place up a bit – which I know is something we all want."

He kept pivoting on his feet a bit so that he could talk to both the committee and the residents behind him. "Now I know the property is next to the park, so obviously that lets out anything loud or too busy I don't wanna bother any family playtime at the park, or make too much noise and upset the plants."

His attempt at a joke got a few chuckles, but his tone was condescending; Maggie got the feeling that he was at a definite disadvantage with those crowded into the room.

"So what I'm proposing for the site is a perfect solution. It's gonna be a golf center. We'll have a little shop inside so you don't have to go all the way to Brentwood to buy your clubs, and we'll have a pro on staff so you can have lessons with simulated golf programs, or practice on your own. Outside, along the back of the property, we'll have a driving range so you can practice your swing in between visits to the Brentwood course. Nothing too big, don't you worry – only five or six lanes." His voice got a little more animated as he brought his hands up toward the crowd, almost as if he were trying to push them away from him. "It'll be up to code and perfectly safe, with a new fence along the property line and lots of netting to keep any stray balls on our side of that line. It'll be great—and exactly what we need to bring a little more class to Caldwell."

The murmurs heard on his last statement no doubt reflected the disapproval in the room.

Mr. Pritchard started rocking back and forth as he glared across the room. "He's an ass," he hissed silently, and Maggie knew that it was a matter of time before the vocal explosion erupted from the old curmudgeon, probably verbalizing what she and everyone else was thinking.

Rich O'Sullivan also heard the murmurs, and spoke to the crowd. "Just a reminder, this is still Mr. McClean's time. Please hold your comments and questions until we open up the microphone to the floor." He then looked at the developer and continued. "Mr. McClean, have you spent any time doing any kind of survey on the needs of the residents here in terms of the business you're proposing?"

Sean looked briefly around the room and back at the committee. "I don't believe that's required by any law. I do own the property – I should be able to do anything I want with it."

Mr. Pritchard sprung to his feet and shook his arm violently as he pointed toward Sean. "Half the property! You only own half the property, and you know it!"

Rich O'Sullivan banged the table with his gavel as he addressed the old man. "Mr. Pritchard, you need to quiet down. You will have an opportunity to speak soon, but may I remind you that future outbursts will mean that you'll have to leave." Carl sat down hard, still breathing *heavily* as he rubbed the top of his thighs with his hands, rocking back and forth.

Maggie patted his arm. "It's okay," she whispered. "You'll get your turn."

She wondered about his outburst as Sean was directed to continue.

He faced the committee while taking a bunch of papers out of the folder in front of him. "The old man's referring to a prior partner who had invested in the property. He no longer owns his shares and is therefore not relevant in this case. These plans are the initial blueprints for the new establishment." He handed a pile to Lucy who was at the end of the main table. "Hand these down the line, girly." Lucy glared at him as she took a copy of his proposal and passed the pile on to her right, rolling her eyes as she picked up her pen to continue with notes.

Maggie wanted to laugh. *"He's so lucky she didn't throw them back in his face."*

Sean continued, oblivious to any offense taken by the young woman he'd insulted. "You'll see that there's plenty of parking so folks won't need to use the lot at the park. And you can see where the fence will be put up – at our expense, of course – for the privacy of those that live along the street."

The committee members all glanced through the sheets in front of them. Rich looked his over and asked, "Is this the official design that's being entered for proposal? Is there a reason why it wasn't turned in prior to the meeting as is requested with your application?"

Sean looked again at his watch. "My partner must not have gotten it in on time. These aren't the current ones. There's a new one I had done recently."

Rich put down his papers and leaned back in his chair. "Might I ask then why you've handed these to us if they're not accurate?"

"I picked up the wrong file; my partner has the up to date one. I called him before the meeting and he's bringing them right down now. Should be here any minute."

One of the other committee members, looking slightly perturbed, addressed Sean. "Can you at least tell us how the new proposal is different than the ones we're holding?"

"Look, it's no big deal," Sean answered arrogantly. "It wasn't my fault. They weren't labeled right--but there's no change in the overall design of the building, only the fence."

"The fence?" asked Rich.

"Yeah, the placement of the fence." He again turned slightly sideward so that he could address both the committee member as well as the others in the room. "It's only gonna affect one house. It's a little thing – and we'll cover the expense."

As all eyes watched, he continued. "The new survey we did – it showed that one small line of bushes was actually over the property line a little, so we'll only need to take those out to make sure the fence is in the right place."

Carl was on his feet before Maggie could stop him. "You're not touching those roses, do you hear me?! You think you can come back here and pick up where you left off all those years ago? You're a scumbag, McClean!"

"Mr. Pritchard!" The gavel hit the table repeatedly as Rich O'Sullivan tried to regain order. Everyone in the room was talking and watching the old man now.

Maggie stood up and tried to take Carl's arm, but he waved her off.

"You'll touch those roses over my dead body, ya hear me McClean?!" he shouted across the room. Maggie looked over at Sean, who stood there with a smug look on his face, almost as if he were enjoying the moment.

"Mr. Pritchard, you're going to have to leave the room – you are out of order!" demanded Rich O'Sullivan. As a town police officer came up the aisle to escort Carl out, Maggie spoke to the man shaking next to her. "Mr. Pritchard, come on. Let's go get you some water. I'll go with you and you can calm down a bit – then you can come back in to talk."

The old man swore and stormed through the two sets of doors with Maggie right behind him. She looked at the officer who she knew and put her hand up. "I'll sit with him. It's okay."

She led him over to a bench on the wall opposite the door and sat down beside him, amazed at how quiet it was out in the hallway. "I know how angry you are, Mr. Pritchard, but I promise your roses will okay. We'll work it out."

"He don't wanna work out nothin'. He's been bad news since the day he was born."

"I know. A lot of folks in town agree with you. But you have to—"

"*You!*" She watched as Carl's face got even redder as he jumped back on to his feet. "What the hell are *you* doing here?"

She followed his gaze to the young man hurrying toward the door and watched him stop short when he saw them.

"Tim?" she asked, seeing the look of shock on his face.

"Maggie – I told you I'd explain later—"

"You know him?" Carl asked, stepping away from her.

Maggie stood frozen. "I didn't know that *you* knew him," she said to the old man. She turned toward Tim, who was shaking his head ever so slightly as his face crumbled.

The old curmudgeon pointed his finger toward Tim. "That man…." he said hoarsely, "that man is my grandson."

"Your *what?*" Maggie looked incredulously back and forth from Carl to Tim. "What is he talking about?"

Tim took a small step toward them, but before he could speak the officer at the door of the meeting room gestured toward him. "Sir, you're needed inside now. Your partner's been waiting for you and the meeting is well underway."

"His *partner*? First Steve and now you?! I'll kill him!"

"Grandad…..Maggie….I tried to tell you…"

"Now, sir," demanded the officer.

Tim looked toward the door where the officer stood waiting. He looked back at Maggie, who stood there staring. She was shocked and speechless.

"I'm so sorry. I….." Not knowing what to say, he shook his head and turned away to follow the officer through the heavy double doors and out of view.

Maggie's eyes stung with tears as she watch the door close. She turned back to the old curmudgeon, who was breathing heavily and sweating. "He's your grandson?"

Suddenly, the old man's hand grasped his chest, and he gasped for air. Maggie recognized the symptoms as he fell to the floor.

"Oh, God!" She knelt beside him and looked up at the officer who was coming back out to check on things. "Get help! He's having a heart attack!"

The officer nodded and grabbed his phone. He called for help as he came to assist Maggie, who knelt beside the old man who she'd come to love. "You can't die, Mr. Pritchard, you hear me?" she whispered to him.

She knelt frozen in time as she watched the officer start CPR on Mr. Pritchard, and the sound of sirens could be heard shortly. She kept looking at the double doors waiting for him to run back out, but they remained close and sound proofed to the outside commotion. She turned her attention back to man on the floor and her tears flowed freely– both for him and the grandson she had just learned about. *"Please,"* she prayed, *"please don't let him die."*

<h1 style="text-align:center">CHAPTER 13</h1>

The ambulance arrived within minutes and carefully lifted Mr. Pritchard off the floor and onto the gurney. Maggie recognized one of the EMTs, Hailey Rice, and asked, "Is he gonna be okay?"

"We'll know more when we get him to the hospital. Does he have any family we need to contact?"

"He has a grandson," Maggie replied bitterly, "but you don't want him. He's the reason Mr. Pritchard had his heart attack. He wouldn't help."

"Do you have contact information?"

The officer spoke up first. "He's in the meeting – I'll go in and notify him as soon as you leave with Mr. Pritchard. Carl had left the meeting in an agitated state, but the grandson's arrival was a definite factor in the attack."

"I can come – he's a good friend and neighbor."

"We'll be taking him to Brentwood. We can't take you in the ambulance, but if you give me your number I'll call you for information if we miss each other at the hospital.

Maggie nodded, wiping the tears from her eyes. "Please take care of him."

"We'll do everything we can, Maggie," said Hailey reassuringly.

As they headed out the door and loaded Carl into the ambulance, Maggie spotted Liz walking in. Liz looked at the old man and realized who he was, and immediately approached Maggie.

"What happened? I can tell you're not okay."

Maggie shook her head, still crying. "I need to get to the hospital. He shouldn't be alone."

She started toward the door, but Liz held her back. "Honey, you're in no condition to drive right now. Come with me – I'll take you."

"But you're here for Lucy."

"I'll text her when I get there. I don't want you driving."

The officer agreed. "She's right. You're too emotional to go on your own. You get going and I'll head in to the meeting."

"Make sure you tell him not to come anywhere near the hospital!" she spit out as they headed outside.

Once in the car and on the way, Liz looked at her with concern. "There's obviously a lot more going on than just the old man. What happened?"

"He had a heart attack – he got so riled up in the meeting they made him leave, so I came out with him. And then……*he* showed up, and Carl collapsed."

"Who? That Sean guy?"

Maggie shook her head, her body sobbing with a new round of emotion. "No…..it was Tim."

"Tim? Your Tim?"

"He's Carl's grandson."

"His *what?*"

"I can't believe it. He arrived, and Carl screamed at him and told me he was his grandson. And Tim – the way he looked at me – I knew it was true."

She cried harder, and Liz reached over to grab her hand. "It's okay – cry all the way if you need to. I'm here. And we'll get Lucy here as soon as she's free."

Maggie nodded, still wanting to block out Tim's face and the guilty anguished expression he had. *How can it be true? And why didn't he tell me?"* She had no answers, only shock. She tried to concentrate on the old man, praying that they could save him. *"Don't let him die that way.....all alone and so angry. Let me get there to be with him."*

As they pulled into the emergency room entrance, Liz pulled over to drop her off. "You go ahead and get in there. I'll park the car and text Lucy, and then I'll be in to wait with you. Have faith, Maggie – from what I know he's one tough old man. Okay?"

She nodded as she got out of the car. "Thanks. You're a godsend."

When she approached the desk in the emergency room she saw Hailey, who waved to her, standing to one side filling out paperwork.

"I'm here for Carl Pritchard," she told the nurse.

"Are you family?"

"No – a friend.....and a neighbor. I was with him when he collapsed."

"I'll let the doctors know you're here. If you have any family contact information that would be helpful."

Maggie was about to say something when Hailey spoke up. "We're working on that, too, Diane – we'll keep you posted. Maggie might be helpful for some of the questions you had when Mr. Pritchard arrived."

The nurse nodded. "I'll have the doctor come out to talk to you as soon as he's free."

Hailey led her over to the waiting area, where several others were seated around the room. "So, can you tell me what happened?"

Maggie nodded, determined not to cry. As she sat down, Liz came hustling in the door, and she waved her over.

"We were in the meeting for the zoning committee – for the property just behind Carl's house."

"That's the old hardware store?"

Maggie nodded. "There's a lot of bad history between him and the owner – Sean McClean – and as the meeting went on he got angrier and more vocal."

Liz chuckled. "He gets really vocal," she told Hailey. "Last year there was a meeting on the community gardens and he went berserk several times. Didn't want a big garden just over his property line."

"This was worse," Maggie said. "This was….personal. Sean explained that his roses were over the property line and they'd need to be be taken out—"

"Woah!" Liz said. "He's gonna take out his roses?" She saw the questioning look on Hailey's face. "Those roses are his pride and joy. He goes nuts if you get too close and spends hours out there taking care of them."

Hailey jotted all this down. "Is that when he had the heart attack?"

Maggie shook her head and sighed heavily. "There's more. Because of his outbursts, he had to leave the meeting. I was next to him so I came out to sit with him. He was so angry – definitely agitated. But then Tim arrived, and he collapsed."

"Tim….?" Hailey asked, pausing with her pencil in hand.

"Tim Collins," Maggie said with tears in her eyes. "He's evidently Carl's grandson. Nobody even knew he had a grandson."

"Do you know why Tim was at town hall?" Hailey asked.

Maggie, determined to stay in control of her emotions, wiped her tears away. "He's apparently Sean McClean's new partner. Tim's father—his name is Steve—was Sean's partner many years ago, and he had married Carl's daughter. At some point there was a huge fight and she left town. They haven't spoken in years."

"Was Mr. Collins there when Mr. Pritchard collapsed? And where is he now?"

"He'd gone into the meeting. The officer at the courthouse was going to tell him what happened."

Hailey closed her notebook and stood up. "I imagine he'll be along any time then."

"But it's his fault! He shouldn't be anywhere near Mr. Pritchard!"

"I understand your concerns, Maggie, and I'll pass them on to the nurse. But he *is* family, so unless Carl refuses or is in major distress, he's entitled to be here."

"He had a damn heart attack – isn't that enough distress?!"

As the words flew out of her mouth, she saw Tim rushing through the door. He went straight to the desk and gave his name, asking about Carl, and the nurse pointed toward her. As their eyes met she saw that same guilty, devastated look in his eyes.

He approached cautiously. "Maggie, I'm so sorry. Please -- tell me how he is."

She looked at him with tears in her eyes, feeling both hurt and angry. "How do you *think* he is?" she said vehemently. "He may be in there fighting for his life, thanks to *you!*"

Liz squeezed her hand and looked at Tim coldly. "He had a heart attack as soon as you walked away."

Hailey looked at Tim and continued. "The doctors are with him – that's all we know. But I'm sure they'll want some information from you." He nodded as she looked down at Maggie. "He's in good hands – and I'll pass on this info to the nurse."

Tim's face crumpled from hearing the news and seeing Maggie, who refused to look at him. "Maggie, I wanted to tell you. I *tried* to tell you Sunday, but then—"

"Sunday?" she said, her head snapping up. "*Sunday?* What about that whole damn day up in Gloucester? Or dinner at Gino's? Did it slip your mind then?"

"I told you it was complicated…"

Maggie shook her head with tears in her eyes. "I don't *care* about how complicated it was. You should have told me who you were and why you were really here!" She could feel the emotion taking over her body as she blurted out, "And I don't wanna talk to you right now!"

As the sobs came, Liz wrapped her arm around Maggie and looked up at Tim.

"Haven't you done enough?"

He shook his head, tears in his own eyes. "Maggie…." When no reply came, he walked across the room and slumped into another chair, elbows on his knees and his head in his hands.

Through the sobs, Maggie could hear Lucy's arrival. She turned toward her sister who rushed over to the chair next to her.

Oh, honey, it's okay…." Lucy's arms wrapped around her as the sobs got stronger. She looked past Maggie to Liz and squeezed her hand. "I came as soon as the meeting ended. Thank you so much for being here with her."

Liz nodded, giving her girlfriend's hand a quick kiss. "I'm glad I walked in when I did." She gestured with her head. "He's over there."

Lucy looked across at Tim, who was sitting up with his elbows on the arms of the chair, clearly wiping away some tears of his own. When their eyes met, he shook his head slightly and mouthed "I'm sorry." She responded by giving her sister a tighter hug. "Shh…." She whispered. "I'm here, sis. It's okay." She watched as Tim looked up at the ceiling, shaking his head. He slumped back, taking his phone out of his pocket, and dialed someone. Lucy could tell from watching that the call wasn't a positive one.

Tim got up and walked over to the desk, and as he and the nurse talked, he kept shaking his head as questions were asked. When she directed him back to the waiting area, he stopped as he passed by Maggie, who still had her head buried in her sister's shoulder. Devastated, he continued back to his chair and slumped down to wait.

About an hour passed. Maggie had stopped crying and sat silently with Lucy beside her. Liz had left to head home to pick up Watson before heading to Lucy's to check on Tramp. Tim sat alone on the opposite side of the room, looking up anytime anyone wandered in or out, and occasionally glancing over at Maggie, but mostly sat just staring at the floor.

"Tim Collins?" A young female doctor stood near the door, a clip board in her hand. Tim noticed Maggie getting up as he approached the doctor and felt her presence nearby even though he dared not look at her. "I'm Tim."

She extended her hand to shake it. "Dr. Kovacs." She turned to Maggie. "Are you," looking at her clipboard, "Maggie Richmond?" When Maggie nodded, she added, "You're the one that was with him?"

Maggie nodded again. "I'm a friend – a neighbor, actually. How is he?"

"He's resting comfortably right now."

"Was it his heart?" Tim asked.

Dr. Kovacs nodded. "He definitely had a heart attack. He's been moved to Cardiac Intensive Care Unit, but he's stable. We'll know more tomorrow, but for now he's holding his own."

"Can I – or we – see him?" Tim asked.

Maggie glared at him, remembering the effect the last meeting had had on his grandfather. Luckily, the doctor spoke for her.

"Not quite yet. I want him to be stable a little longer before having you in. Are there any other family members who need to be contacted?"

Tim shook his head. "I called my mom – his daughter. She told me to keep her posted."

Maggie looked at him. "She's not coming?"

"I tried, Maggie. I told you it was complicated."

Maggie shook her head, and then turned back to the doctor. "Is there a waiting room on the cardiac unit?"

Dr. Kovacs nodded. "There is – up on the third floor. I might suggest that you both go home and get some rest, though. We have numbers for both of you if there's any change. Like I said, we'll know more tomorrow."

Lucy came up behind Maggie. "She's right, honey. Why don't we head home and try to get a little rest. I'll drive you back in the morning."

Maggie looked at Tim, and not wanting to have to be alone with him, nodded. She extended her hand to Dr. Kovacs. "Thank you for all you're doing. I'll be back in the morning."

"Stop at the front desk and they'll direct you up. I'm on duty tomorrow as well, so I'll let you know as soon as we know more."

Without a word to Tim, she walked past with Lucy and headed out the door.

<h1 style="text-align:center">CHAPTER 14</h1>

Maggie woke up early the next morning to the smell of fresh coffee. She couldn't remember exactly when she fell asleep, but between the crying and the worrying it wasn't more than a few hours ago. She got up and went to the bathroom, stopping to look at her swollen and bleary eyes as she brushed her teeth. *"I look like hell,"* she thought.

Lucy and Liz were in the kitchen, both looking equally tired. Lucy handed Maggie a mug of coffee. "Drink this. It'll help."

Maggie took a long sip, grateful for rich taste and the warmth flowing down her throat. "I gotta call work and tell them I can't come in."

Lucy shook her head. "Already did. I talked to Charlotte and she said not to worry. Now go and curl up on the couch and drink your coffee."

Maggie sank down into the plush couch cushion and curled her legs under her. "You always know what I need. Thanks." She sat there in silence, sipping her coffee and trying not to see Tim's face over and over again. Tramp climbed up and nudged her hand, wagging his tail slightly as he looked up with concerned eyes. "Hey, boy," she whispered. "you always know, too, don't ya?" She put her coffee down and wrapped her arms around him, and he gently licked her face as more tears came.

Lucy joined her as Liz stayed behind to do the dishes that had been sitting in the sink from the night before. "You wanna talk about it?"

Maggie shook her head. "Not yet," she said. "I just wanna have some coffee and then head back to the hospital."

"You do realize you're gonna have to see him again?"

"Seeing him and talking to him are two different things."

"Fair enough. Do you want me to go with you today? I can call off work."

Maggie shook her head. "No, don't do that. I'll be okay."

"So, do you want the rundown of what happened at the rest of the meeting?"

"I don't even care right now, sis. Maybe later."

Lucy patted her hand. "I understand."

Liz walked in with a piece of toast with peanut butter and sliced banana on top and handed it to Maggie. "Here, eat this. You need something in you before heading out."

Maggie tried to hand it back. "I'm really not hungry, but—"

"Liz is right," Lucy said, grabbing the plate and holding it. "You need to eat. Now's not the time to screw up your normal routines. Come on...."

Maggie rolled her eyes and took a bite of toast. She had no appetite whatsoever, but knew that Lucy would sit there until she'd eaten. She ate mechanically, not aware of tastes or smells or textures of the food. When she was done, she took the final swigs of coffee. "There? Happy now?" She looked at Lucy with disproval as she stood up. "I'm gonna go get dressed and I'll be ready to go in ten minutes."

Maggie emerged in a pair of jeans and a tee shirt. She had a sweatshirt in her hand and a tote bag with a notebook and a couple of books. As she went into the kitchen for her water bottle, she looked at her sister still sitting on the couch.

"Sorry I was snappy. I guess none of us got much sleep, huh?"

Lucy smiled and got up to give her a hug. "Don't worry about it. Are you sure you're okay to drive yourself?"

"Hmm-hmm," Maggie answered. "Oh, wait! My car's still up at town hall."

Lucy shook her head as she reached over to grab an apple out of the fruit bowl. "No it isn't. Liz drove me up to fetch it after you fell asleep." She stuffed the apple into the tote bag. "Now take this and promise me that you'll eat it later. And don't worry about Tramp. I'll take him for a walk."

Maggie gave her a long hug, so grateful for the sister that knew her and loved her so well.

"Thanks, sis. You're the best."

She patted Tramp and gave him a goodbye kiss and headed for the door.

"And Maggie?" Lucy called after her. "Give that old curmudgeon a hug from me, okay?"

Maggie nodded, her eyes getting misty from the nickname for the man that so many in this community loved. And for the grandson that no one in the community had even known about.

When she got to the hospital the front desk employee gave her directions up to the third floor, and after grabbing some coffee in the cafeteria she found the elevator and followed the signs to the cardiac intensive care unit. She stopped at the nurses' station to ask about Carl's condition, as well as where the waiting room was.

"Are you family?" the nurse asked.

"A good friend and neighbor – I was with him when he collapsed."

"I'm sorry. Only family is allowed in on this unit. But I can tell you that he's stable."

"Look, I understand your policy, but he *has* no family that he's close to. And I hate to think of him all alone."

"He hasn't been alone; a family member was with him most of the night."

Maggie scoffed. "Are you talking about Tim? Do you guys realize that he's the reason Mr. Pritchard *had* his heart attack?"

"Miss Richmond, I'm afraid I'm not at liberty to discuss any details," the nurse replied automatically. "It's patient privacy."

She shook her head. "Can I at least stay in the waiting room and talk to the doctor? Is Dr. Kovacs on by any chance?"

The nurse nodded. "She'll be making rounds soon if you'd like to wait. I'll be sure to tell her that you're here."

"Thank you," Maggie said curtly. "And please take care of him – especially if his grandson is with him."

She stormed down to the waiting room and sat in a chair in the corner of the room, placing her coffee on the table. She was grateful the room was empty. She felt so helpless, wanting to be with the old man to keep him company, and hating that Tim was alone with him. *"What if he wakes up and sees him? It might truly kill him this time."*

Tim. Even his name brought up so many conflicting emotions. Just a couple of days prior she was all excited about where their relationship might go. And now she felt like she didn't even know him. *"It's your own stupid fault; you never should have jumped into a relationship. You were too ignorant to see the signs – all that 'complicated' talk."*

She shook her head and reached into her bag for her water bottle, choosing to hydrate a little as her coffee cooled off. *"That kind of talk is not healthy,"* she said to herself. *"Just let it go for now and focus on what you can control."* She realized she had no desire to lose herself in a book, so she picked up a magazine off the table and flipped through it absently, preparing herself for a long wait.

Within minutes, however, the silence was broken by a quiet voice.

"Maggie." She froze, staring at a photo of a couple holding hands in the magazine, knowing that she had to face him, but feeling totally unprepared to do so. When she finally looked up at him standing in the doorway, she could see how tired and worried he looked. His hair was all disheveled and the stubble on his chin proved that he had been here for the night. He had the same clothes on, although he'd taken the jacket and tie off at some point. His shirt was hanging out of his pants and everything looked wrinkled.

"You look like hell," she said bluntly, not caring about how it came across.

He smiled weakly. "Been a long night – he's doing okay, by the way."

"I'm guessing he slept through the night," she said icily. "I doubt it would have gone well had he woken up to you sitting by his bedside."

"They had him sedated pretty well. I told Dr. Kovacs everything about last night -- and she still decided to let me stay with him. I would've stayed out here otherwise."

"Did she say how he was? They wouldn't tell me anything at the desk."

"They just took him down for a few more tests, and then she'll have more details. But she thinks he's gonna pull through okay."

Maggie's eyes filled with tears. "Thank God for that."

"Look, if you don't want me here I'll leave. I don't wanna upset you any more than I already have." Maggie could see his eyes filling up as he continued. "I am so sorry that I hurt you – I wish to God that I had told you earlier."

"But you didn't. You made a choice not to be upfront, and every choice has consequences."

"Can I at least sit? For a few minutes? You don't have to talk to me – I just don't wanna be alone right now."

Maggie shrugged. "It's a free country," she mumbled, flipping through another few pages of the magazine to an ad for a yoga place. It reminded her to let go of stress, so she took a deep breath, held it, and let it out slowly. She looked over at Tim, who had his head back against the wall with his eyes closed. She tried hard to empty her heart of the anger enough to at least offer a small bit of support.

She spotted her coffee, which she hadn't yet touched, and picked it up. She got up slowly and closed the gap between them, and when he opened his eyes in surprise she handed him the coffee. "You could probably use this more than me right now."

When his hand brushed against hers as he took the cup she pulled back instinctively. His eyes met hers for a moment and she looked away quickly.

She returned to her seat as he took a long sip. "Thanks, Maggie. It means a lot."

She sat there, not bothering to pick up the magazine again, knowing the distraction would be futile. Without looking at him, she spoke. "Look, much as I want to run and hide from you right now, I know I can't. Not if I wanna stay healthy myself."

Tim leaned forward and answered softly. "I never wanted you to be hurt – and I wish to God that Lucy hadn't gotten home when she did on Sunday."

Maggie, remembering the conversation just before Lucy barged in, finally looked at him. "You were gonna tell me then, weren't you?"

He nodded. "I had to. I knew you'd be gone for a couple of days before the meeting, and I wanted you to hear it from me.…..not like you did."

Maggie remembered back to how reluctant he was to leave on Sunday night. She sighed. "That's why you called me in Boston on Monday?"

Tim nodded. "I hated the idea of telling you on the phone, but I was running out of time." He ran his hand though his tousled hair and sighed. "Tuesday Sean had a meltdown and needed new plans drawn up right away, and I was up half the night getting those ready." His eyes softened as he looked at her. "That's why I texted you about seeing me after the meeting. I knew it was going to be a shock."

Maggie looked down at the floor. "That's an understatement."

"I wanted to rush in and throw the plans in Sean's face and come right back out. But then there were questions, and by the time I came out you were gone, and then the officer told me what happened." Tim was fighting back tears. "Maggie, I know I screwed up. I don't even remember driving here, but all I could think of was that I'd just lost the two people in my life that I wanted most to know."

Maggie was about to respond when she saw Dr. Kovacs entering the room. "Tim," she said quietly, gesturing with eyes toward the door. As they both began to stand, Dr. Kovacs put her hands up to have them remain seated.

"Don't get up," she said, "It gives me an excuse to sit for a few minutes." Dr. Kovacs sat across from them, a clipboard in her lap and looking exhausted.

"How is he?" Tim asked.

"We had to do a double bypass. He's still weak, but I think he'll pull through fine. He seems to be a tough old guy."

Maggie nodded, her eyes brimming with tears. "We call him the old curmudgeon."

Dr. Kovacs chuckled. "He lived up to that nickname early on, which is why I chose to sedate him for the night. He needed the rest, and it was obvious that he was in some distress."

"That's my fault," Tim responded.

"Not entirely, Mr. Collins. From what the EMT report said he was clearly already extremely agitated before you arrived. You were the final straw."

"Is he still sedated now?" Maggie asked.

"He should be coming around in the next hour or two. And Maggie," Dr. Kovacs continued, "I think he'd like you to be there when he wakes up."

Tim was about to say something, but stopped himself. Dr. Kovacs looked directly at him and spoke gently. "Look, I appreciated your honesty last night and I knew it would be safe to have you in there with him sedated. I think you needed to be with him. But when he wakes up, I need to know that he's going to stay calm, at least for a while – and I'm not sure what effect your presence might have on him."

Maggie was suddenly concerned. "Will my being there bring it all back?"

"Possibly, but I'm willing to chance that since you seem to have a pretty good relationship with him. He'll be a little fuzzy as he's coming to, but if there's any major reaction the nurses will be in to boot you out, believe me."

"You should be with him, Maggie. Way more than I should."

Dr. Kovacs nodded. "Tim, you've been here all night. Now would be a good time to go home, get some rest and have something to eat. Then we can look at the best way to proceed with a visit."

Maggie watched him as he sighed heavily and agreed. He glanced over at her and smiled. "I know he's in good hands with you. I'll be thinking of him." As he got up and turned to leave, he added, "I'll be thinking of you, too."

CHAPTER 15

Maggie sat beside Carl's bed and found herself reflecting back on the night she and Tim were eating pizza and calzone. She remembered him starting to tell her something about why he was in Caldwell, and how everything was related. She wished now that Lucy hadn't gotten home when she did – maybe it still would have hurt, but at least the shock might not have been as bad.

"Keep that damn dog away from my flowers," she heard to her left. Carl was looking at her and shaking his finger weakly from where his hand lay on the bed beside him.

Maggie smiled, fighting back tears to see him coming to. "Morning, Mr. Pritchard. It's good to see you awake."

He looked around the room, confusion on his face. "Where.....am I?"

"You're in the hospital. You're gonna be okay, but you have to rest."

"I've gotta go tend to my roses..." he said stubbornly.

"Your roses are safe and beautiful right now," Maggie said, trying to keep him talking about anything but what had happened. She thought back to when he was talking about his roses as the surveyors worked. "I especially love the Rainbow Niagaras this time of year".

Carl closed his eyes and smiled. "They were Ruthie's favorites...."

He was out again for a little while, and then he opened his eyes again and spoke to her. "I should've saved his letters."

"Do you mean *her* letters?" Maggie gently replied, thinking he was still talking about his wife.

"No, Tim's letters....he wrote me so many. I should've saved them."

Maggie was a bit nervous now, but luckily a nurse was coming in to check on him.

"He came to visit me, you know – or was it a dream?" He looked at the nurse on the other side of the bed. "Are you the dream lady?"

She smiled down at him. "No, I'm the nurse, Mr. Pritchard. I'm checking in on you. But you can tell me about your dream if you want."

Carl lay back and smiled as she took his pulse. "He talked about Caldwell. He loves it here......I think he loves her, too...."

Maggie sat listening, trying to figure out what was real and what was post surgical delirium.

The nurse kept him talking. "It's a nice town, isn't it?"

The old man nodded, but then his expressions got serious. "It's my fault he went away... I should have saved his letters...." He turned his head toward Maggie again. "Nobody knows him, and it's my fault..." His eyes closed and he stopped talking as he fell back asleep.

"What was that all about?" Maggie whispered to the nurse.

"Totally normal – don't worry. Lots of patients say odd things when they're coming out of anesthesia."

"Will he get more agitated when the drugs wear off?"

"Possibly. He may not remember right away. Every patient is different. He'll probably sleep a little bit now, and then be in and out some more. I'll be back in a little while to check on him. If you need anything just press that button on the remote."

Maggie nodded as she left watched the old man sleep. *What were you saying? Do you remember him being here? What letters? And what's your fault?* She had so many questions she wanted to ask him, wanting desperately to understand what he was saying. But none more than what he meant by "I think he loves her..."

Her phone vibrated to bring her back to reality. She read a text from Lucy, saying that she'd stopped by the garden on the way to work and filled in the ladies. They would handle her plot for tied day and they sent their love. *"Lucy, what would I do without you?"* she answered back. She got a smile emoji back, along with "See you tonight – will fill you in on the meeting."

Maggie realized that she had no idea what had transpired in the meeting after she left with Carl. She wondered what the residents had to say and how Sean reacted. How did they respond to Tim's entrance? So many questions, and no answers.

She was too tired to read, but didn't dare lean back to close her eyes. She grabbed her crossword puzzle book and had completed three puzzles before she heard Carl starting to whisper again. She quickly put her book down and waited to see if he'd wake up again.

His eyes fluttered open and he looked around the room. "What is this place?"

"You're in the hospital, Mr. Pritchard."

He turned to look at her and smiled. "Where's my tomatoes? You make good tomatoes."

Maggie laughed. "I didn't pick any today, Mr. Pritchard. But I'll bring you some. I promise."

His eyes opened wider. "I gotta go take care of the roses." He appeared to be trying to lift himself up, and Maggie could see his machine blinking and heard a bell ringing out in the hall.

"Mr. Pritchard, you can't get up. You need to rest."

He shook his head, mumbling about his roses as the nurse came back in.

"Mr. Pritchard, what can I help you with?"

The old man settled back, but his eyes were still wide open. "My roses…"

"His roses are his pride and joy," Maggie whispered. The nurse nodded with understanding.

"Your roses, Mr. Pritchard --- they are beautiful today. I have someone taking care of them for you, so you don't have to worry at all."

Maggie watched the old man relax. His index finger tried to

gesture toward her from beside him. "Be careful with Mr. Lincoln – he's tough some days." He closed his eyes again and was back to sleep.

The nurse smiled at Maggie. "It'll be like this for another hour or so. Then he should be back. In the meantime, do you know anyone who knows about roses? You might wanna give them a call."

Maggie knew immediately who to contact. As the nurse left again she texted Liz. "I need someone who knows about caring for roses. Can you help?" Liz was working on getting her certificate as a Master Gardener and taking classes in greenhouse management.

The reply came quickly. "You bet – what's up? How's the patient?"

Maggie texted back the situation, and Liz replied that she and Lucy would stop by after work at Carl's house to check on them. Maggie smiled. "You're the best," she replied with heart emoji and leaned back. She would definitely need to make sure Carl's roses were taken care of while he was in the hospital. If Sean and Tim didn't kill him, his roses dying definitely would.

The next time Carl opened his eyes he seemed more alert. "You're still here," he said to her softly. "My tomato pal."

"I'll stay as long as you want me, Mr. Pritchard."

He looked around the room and then back at her. "Where's your damn dog?"

She laughed. It felt good to laugh, and he so often made her laugh. "He's probably home fast asleep."

Carl nodded and closed his eyes. "He's not all that bad…..for a dog."

"Mr. Pritchard, that's the first time you've ever said something nice about Tramp."

"You're a good neighbor, Maggie Richmond. I'll make an exception for you."

"I feel honored – I'm sure Tramp will, too."

She saw him shaking his head and muttering to himself. "That can't be right."

"What can't be right, Mr. Pritchard?"

"I swear he was here….but he couldn't have been, could he?"

"Who is that?" she asked nervously.

"My grandson…" He looked at her and smirked a little. "Bet you didn't know I had a grandson, did you? That's 'cause nobody around here did."

Not wanting to cause any sudden bursts of memory, Maggie answered gently. "Why don't you tell me about him?"

"Not much to tell. I never even got to see him. She moved away and blamed me for everything."

"Who moved away?"

Carl lay in his bed rocking his head forward and back ever so slightly, as if deep in thought. "Sharon, my daughter. She moved away before Tim was born and said it was my fault."

"What was your fault, Mr. Pritchard? That seems like a long time ago."

"I told her to come home…He wasn't nice to her. But she went… and it made her mother cry." He started nodding to himself and closed his eyes. "It was my fault. I ruined everything."

Maggie patted his hand. "That must have been really hard on both of you – on all of you."

Carl kept thinking out loud, struggling to remember. "He looks like his picture, you know."

"Who's that?"

"Tim….my grandson. Did you know I had a grandson, tomato girl?"

Maggie hoped the nurses weren't far off, as Carl seemed to be slowly regaining pieces of memory.

"You said he looks like his picture."

"I opened one of his letters. Still have that picture." He shook his head. "I should've saved them."

"Why didn't you save them, Mr. Pritchard?"

"He looks *just* like him, you know."

"Like who?"

"His father – Steve……he took them both away."

"You said he wasn't nice."

Carl shook his head. "He was a bad man…." He looked at Maggie sadly. "Why did she go with him? He was so mean to her."

"Sometimes we love the wrong people."

"He didn't love her, you know. Only his work – and himself. He's just like his buddy—"

Carl stopped talking and Maggie could see him tense up. He moved a bit and the bells started ringing in the hallway again. He looked at her with clear eyes and whispered, "That Sean McClean kid."

The nurse was in the room quickly and calmed him down. She checked his vitals and talked gently to him. "I think it's time for you to take a little rest now, Mr. Pritchard. You're doing a great job remembering, but let's talk about it later. Let's think about those roses for now and how beautiful they'll be when you get back home."

Carl closed his eyes and nodded. The nurse looked over at Maggie. "Might be time for you to head out – sounds like he's getting closer to clarity, and we don't want to rush that until his heart is a little stronger."

"I understand – thank you for always being close by. I was really nervous that his memory would trigger another heart attack."

"He's doing fine, Maggie. You're a good friend. Dr. Kovacs has okayed your name to be on his visitor list, so you won't get any hassle next time you come."

Maggie gathered her things and stood up, patting the old man on his hand. "You rest, you old curmudgeon, you. I'll be back tomorrow."

As she was heading for the elevator, Dr. Kovacs came out of another patient's room and smiled. "How's the patient? I hear he's coming back slowly."

Maggie nodded. "I'm not sure I understand some of what he's saying, but there are moments of clarity. He did just remember the name of the guy he hates. I hope he'll be okay."

"He'll most likely sleep awhile. We'll be taking him down for another test shortly, and if all goes well then we'll transfer him from the ICU to another room tomorrow."

"That soon?" Maggie asked.

"He's progressing as he should be. I'd say he'll be in the hospital for another 7-10 days. And then he can get back home."

Maggie shook her head. "He lives alone, doctor. The situation that caused all this stress is literally right outside his back door – is that really going to help him?"

"Well, we'll have to discuss that more with the family. Mr. Collins did insist last night that I add your name to the visitor/contact list. He said you were probably closer to his grandfather than anyone else right now."

"He did that?" Maggie. "I'll … have to thank him. I really am fond of Mr. Pritchard – we've talked almost every day for the past year or so. He may be a grumpy old man, but he's nice under that rough exterior."

Dr. Kovacs smiled. "Well, it seems pretty clear that he thinks highly of you."

"I am concerned, though, about what will happen when he leaves here."

"If what you say about him being alone and his home environment are true, then we might look at another facility that can do some cardio rehab. Again, we can talk about that in the next few days. We'll most likely want to meet with you and Mr. Collins in another day or so."

"What? Both of us?"

"He's family, and you're a friend. He also mentioned that you were a social worker over at Caldwell Manor. That might be an asset to have you as part of Mr. Pritchard's recovery team."

Maggie walked out to her car and wondered about the different pieces of the puzzle, as well as the one person who might be able to help her put them all together. She just wasn't sure she was ready to talk to him again.

When she got home she was surprised to see Lucy's car out front and her bedroom door closed. *"I thought she'd gone to work."* Maggie gave Tramp a little attention but was feeling more and more restless. There were so many questions swirling around in her head and she was frustrated to have no answers. She looked in the refrigerator to see if anything interested her, and realized she didn't want to eat. *"Maybe I'll go for a run – that will clear my head."*

She was getting her other shoes on when Lucy emerged from her room. "Hey, you're back. How is the old guy?"

"He's in and out of this weird delirium stage, but he's doing okay. What are you doing home?"

"Got to work and realized I was useless – came home and took a little nap." Lucy saw the shoes and stopped en route to the kitchen. "What are you doing?"

Maggie looked down, lacing her running shoes. "Going for a run. Need to clear my head."

"A run? Maggie, you haven't gone for a run in years. What's going on?"

Maggie stood up defiantly. "Look, I don't need the sergeant routine right now, okay? I have a lot on my mind and I need a little run, that's all."

"Like hell it is! You know that's a trigger behavior for you." She took a step toward Maggie. "Look, I know you're going through hell right now – but remember that your recovery has to come first. Call Natalie and make an appointment or sit and talk to me. Or we can go for a walk if you really need to get out – but for God's sake, don't let him or anything else give your eating disorder that power back."

Maggie walked past her and opened the door. "Leave me alone. It's just a friggin' run."

She went out and slammed the door behind her, but then found herself frozen on her front porch. *Just go for the run, Maggie – don't listen to her.* As the old tapes started to play in her head she knew her sister was right. If she started down that path again she wasn't sure she'd have the strength to fight back. *I want to scream right now!*

Instead, she turned around and went back inside, quietly closing the door behind her. Lucy came flying out of her room with her running shoes on. She was still in her pajamas.

"You were coming after me like that?"

"Damn right. I didn't know which way you'd head and I had to be sure to catch you. You going for a run alone inside your brain right now is a dangerous place."

Maggie walked past her and slumped down on the couch, kicking off her shoes.

"So what made you come back in?"

Maggie glared at her. "I hate it when you're right."

Lucy kicked off her own shoes and sat down beside her. "I'm really worried about you, sis. I'm so scared you're gonna relapse, and I don't know what to do to stop it."

Maggie leaned her head back and closed her eyes. "I feel like my whole world is out of control right now. I have no answers – only a million questions."

"So your brain goes automatically to that old default tape that lies about how to get that control back."

"Something like that."

"Look, I know you're hurting right now. Finding out that Tim was his grandson *and* Sean's new partner – while dealing with the old guy having a heart attack – it's no wonder that you're feeling crazy."

"I wanna hate him so much right now."

"He should have told you. No excuses."

"He started to – just before you came home Sunday."

Lucy pondered a moment as she remembered. "It did look like you guys were having a serious talk. I'm sorry I interrupted that…..but he still should've told you."

"I know. He apologized numerous times for that."

"So you guys did talk?"

"We were civil. He'd been at the hospital all night, so I gave him my coffee."

"I would've thrown it in his face."

"I don't know – he looked so beat. I might *want* to hate him, but…"

"But you still care about him a lot, don't you?"

Maggie nodded as her eyes teared up again. "He stayed with him all night."

"So what else did you talk about?"

"Nothing really. The doctor sent him home and I took over. Tim insisted that my name be added to his visitor list."

"That's something, I guess. So you said Pritchard was in and out – did you guys talk at all?"

"There were moments of clarity but he was mostly out of it. He knew me – called me his tomato pal. He even said something nice about Tramp."

Tramp heard his name and came up and put his head on her knee. "Yeah, I think he likes you, boy." Tramp wagged his tail slightly, happy for the attention. "He also remembered his roses, and twice wanted to get up and leave. I'm so glad Liz is willing to go and check on them."

"She's happy to do it. So did he remember what happened?"

Maggie shook her head. "Not totally. He did remember Sean at the very end, but I don't think he'd remember last night yet. They scooted me out at that point and wanted him to rest some more."

"So what *did* he talk about then? You said he was in and out of delirium."

"Lucy, it was so weird, some of the stuff. He talked about Tim writing letters, and how he should have saved them. He said it was his fault that he went away. Then he talked about his daughter and how she left and that her husband was a bad man. It sounded like he knew Tim was there on some level – said he was talking about how much he likes Caldwell, and how he thought he might be in love…"

"He said *what?*"

"That's just it. I don't really know what he was saying. I left feeling so confused."

"I know you don't wanna hear this, but it sounds like there's only one other person who might be able to shed some light on all of this. You need to talk to him, Maggie."

"I know. My stomach's been churning at the thought."

"Look, Natalie's always telling you that you have go through the crap to get rid of it."

"I see her tonight. I'll be sure to tell her that you're quoting her."

"She'll be honored, I'm sure. And she'd agree that you need to face him if you're gonna get any answers."

Maggie nodded, knowing that she was right. "I guess I should go track him down."

"Wait, don't you wanna know what happened last night at the meeting?"

Maggie straightened up. "Wow. I'd totally forgotten the meeting was still going on when I left."

"It was like a circus after you left. Of course, no one knew what was going on out in the hall or the meeting would've ended I'm sure."

"So…what happened?"

"Well, Sean went off on the old man after you left. Said 'He's had it out for me all these years, and can you believe that guy?' Totally outta control."

"Sounds like Sean. God, he's arrogant."

"So when Tim finally came in, I thought Barb, Brooke, and Colleen were gonna lose it. We didn't even know about the grandson part yet – we couldn't believe he'd be Sean's partner. He looked like hell, Maggie. You could tell he wanted to give Sean the file and leave, but then the committee started to ask him questions."

"That's what he told me, too."

"Point is, even though he seemed really distraught, he was very professional. He answered every question about the new survey, with Sean butting in on every single answer, like he knew everything. Tim even corrected him a couple of times. Sean obviously doesn't know what he's talking about – I suspect he brought Tim on because he didn't know anything himself and needed someone competent."

"So did the residents get to talk at all?"

"Not last night. Teagan's dad was great. Right after Tim left he told Sean that it was clear that he wasn't prepared for the meeting and hadn't done his homework in terms of knowing what the community needed. They tabled the discussion until the next meeting and asked that he return with real data."

"That must have gone over well."

"He went nuts. I mean, does he not get that the committee can say yes or no to his proposal? He was cursing up a storm when he left. I think the whole room was ready to give Teagan's dad a standing ovation for shutting him down. He sure hasn't made any friends in this town."

"I don't suppose they were too happy with Tim, either."

"Remember, not everyone knows Tim. Most of the chatter about him was how he seemed to be the brains of the two, but questioned why anyone would want to work with Sean."

"I'm sure the ladies will have a lot to say tomorrow." She sighed wearily. "I guess I'd better go see if he's over at the B&B. This isn't a conversation for texting."

"If he's not there, he's probably back at the hospital."

Maggie nodded as she got up. She picked up her running shoes and threw them back into the closet, grabbing the flats she had been wearing earlier. Before heading out the door again, she turned back to Lucy. "Thanks for looking out for me. I know I'm not in a good place right now. Without your support I'd probably be dead by now."

Lucy came over and gave her a hug. "Go and talk to him. Maybe he'll have some answers that will make things a little easier to handle."

"I sure hope so, sis."

CHAPTER 16

Maggie saw Tim's car parked by the B&B garage apartment and knew he'd be there. She climbed the stairs slowly, not really having any idea on what to say. At the top she paused a moment, took a deep breath, and quietly knocked on the door.

Tim opened the door and froze. "Maggie. I didn't…wait, is he okay?"

Maggie nodded. "He's doing okay. In and out a lot, but they said that's normal. Dr. Kovacs seems to think he'll pull through fine."

He sighed with relief, and then opened the door wider to let her in. "I'm sorry, come in."

She entered the studio apartment that Barb had recently renovated. It was a bright, airy room with a small kitchenette on one side with a small microwave and a two burner stovetop. There was no oven as renters were invited to eat at the main B&B. There was a small table by the window with two chairs; right now it was covered with a pile of blueprints and Tim's computer. A loveseat and a chair finished off the main room with a small bookshelf between them. The bathroom and a small bedroom could be seen off of the main room.

"Barb did a great job on this," Maggie said, slowly taking it in.

Tim nodded. "It's been a perfect spot. Can I get you something? Coffee, or water? And please," he said gesturing toward the loveseat, "have a seat."

"I'm good right now, "she said, sitting down on the chair. Tim sat on the loveseat closest to her. "Sorry to barge in, but I felt like I really needed to talk – my head is starting to play mind games with me and I need to try and make sense of some of this before it gets worse."

"I haven't been able to stop thinking about you – or him. I hate not being able to go today." When Maggie looked at him perplexed, he continued. "Dr. Kovacs called a little while ago. His memory's getting clearer, so they want me to wait until tomorrow to give him a chance to get a little stronger."

"I'm sorry – I know that must be hard. The last thing he remembered before I left was Sean, and he definitely got more agitated."

"So he remembered what happened?"

"Not the meeting, or..."

"Or me showing up?"

She shook her head. "It's only a matter of time, Tim. The doctor says sometimes a patient will block out what happened right before the heart attack. But he had some real moments of clarity, and there's no doubt that the Sean McClean feud goes back a long way." Maggie was starting to grasp how complicated the situation was.

Tim sighed, running his hand through his hair. "You don't know the half of it."

"I can only imagine," she said with understanding. "He was rambling about so much stuff this morning – I couldn't tell what was real and what was the delirium, but it was crystal clear that he hated Sean."

"He has every reason to. He destroyed our family," Tim said angrily.

"Then why in the world would you be *working* with him?"

Tim looked at Maggie and sighed. "I inherited the mess from my father."

"I'm sorry – is he—"

"Dead?" Tim said flatly. "Last year. The alcohol finally beat him."

He added, "And you don't have to be sorry. He was a lousy father and a worse husband – and that was when he was sober. Most of the time he just sat there with his alcohol."

"And your mom?"

Tim's eyes got a little misty as he shook his head. "I really thought she'd finally be free when he died. But she's a bitter, depressed shell of a woman. I think she regrets every choice she's ever made and has no idea how to rectify it. I haven't been able to help her – every time I try she pushes me away."

Maggie teared up at the anguish Tim was feeling, knowing that this had been his whole life. "I imagine it's a coping mechanism that helped her through all these years."

Tim looked at her surprised. "I guess I never really thought of it that way."

"Tell me more about how you ended up as Sean's partner."

"When the will was read I found out that I owned half of the old hardware store. My dad had bailed Sean out years ago when Henry died and he ended up as co-owner."

"So that's what Carl was yelling about during the meeting. He was screaming at Sean that he only owned *half* of the property. Nobody knew what he meant at the time."

"Well, shortly after my dad died Sean showed up again to let me know that there were a whole lot of tax payments and penalties that needed to be paid on the property and that my dad owed him a boatload of money."

"Let me guess – he didn't have the money."

Tim shook his head. "Bingo. He managed for a while, I guess. But he was going to lose the place and needed me to bail him out—just like my dad did years ago." Maggie scoffed and Tim raised his hands in exasperation. "Trust me, I knew he was a snake. But he said he had a great idea on what to do with the property to turn it around and make some money. I should have signed over my half and told him to get lost."

"So why didn't you?"

"Because I knew it was in Caldwell – and I knew I still had a grandfather right across the property line. I've been trying to connect with him for years but he's as stubborn as my mother. I guess that's where she gets it from."

"You came because of him?" Maggie asked, tears filling her eyes.

He nodded, blinking back his own tears. "My mother had told me a few things about him. She told me about growing up in the old house and working with Sean at the store. She told me how much he hated my dad – who was just like Sean -- and that he wasn't welcome in his home. I think she blamed him for my dad's drinking. I know they moved away before I was born."

"He talked about her this morning," she said gently as his eyes met hers. "He said it was his fault that she left. He also said that he should have kept all your letters." As she watched she saw tears rolling down Tim's cheek.

"He....he said that?"

She nodded. She moved over to the loveseat, unable to keep from comforting him as the truth of his story was finally coming out. She rubbed his back while he cried a short while, and then he finally wiped his eyes and faced her.

"Tell me everything he said – please."

She nodded, not knowing where to begin. "He said he knew your dad was mean, and he begged your mom to come home before you were born. When she left and cut off any contact he felt horrible--so did your grandmother."

"I never got to meet her. My mom always said she was a good person. I know she went to see her a few times once the dementia hit and she was in the Manor, but she didn't know her anymore. I think she blamed him for that, too. I think her funeral was the last time she was in Caldwell."

"I think your grandfather's been carrying that guilt around for a long time. He...talked about you, too."

Tim straightened up and grabbed her hand. "Me?"

"I think he knows you were there, Tim. He kept asking if it was a dream."

Tim shook his head. "I thought he was totally out of it."

Maggie was aware of how warm his hand was on hers, and while part of her wanted to pull away, she also craved the contact. "He said you talked about Caldwell, too."

Tim's eyes got brighter. "I did. I told him everything I had discovered in this little town – Gino's, the cemetery, Grandma's grave, and the house…I had no idea he was hearing me."

"He said you loved Caldwell." She left out the part about him being in love and continued on. "Tim, tell me about the letters you wrote."

Tim sat back, his eyes full of tears. After a moment he got up quietly and went into the bedroom, and emerged with a pile of letters tied together, handing them to Maggie. "They're all here. He sent them all back."

He sat back down as she held them tenderly.

She could see a Maine postmark on some, and a Gloucester postmark on a few. "He kept one though, didn't he?"

"How did you know that?"

"It's the one with your photo – he opened that one--and he said he still has it. Tim," she said, reaching over with one hand to hold his. "He told me that he should have saved them all."

He squeezed her hand gently as he wiped his eyes with his other hand. "Thank you for telling me that. It means more than you know."

She nodded, blinking back her own tears. "Thanks for your honesty and filling in the gaps." They sat in silence a couple of minutes, and then Maggie asked, "Will you be okay? I actually have a counseling appointment I need to get to."

"I'll be fine. I think I need a little time alone anyway."

He walked her to the door and she smiled a bit. "It'll work out with him – you just gotta give it some time."

As he opened the door his eyes met hers. "And what about us? Is there still a chance that we might work out, too?"

"I don't know," said Maggie tentatively. "I need some time, too. These last few days have been a whirlwind."

"Take all the time you need. I'm not going anywhere."

CHAPTER 17

$\mathcal{M}$aggie had an intense therapy session with Natalie, but she knew it had been perfectly timed. Even though she felt drained and wanted to head home, she also knew that visiting Cassie would be good for both of them. She found her in the art room finishing up the painting of the cemetery. Cassie was so focused on her work that she wasn't aware of Maggie's arrival until she was next to the girl. The painting was beautiful - all the warm colors of autumn provided a beautiful contrast with the simple gravestone and stone bench.

"It's beautiful," Maggie whispered.

Hearing her, Cassie spun around. "Hey! I didn't know you were coming today. I'd hug you but I'm covered with paint."

"Consider it a virtual hug, then." Gesturing toward the painting, she added, "I can't believe how realistic that is. It's simply gorgeous."

Cassie smiled at her work. "It's been really good having a creative therapy. I thought I'd go mad not being able to dance, but painting has nurtured that artistic and expressive part of me. I've been doing some other stuff, too – wanna see?"

Maggie nodded, and Cassie left her brushes beside her easel and led her over to a table. "They're nothing really – we had gone out for a nature walk and we all got to collect some stones. I decided to paint on mine."

She had about a dozen flat stones in front of her, all done as different flowers in bloom. There were roses, daisies, lilacs, and sunflowers.

"Cassie, these are amazing!"

Cassie shrugged a bit. "They're nothing special."

Maggie looked at her and shook her head. "Don't put yourself down – you have a real gift, you know that?"

"I suppose," said Cassie shyly. "It gives me something positive to obsess on when I'm bored. Hey, do you mind if we chat while I clean up? I don't want the paint to dry on the brushes."

Maggie nodded and followed Cassie as she worked. "So anything else new?"

"My therapist says I can go home this weekend."

"That's awesome news! How are you feeling about that?"

Cassie sighed as she dried off her brushes. "Not gonna lie – there's a part of me that's scared to death about it."

"I know. I remember feeling the same way. It's okay to be scared. You've been in this safe place that's offered some protection from your eating disorder. Going back into the world can be intimidating, but they wouldn't send you out if they didn't think you were ready."

They sat down on a couple of stools in front of Cassie's rocks. Maggie picked a few up and held them as she listened to Cassie talk.

"I guess I'm scared of all the free time I might have. That's when my brain starts talking again. Teagan said I could go and volunteer with her at Caldwell Manor, but I'm not sure that's for me. Besides, I wanna spend some time with my Gram, not work there with all the other old people."

Maggie chuckled. "Hey, that's what I do--and it's not for everyone."

Cassie fingered the outline of one of the daisies as she spoke. "I know I'll be coming here a few days a week, but that still leaves a whole lot of days every week with no school, no dance, and limited counseling. As much as I hated the structure when I got here, I think I'm gonna miss it when I leave."

Holding Cassie's rock reminded Maggie of possible solution to her fears.

"How would you feel about a paying job that allowed you to be creative?"

Cassie looked intrigued. "A paying job?"

Maggie nodded. "You've been in Brooke's Treasures, haven't you?" When Cassie nodded, she continued. "Brooke is looking to hire someone to help her in the store – both with customers and also creating things that can be sold. Something like these rocks would probably sell really well."

"These?"

"Hmm-mm. Brooke said it would only be about ten hours a week, which sounds like it might be perfect for you. And Brooke is one of the nicest people I've ever met."

"That place always has a peaceful vibe inside. And I like some of the stuff she sells."

"She's already told me that she'd consider you. If you don't mind, could I bring a few of these to show her? Just to give her an idea of your talent?"

"Sure. Like I said, they're no big deal. But why would she hire me?"

"Because I vouched for you. And I think it would be a great fit for both of you."

Cassie looked down at her flowers and smiled. "I'm….not used to having people do nice stuff for me. But thanks….you know, for looking out for me.

"Hey, it takes time to love yourself again. You'll get there."

Cassie chuckled. "That's what Teagan says, too."

"Does she know that you're heading home?"

"Not yet, but she's coming tomorrow to visit. I'll tell her then." Cassie hesitated for a moment. "Can I….ask you something?"

"You know you can."

"It's about Saturday. Much as I'm looking forward to being home, I'm a little nervous about my folks coming to get me. I think they're gonna make a huge deal out of it and talk about it all the way home, and I…."

"You're afraid you'll freak out on the way?"

Cassie nodded.

"If you're asking me if I could drive you home, I'd love to."

"Really?" Cassie's face lit up and it was astonishing to see how different she looked then when she first arrived. Her cheeks were filling out again and the dark circles under her eyes were gone. She looked truly happy again when she smiled.

Maggie nodded. "As long as your folks are okay with it. How 'bout if I brought Teagan along as well?"

"That would be awesome. I'll talk to my mom about it tonight, but I think she'll be okay with it."

Maggie looked at the clock on the wall and knew that visiting hours were almost over. "I guess I better get going before they kick me out. Glad I could stop in."

"Me, too. You've helped me more than you know."

"Thanks. I needed to hear that. Believe it or not, you've helped me, too. You remind of where I've come from, and how easily I could make choices that would lead back there."

"Did something happen?" asked Cassie genuinely, concern in her eyes.

"I had a rough day – but between my sister, therapy with Natalie, and a visit with you, I'm feeling much better. Sometimes we need to recenter ourselves and not listen to those nasty little voices in our heads. Anyway, which rocks should I take to show Brooke?"

"How about one of each flower? That way she can see which ones she likes best," offered Cassie.

"Good idea. Would you mind if I also took a photo of your painting as well?"

"I guess….but I can't imagine anyone wanting to buy a cemetery picture."

Maggie turned to her. "Actually, I know one or two people that would love that painting. I might even buy it myself to give to one of them. I'll talk to Brooke in the meantime."

"And I'll talk about the job in therapy to see what Natalie thinks."

"Sounds like a plan. Have a good night, Cassie."

"You too, Maggie. And I hope tomorrow is a better day for you."

"It will be," answered Maggie confidently. As she left, the stain glass Phoenix reminded her that fresh starts are always possible.

By the time she got home, she found Liz and Lucy in the kitchen making spaghetti.

"Hey," her sis said with a smile. "You look better than when you left."

Maggie nodded as she came in and picked up a piece of green pepper off the cutting board, biting into it with a satisfied crunch. "Nothing like plowing through the crap to make you feel better."

Lucy grinned. "Have you eaten yet? We're doing spaghetti with a veggie sauce."

Maggie took a long whiff and shook her head. "No, I haven't eaten, and that smells heavenly." She looked past Lucy to where Liz was sautéing onions. "Hey, thanks for taking a look at Mr. Pritchard's roses. I owe you big time."

"Happy to do it. He's got some gorgeous rosebushes back there. Some of them look really old. You can tell he spends a lot of time with them."

"I think it must be his favorite hobby. He wanted to get up and leave the hospital to take care of them."

"Well, you tell him that I'll take care good care of his beauties until he gets home."

Lucy looked up from the celery she was chopping. "So, I take it you found him?"

Maggie nodded. "It was a good talk. I'll fill you guys in over dinner."

"I'm glad you had therapy right after."

"That's funny, Natalie said the same thing. Let's just say I'm pretty drained, but in a good way. I'm gonna change and curl up with Tramp for a few minutes if you don't mind. I'll do the dishes later since you guys are cooking."

"Sounds like a great trade off to me."

Maggie changed into lightweight pajama pants and a tank top, and sat down on the floor between Tramp and Watson. "How's my favorite guy and his best buddy?" She gave them both head scratches and got thank you kisses in return. *"Nothing like a dog to feel uncondi-tionally loved forever."* "You're such a good boy," she whispered to Tramp, "and you, too, Watson."

Over dinner she told them about her conversation with Tim.

"Wow," Lucy said, as the briefing ended. "Sounds like old man Pritchard's had a lot to feel grumpy about all these years. I feel sorry for him."

"It does explain a lot, doesn't it?" Maggie said as she twirled her spaghetti around her fork and took a delicious bite. "Hmmm....I so grateful to appreciate how good this tastes."

Liz nodded in agreement as she dipped her Italian bread into some sauce. "Sounds like he's been super lonely, too. No wonder he hangs out at the cemetery every weekend talking to his dead wife."

"That reminds me!" Maggie said, putting her food down and reaching across Tramp to grab her purse on the floor. "Wait till you see this."

She grabbed her cell phone and brought up the photo of Cassie's painting and passed it over.

"Woah," Liz said. "That's so realistic."

Lucy nodded. "Who the hell painted this? It's gorgeous."

"Cassie, believe it or not. I don't think she realizes how talented she is." Maggie reached in and found the rocks in her purse and placed them on the table. "She did these, too."

They each picked up a rock and marveled at the detail. "She's really good," Liz said.

"Right? I'm gonna show these to Brooke – I can't imagine that she won't hire her to help in the store this summer."

Lucy nodded as she twirled the last few strands of spaghetti onto her fork. "She'd be perfect for Brooke's shop."

Liz was looking at the photo of the cemetery again. "I still can't go over how good this one is."

"I may buy it from her – I think that maybe Carl or Tim might like to have it."

"That's a wonderful idea."

"I don't know if Cassie will consider selling it, but I hope so. It'll be one less thing to cart home."

"Does that mean she's coming home soon?"

"Probably next week. She's scared, but I think she's ready."

"You've been so good for her recovery, sis."

Maggie smiled. "That may be, but she's been really good for mine as well."

CHAPTER 18

The next morning Maggie and Tramp headed for the gardens, stopping to pick up Mr. Pritchard's newspaper on the way. "Maybe I can bring it to him tonight, boy," she told Tramp as she tucked the paper into her bag. She surveyed the house as she walked past; it somehow looked lonelier with its owner away.

The ladies had been anticipating her arrival.

"You okay, honey?" Barb asked, giving her a big hug as she arrived.

Maggie nodded. "It's been a long couple of days, that's for sure—bit I'm managing."

"How's our favorite old grump?" Brooke asked.

"The doctor says he's doing well. He'll be leaving the ICU today if all goes as planned."

"We were dying to talk to you after the meeting," Colleen said. "Then we heard what had happened and we've been worried sick about you. Glad he's gonna be okay."

"So did you have any idea about Tim being his partner?" Brooke asked.

"Never mind the partner," Barb said. "Lucy told us about who he really is. Considering how shocked we were, I can only imagine how devastating it must have been for you."

Maggie took a deep breath and let it out, tired of her eyes getting misty when she thought about him. "I think I was as shocked as Mr. Pritchard. I had no idea."

"He never said anything?" Colleen asked, coming to stand next to her and Barb.

Brooke joined them as Maggie shook her head. "You poor kid. So what did he think, that he could just waltz into town and maybe his grandfather wouldn't know him?"

"No, it's not that at all," Maggie said. "He agreed to work with Sean *because* of his grandfather. He had hoped that maybe being closer he might have a chance to meet him."

Colleen looked confused. "But didn't you say he hadn't told you?"

"We talked later yesterday. I couldn't let it fester inside of me."

Barb rubbed Maggie's back lightly. "He told me a little bit last night. He came over to see if he could grab a little dinner and take it back to his apartment. I pulled him into the kitchen and made him eat with me – he looked pretty drained, too."

"So, what's up?" Brooke asked. "There has to be a story."

Barb gestured for them to get back to their gardens. "There is a story – and it's a long and complicated one. Maggie can share it when she's good and ready." She winked at her young friend. "I don't know much, but I know that he appreciated your visit more than you realize."

"Thanks, Barb," Maggie whispered. "And you two," facing Brooke and Colleen, "I promise I'll give the full run down soon. I'm still trying to sort it all out first."

"It's okay," Brooke answered. "We're not going anywhere. Besides, Sean's performance will give us plenty to talk about until you're ready to tell us about Tim."

"Wasn't he an ass?" Colleen said. "Maggie, you really did miss McClean in action."

"Lucy filled me in. I heard that Teagan's dad shut him down pretty well."

Brooke laughed. "He shut him down – but didn't shut him up. I can hardly wait for the next meeting. It's gonna be a long two weeks for that jerk."

"If it helps at all," Colleen chimed in, "Tim was so professional when dealing with him. I'll never understand why he'd want to be his partner, but it was clear that he's the only one that really knew what he was talking about. And Brooke, it's gonna be a long two weeks for all of us."

Maggie suddenly remembered something. "That reminds me, Brooke. Next week Cassie will be home. I mentioned the job possibility to her." She took her gloves off and dug her phone and Cassie's rocks out of her basket. "Take a look at these," she said, handing them each a rock.

"They're so intricate," Colleen said. "How did she do this on rocks?"

Barb studied her rock. "The detail's amazing. She's very talented."

Brooke agreed. "I think these would sell. And if she could find bigger rocks, they'd make great garden accents."

Maggie smiled and held out her phone. "Look what else she did." The ladies passed the phone around and were amazed by the painting.

"Tell her to come and see me as soon as she's home," Brooke said eagerly. "I want to hire her immediately."

"Really?"

Brooke nodded. "With talent like that I can only imagine some of the stuff she could help me with."

Maggie took the rocks and phone back and thanked Brooke. "I think you two will really hit it off. She's ready to have something to do on the days she's not doing outpatient therapy."

"Good. Saves me from having to advertise and interview people."

"Thanks, guys, for not pushing about Tim. I'll fill you all in as soon as I know more myself. But now, I'd better get the garden dealt with so I can get to work on time today."

They all continued, chatting as they worked. A couple other residents showed up as they were finishing up. Maggie smiled to see how much busier it was getting now that produce was ready to pick daily.

"Ya know, ladies" she said as she stood up. "We should be so proud of this place. It was exactly what this town needed."

Brooke nodded. "Not sure the same can be said for the property next door."

Barb laughed. "I'm ready to bet money that the zoning committee will vote it down, no matter how good Tim was in there."

Colleen chuckled. "I wish they'd sell it instead. Sean's idea is crap."

"I don't know," Maggie replied. "If someone else bought it who knows? Might be an even worse plan."

"Worse than Sean? Honey, there ain't nothing worse than that guy."

* * *

AN HOUR later Maggie pulled in to Caldwell Manor. She had gotten into the habit of looking across the street to if Tim's car was parked by the garage, and today it was not. *"I wonder if he's gone to the hospital?"* she wondered. She made a note to call Dr. Kovacs later in the day to see how Carl was doing. *"But for now, I've got other stuff to deal with."* She headed in to find Melvin approaching his daily lookout seat by the door.

"Morning, Miss Maggie! We missed you yesterday."

"Aw, thanks Melvin. It looks I caught you coming late to your post by the door."

He grinned and patted his stomach. "Pancakes for breakfast. I was the last one to leave."

She chuckled. "Hmm, they are good, aren't they?"

He nodded as she headed down the hall. She loved the residents here, but had a soft spot for Melvin.

She passed by Charlotte's office, who waved her in as she wrapped up a phone call. "Hey, how are you holding up? I also heard about Carl – how is he?"

"He's doing okay. Supposed to be leaving ICU today, so that's progress. I'll be okay, too. Just working some stuff out."

She filled her in on the past twenty-four hours and Charlotte sat entranced by the details.

"Wow, you've had one hell of a day, lady. You sure you're okay?"

"Are you asking as a friend or a nurse?" Maggie asked with a smirk.

"With the emotional roller coaster you've been on, maybe more as a nurse. I'll be keeping an eye on you, trust me."

Maggie chuckled. "Join the club. My sister Lucy can be an army sergeant. I saw my therapist yesterday and visited Cassie as well, so right now I'm in an okay place. Working really hard to keep it honest – I can hear the old tapes playing in my head again, and I don't wanna start listening to them."

"Good," Charlotte said. "That makes me feel better. How's Cassie doing?"

Maggie smiled. "She's doing really well. Coming home this weekend."

"I know Teagan had asked in a meeting about her coming to volunteer here. I know Ida would love it, but I'm not sure about Cassie being here."

"Cassie said the same thing. Old people aren't really her thing--but it looks like she's gonna work for Brooke Martin down at the store. She's an amazing artist and Brooke is excited about having her help out.

"Now that I can see. That place is a lot more peaceful than our activity room."

Maggie's phone vibrated and she quickly read a text. "It's Tim. He wants to know if I can make a meeting at the hospital later today. God, I'd have to leave early again."

"Just go," Charlotte said easily. "Things are pretty quiet right now. I know we'll have to work on getting the empty bed filled now that Alice Kennedy moved, but it can wait a day."

Maggie got up to leave, but then had an idea and turned around. "Would that bed be available as a short-term respite?"

Charlotte sat back in her chair. "Probably. We've had some before. What are you getting at?"

"What about Mr. Pritchard coming here?"

Charlotte paused before answering. "I'd have to look at it. I know we could handle the cardiac rehab, but I don't know about the insurance. And quite honestly, this place doesn't have a lot of great memories for him. He might not be at all interested."

"I know that. But it's close to home, and I'm here – and he knows me. It might be something to at least look at."

"He might get more extensive help in Brentwood--but we won't rule it out."

"Thanks. I'll have more information after the meeting today. Can we can talk tomorrow?"

"Sure. So are you gonna text him back?" grinned Charlotte.

"Yes, but about the meeting. Things are still fragile between us right now."

"Just be yourself--and take it slow. But I'm glad you said fragile and not broken."

"Is there much of a difference?"

Charlotte leaned forward and smiled. "Of course there is. Broken is broken, and can't always be fixed. But fragile things can, when handled delicately. Now get to work, Miss Richmond." She smiled as she picked up her pen and opened a file.

Maggie smiled as well. *I guess I know where she stands on what to do about Tim.*

She sent him a message saying that she'd be able to attend, and added "Hope you're doing okay" at the end of her message. After their talk yesterday, she was a little more hopeful today that Charlotte was right.

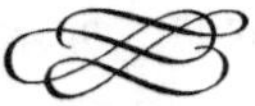

CHAPTER 19

Maggie left Caldwell early enough to visit with Carl for a few minutes before the meeting with Tim and Dr. Kovacs. He appeared to be dozing, but the television was on, so she quietly said his name. His eyes fluttered opened and he looked over at her. "Yeah?"

She took a few steps closer and he smiled a bit. "Well, it's my tomato pal. Did you bring the damn dog with you?"

Maggie chuckled as she pulled her chair closer to the bed and sat down. "No, you'll just have to wait until you're out of here to see Tramp, I'm afraid."

"I hope he hasn't been digging in my roses."

"Nope, not a single paw. And your roses are being well taken care of, Mr. Pritchard. I have a friend who works over at The Green Thumb Gardening Center looking after them – she said that even Mr. Lincoln is thriving."

The old man nodded his approval. "Anyone that can tend to Mr. Lincoln is okay in my book. So, did you bring me any tomatoes? The food here is lousy."

"You must be feeling better if you're complaining again."

"It's bland and looks like everything went through a blender. I wouldn't mind a nice juicy tomato sandwich."

"If your doctor okays it, I'll bring you one next time I come."

"Don't bother. I'm gonna go home tomorrow."

"You are, are you? Did Dr. Kovacs tell you that?"

"Nope, don't need no doctors. I'm feeling a little tired, but I'm fine now. I still can't remember everything."

"You still don't remember what triggered your heart attack?"

"Last I remember I was going up to the town hall for something. Then I had a weird dream about – oh, never you mind about that – and I remember you being there. Doc says it'll come back soon enough."

Maggie nodded. "It will. And whatever you remember, know that everything will be okay. You have lots of people that are here for you and want you to get better."

"Pfft. Who would care about an old curmudgeon like me?"

"Mr. Pritchard, it's a term of endearment. It's an acknowledgement that yes, we know that you're a grumpy old man, but we all still love seeing you walk around town and complain about everything."

"I guess I never looked at it that way. So… if I need a ride home tomorrow, can I call you?"

"Mr. Pritchard, you can call me any time and I'll be happy to help you. But I don't think you're heading home quite that fast. I suspect you'll be here a little longer – maybe a few more days."

"Well, that friend of yours better be okay watching my flowers a little longer then. I'll take over as soon as I'm home."

"You really think so? I imagine you're still pretty tired during the day, am I right?" When she saw the old man scowl, she continued. "How about I go track down your doctor and try to get some answers for you. Then I'll come back in a couple of days and let you know where things stand, okay?"

The old man looked at her for a moment, considering her proposal.

"You gonna bring me that tomato sandwich?"

"If the doctor says okay, absolutely."

"Sounds like a fair deal then. I'll stick around until then at least."

Maggie stood up and reached over to pat his arm. "Now you get some rest, and keep that television on. I think Jeopardy is on tonight, and you can exercise that brain of yours to keep it sharp."

"Don't forget the sandwich, tomato pal."

Maggie grinned. "I'll see you soon, Mr. Pritchard."

As she walked out, she turned to back to see him looking up at the television, and he had a smile on his face. She found Tim already seated with Dr. Kovacs in the cafeteria. There was a cup of coffee in front of the empty seat.

"I think I owed you one," Tim said softly as she sat down. She gave a little smile, and for the first time since Carl's heart attack she felt those butterflies in her stomach flutter ever so lightly. Dr. Kovacs had a bottle of water, and Tim had another cup of coffee.

"Sorry I'm late, "Maggie said. "I stopped in to see him for a few minutes."

"How's he doing?" Tim asked.

Maggie chuckled. "He's definitely on the mend. He's complaining about the hospital food and says he's going home tomorrow because he's feeling fine. He also wants a tomato sandwich." When the other two laughed, she looked at Dr. Kovacs. "And you better alert your nurses tomorrow morning to be on the lookout, because he might very well try to get up and walk out of here."

The doctor laughed. "That's a good sign when they want to leave. Did he talk to you at all about his heart attack? As of earlier he still had no recollection of the event."

Maggie shook her head. "He remembers walking up to town hall, and then waking up here." She looked at Tim and added, "He did say that he had a weird dream – I suspect it was about you and he didn't want to tell me. Remember, in his mind no one knows about you."

Tim looked downcast. "I'd really love to be able to see him. But I know for now it's not in his best interest."

Dr. Kovacs nodded. "I know it's hard waiting, Tim, but I really want him to remember the incident on his own if he can. Then we can work on bringing you in for a visit."

"Whatever you say – I just want him to get better."

"Well, that's why I wanted to talk to both of you. I believe that within the next week Carl will be ready to leave the hospital. However, it's my understanding that he lives alone?" They both nodded. "That's a definite problem, unless someone could stay with him. Ideally, it should be someone who can help him with all of his activities of daily living – dressing, showering, and cooking – and I'm more than concerned that he may not be willing to accept the help."

Maggie laughed out loud. "I'm sorry. I'm trying to picture the poor soul who has to try and get him to do *anything* he doesn't want to do." Getting more serious, she continued. "I really don't think that he can be alone for a while yet, but he needs more than someone that can help at home. He needs some rehab where people will help him to face the challenges ahead."

"I can tell you've had some experience in the field."

"Being at Caldwell Manor, I've had my share of stubborn old folks come through, and it's a team approach that works best for them."

"I agree with Maggie," Tim said. "I'd be really nervous about him being home all alone; even it's where he says he wants to be."

The doctor took a sip of her water. "I agree with both of you. I can have the social worker here inquire about empty beds at the Brentwood Rehab and Skilled Nursing Center. If they don't have anything open there, I think we can find something between here and Boston."

"Actually," Maggie said. "It might be possible for him to have a bed right at Caldwell Manor, just a couple of blocks from his house."

"I didn't realize that they were a skilled nursing facility."

"Technically it's not our focus. Most of the residents are long term placements – but we have had short term respite stays."

"We'd have to really look at the services available to assess whether it would even work,' said Dr. Kovacs.

"We have a whole team of therapists that we contract out for – physical and occupational therapy, speech therapy when needed, and a psychologist / chaplain for emotional and spiritual needs."

The doctor rose an eyebrow in surprise. "That sounds like a good team – as long as they're trained in cardio rehab it's something we can consider. Can you send me the info?" Dr. Kovacs said as she reached into her pocket and handed Maggie a business card. "Then I'll pass it on to our social work department."

"I'd be happy to. Personally, I'd love to be able to bring Mr. Pritchard back to Caldwell. He knows me well and I'd see him every day. There are activities throughout the day that are well planned and well attended."

Dr. Kovacs nodded as she stood up. "Okay, I'll wait to hear from you, but we need the other options checked out." She turned to Tim and shook his hand. "Thanks for being patient, Tim. I hope you can reunite with your grandfather soon. I'll call in a couple of days with more information about our plan in moving ahead. Maggie, thanks so much for coming in. I look forward to hearing from you."

"Glad to help. Oh, about that tomato sandwich. Could Mr. Pritchard eat one if I brought it? I've been giving him extra surplus from my garden and he really likes the tomatoes."

Dr. Kovacs laughed. "I'd say he's definitely feeling better – and yes, feel free to bring one in. Let the nurse know, too. That's a nice gesture, Maggie. I can see why he likes you."

After she left Tim looked at Maggie rather shyly. "Would you stay for a little while to finish our coffee?"

Maggie nodded and took a sip. "It tastes wonderful. Thanks for getting it for me."

Tim smiled. "So.....that part about Grandad coming to Caldwell Manor – do you think it's viable?"

"I think so. We recently had a patient move out, and I think I can get the insurance company to approve a short term respite stay. I'd say the biggest problem is trying to convince him to agree. The Manor is not one of his favorite places in town."

"Still, it'd be nice to think he was right across the street. Maybe at some point I could even finally visit."

"He *will* remember, Tim. I hope that after he does you two can have a fresh start. You've both missed out on a lot of time together."

"That's what all those letters were for. I really wanted to have some kind of relationship with him, even if my mom wasn't open to reconciling. I kept praying that maybe the next one I mailed wouldn't be returned."

"That must have been hard."

"Hey, it's like you said. Every choice has a consequence. My mom's choice is my consequence, I guess."

"Doesn't seem all that fair, though."

"I guess life isn't always fair, is it?"

Maggie sat quietly for a second, not sure she wanted to talk about their relationship quite yet. "So what did you do today? I'm sure you didn't sit here at the hospital all day."

Tim sat back and ran both hands through his hair as he stretched. "Not the most peaceful day. This morning I had a meeting with Sean over at the old hardware store."

"I bet you got an earful."

"Yeah, you might say that. He was walking around picking things up and throwing them. It was like watching a toddler having a tantrum."

"I wonder if they heard him from over in the gardens."

"I can't say we got anywhere, though. I tried to suggest that we address the concerns that the committee had, but then it was an 'everybody in this town is out to get me' speech. I just sat there in the quiet after he stormed off."

"I bet that building is pretty gross inside, isn't it?"

"Structurally, it's in really good shape. But yeah, everything inside needs to be gutted and redone." He got quiet for a minute. "I went out the back door and just stood there looking around. It's a pretty peaceful spot out behind the building."

"Ah, part of it is kind of a jungle, isn't it?"

Tim grinned. "Yeah, it's definitely a little overgrown. I'm surprised the town didn't take it over years ago."

"Maybe they didn't want to do battle with Sean McClean again."

"Well, that's understandable. Ya know, I stood out and looked over at the gardens and my granddad's house, and I got really angry at Sean – and my mom, too."

"How so?"

"I could have grown up here. That house might have been my home…..and I really feel like I was robbed of what might have been an amazing childhood." He grimaced as he looked at Maggie. "I might have even known you way back then."

Maggie looked at him sadly. "Possibly."

Tim held her gaze a moment, and then sighed heavily. "At any rate, I decided at that point that I really need to get out of this partnership with Sean. I can't stand working with a man who isn't capable of caring about anyone but himself, and I don't want to be associated with him."

"That's sounds like a pretty big challenge."

He nodded. "It's one I'm ready to tackle," he said with determination. He paused a minute as he looked out the window. "Of course, there's an even bigger challenge I'm taking on as well."

Maggie looked at his face staring out at the swaying trees. "Be patient, Tim. The relationship with your grandfather is right there. Give it time and you'll have what you want."

Tim slowly turned back to face her. "I hope you're right about that. But that's not what I was talking about."

"No?"

He shook his head. "I was talking about you. And how I'm determined to earn your trust back."

Maggie looked into his eyes tenuously. It still hurt a lot.

He took her hand gently, and with his other hand cupped her chin and gently raised her face to look at him again. "I believe it's there, just like my grandad. I'll be as patient as I have to be to get us back to where we were."

Maggie spoke softly. "And where was that?"

"Back to where we were falling in love. At least, that's where I was. I still am, Maggie."

He dropped his hand from her cheek, but continued to hold the other across the table.

She looked down at it, wanting so hard to be back up on the beach in Gloucester. She finally looked up to meet his gaze. "You weren't alone. It's just that—"

"I hurt you. I know that. I know how important honesty is to you."

Maggie nodded. "Those walls are back up right now."

"I understand. Really, I do. But I can promise that I'll never lie to you again. I mean that. I'm praying that you can at least try to stay open – just a little bit."

Maggie eyes filled with tears as her heart tugged inside of her. She looked across the table at him and smiled weakly, squeezing his hand gently. "I can try."

For the first time in what seemed like forever, she saw that dimple appear as he smiled back at her.

CHAPTER 20

Saturday morning Maggie woke up bright and early, and after getting dressed, she grabbed Tramp's leash. "Want to go for a little walk?" Seeing the leash and hearing his favorite word aside from "dinnertime", Tramp trotted eagerly over to the door.

On their way to the garden they passed by Carl's house and picked up the newspaper. "Maybe I should bring him the pile when I see him tomorrow. What do you think, Tramp?"

The beagle stood at the end of the driveway looking expectantly at the house for the one that was usually standing there in his flannel shirt.

"I know, Tramp," she said. "He'll be home soon enough. And he *likes* you." She gave him a pat and he licked her hand, almost as though he understood. "Come on, let's go pick some tomatoes for our buddy."

She'd gotten here earlier than the others. Barb was probably serving breakfast to her guests, which made Maggie wonder if Tim was over at the house right now. She dwelled on his words as she worked, wanting so much to give him a hug and wipe out the past week's heartache. She believed him that he was sorry, and that he was falling in love. And she wanted to do the same. *"I just have to take it slow; I know now that he didn't mean to hurt me."*

She found a few ripe tomatoes on the vine, and pulled off several, along with some zucchini, cucumbers, and peppers. She pulled a few weeds that tenaciously tried to keep popping back up, and then got the hose that was attached to the spigot and watered her plot. In no time she and Tramp were heading home, and Maggie was thankful for once that the only two people she saw were a couple jogging at the other end of the park. *"Sometimes I'd give anything to be able to run again,"* she thought, *"but I'll focus instead on everything that recovery has given me."*

When they got back Lucy was just getting up. "You were out early." Her eyes narrowed a bit, and she looked down at Tramp. "Did she make you run?"

Maggie rolled her eyes a bit and glared at her sister. "No, I did not. We walked at our normal pace and did our normal gardening routine. And here, I have proof," she said as she lifted the basket of produce.

"Those look gorgeous. I might steal a tomato right now and make us grilled cheese and tomato for breakfast. What do you say?"

Maggie thought a moment and nodded. "That actually sounds delicious. But make sure you leave one tomato alone." When she saw the confused look, she added, "I promised Mr. Pritchard that I'd bring him a tomato sandwich tomorrow when I go."

Lucy laughed as she started preparing the meal. "He must be feeling better. I'm glad. So are you heading over to Brentwood right after breakfast?"

"Yup. It's Cassie's big day today. I'm going to swing by and pick up Teagan on the way. She helped Cassie get to the Phoenix – it's only fitting that she gets to celebrate her leaving."

"Is Cassie excited?""

"Excited, scared, and a little sad I suspect. I think she's ready to face the next phase and tackle being back in the midst of life."

"So why are you bringing her home instead of her folks?"

"That's what she wanted. Cassie didn't want them making a fuss."

"That makes sense. So did they do the family therapy like we did when you were there?"

"Yup, it's still required, although I think it's only once a week now.

I hope Cassie's family can give her the same strong support that you, mom and dad gave to me."

Lucy finished grilling the sandwiches and placed one on the plate she'd gotten out for Maggie and one for herself. "I hope it works out for her. I suspect we'll maybe see Cassie right at this table from time to time."

"I think so," she said, taking a bite of the sandwich. "Hmm...... nothing better than fresh tomatoes. I can hardly wait to watch Mr. Pritchard take his first bite tomorrow."

"So were you at the hospital long? I know when I got home you'd already gone to bed."

"I was wiped out. It was a long day. I had that meeting with Dr. Kovacs – and Tim."

"I imagine meetings with him are a little emotional right now, huh?"

Maggie nodded. "He's trying so hard, and my head believes him – I just can't get the heart to quite let him in yet."

"Give it time. I don't think he's going anywhere."

"That's basically what he said." She took another bite of the sandwich and licked her fingers. "Hmm. This is a really good breakfast, sis."

"Not to sound like your drill sergeant or anything, but are you managing okay to keep your routines?"

Maggie nodded. "For the most part. I can usually recognize the old tapes when they start to play in my head. And I'm eating okay – maybe not as well as normal, but I'm at least still being mindful."

"Good – and you know I only bug you because I love you."

"Trust me, I give thanks every day that I get to live with you. I know someday that might change if you and Liz ever decide to get married, but I'm grateful for how things are now."

Lucy grinned. "You know you could still live with us. Liz adores you, and Watson loves Tramp." She got up to take the two plates over to the sink, and then turned around and smiled. "Besides, maybe it won't be only me getting married someday."

Maggie rolled her eyes. "I think Tim is way more patient than you are. Listen, I gotta go pick up Teagan so we can go get Cassie. Thanks for breakfast."

"Have a good day, sis. Liz and Watson will be here tonight. We'll check in on Mr. Lincoln and the other roses once she gets here. If you're home maybe you can walk over with us."

"I might like that – thanks. Maybe I can cut a few roses to bring to him tomorrow."

"Might cheer him up to have some of his babies nearby."

A few minutes later Maggie saw Teagan waiting for her as she pulled into her driveway. She hopped in the passenger seat and got her seatbelt on. "Thanks for letting my come along. I'm so excited for her."

"Me, too. It's a big step."

"I know I've said this before, but I'm so grateful that you were there at that meeting when we first talked about the Phoenix. I think she was shutting us all down until you spoke up."

"I was glad to be there. Sometimes it takes someone who's walked the same path to finally make that connection."

"When I see how together you are now, I wonder if Cassie will be in the same healthy place in a few years."

Maggie laughed. "Remember, you can't compare one person's recovery to another – everyone has their own path. And as for that part about me being so together? Trust me, I still struggle some days."

Teagan looked concerned. "Are you okay, Maggie?"

"Yeah, I'm okay," she said. "I've been trying to figure out how dating fits into the whole equation, and some days are tougher than others."

Teagan laughed. "Now that's a problem I'll never have – and I like it that way."

"Hmm….life might have been easier if I'd been ace or aro, but I can't deny that I have real feelings for Tim. So how do you like working more hours during the summer?"

"I love it. Seriously, I was born in the wrong era. The folks at the Manor are like extended family."

"I hope you have a *few* friends your own age."

Teagan smiled. "I do – and that hadn't been the case the last few years – I mean, aside from Brian. But he's more like than a brother than anything."

"He's the one that comes in to cook?"

"Yup – and he's loving it. He's a natural with the residents and he gets them sharing all their recipes from childhood. I love the days when he comes in and helps."

"I know that Cassie is also on that list of good friends now."

"We've gotten so much closer. I'm really looking forward to senior year and being able to do one more show together."

Maggie frowned a bit. "You do know that Cassie might have to really look at the show and whether it's a healthy choice for her, right?"

Teagan nodded. "Yeah, she's been talking about it. She knows that she'll likely have to choose between the show and the dance studio, or maybe neither. I told her I'd be there for her no matter what. I only want her to get better."

"That's exactly what she needs," Maggie said. "I know she's mentioned a few of the cast have been to visit her, too – that's nice."

"Yeah, I set that up. They were asking about her, and I thought it would be beneficial for her to see that she really does have friends here in Massachusetts."

As they drove the rest of the way to Brentwood they talked about favorite Broadway shows, books they were reading, and favorite summer foods. The topic of the community garden came into the conversation.

"I know you helped Colleen and the others to get that going," Teagan said. "It's been a great addition to Caldwell."

"I agree," Maggie said. "I love the camaraderie that's developed between different residents as they chat while working. I mean, look at me and the three ladies that started it. We're all as different as can be, and yet I love seeing them every single day."

Teagan nodded. "That's what theater did for me this past year. I wish we could have a summer show somewhere to stay connected. I made some good friends on the stage."

"That would be a good fit for Caldwell – aside from Colleen's studio and a few things at Brooke's shop, there's not much else for the arts here in town."

"Nope. I suppose we can have the golfers quote Shakespeare or sing once the driving range opens."

Maggie chuckled. "Now that I'd like to see. I wouldn't want to be your dad right now. I'm sure facing off against Sean McClean isn't a top agenda item."

Teagan grinned. "On the contrary – he can hardly wait for the next round."

"The next round? Now that's funny."

They arrived at the Phoenix Center and signed in, then made their way to Cassie's room. She was sitting on her bed with a sketch book and a pencil in hand. "Hey – you're here."

They both gave her a hug and admired her sketch. It was a copy of the phoenix bird that made the stain glass window on the front door.

"That's really good, Cassie," Teagan said.

"A nice reminder?" Maggie asked.

Cassie nodded. "I remember the day I came here and how scared I was. And then when I got to the front door that phoenix was so striking. It made me feel that I could do this. I didn't wanna forget that memory."

Maggie looked around at the few items she had to bring with her. "You know, it's just as striking on the way out – maybe more so. You ready?"

Cassie closed her book and got up, grabbing a little stuffed monkey off of her pillow.

"Aww, that's cute," Teagan said. "Old childhood friend?"

Cassie shook her head. "Actually it was a gift from Philip shortly after I got here. I called him 'Monkey' when we were little 'cause he was always trying to climb stuff. He didn't want me to forget him while I was here."

"I'm sure he's looking forward to having you back home. As are your folks."

"Yeah, I think my mom was a little hurt that I asked you guys to come get me – you know how moms are."

"Well then," Maggie said, "let's not waste any time getting you back home. I'm sure she's eagerly awaiting your return."

Cassie only had one small suitcase, and then one tote bag filled with assorted books and toiletries that were allowed. Her last bag contained a bunch of art supplies and various things she had made while at the Phoenix.

"Wait," Cassie said, before they started to pick them up. "I have a little something I want to give to both of you."

She reached down between her bed and the wall and pulled out the cemetery painting she had done. She held it out toward Maggie. "I know how much you liked this – I'd really like you to have it. I don't really think it's something I'd hang up at home."

Maggie smiled and took it gently. "Actually, I was hoping that you'd be willing to sell it to me. I really want to give this to Mr. Pritchard – you happened to paint his wife's gravestone and bench, and I think he'd cherish it."

"But then I have nothing for you."

"How 'bout you let me keep those rocks you painted? I absolutely love them."

"Okay – if you're sure. Or I can paint you whatever you might want instead. I really don't know if I'd be going home today if it hadn't been for you."

Maggie gave her a big hug. "I'll always be here for you. You have number, and you can call anytime day or night. I mean that. "

Cassie then reached into her art bag for a smaller canvas which she held out for Teagan. "This is one I did for you. My memory's not as good on this one, but I hope it's close enough for you."

Teagan turned it over and immediately teared up as her hand went to her heart. It was the other end of the cemetery, with a small gravestone under a tree, with a beautiful white angel perched on top. On the stone Cassie had painted the name 'Joanne'. "Cassie, this is beautiful – and the angel's pretty damn close."

"You like it then?" Cassie asked tentatively.

"I love it. Thank you so much." She wrapped her arms around Cassie who gave her a warm heartfelt hug in return.

Cassie's eyes were misty as pulled away. "Thank *you*. For being a friend when I didn't want one, and for caring enough to point out what I didn't want anyone to see."

"I'm glad that it made a difference. And that you're in such a better place than when you first got here."

"Well, without you and Maggie, I might not be. I just wanted to somehow let you both know how much I appreciate all you've done for me."

Maggie picked up Cassie's suitcase. "Let's get you home, girl. We have the rest of the summer to hang out together."

With that, the three of them carried Cassie's belongings down to the door, waiting as Cassie said goodbyes to various residents and staff. As she got to the exit, she lovingly reached out and touched the deep blue phoenix bird on the door, and with a smile, turned the knob and headed out to face the world.

* * *

WHEN MAGGIE GOT HOME LATER in the day she was greeted at the door by both Tramp and Watson. Liz was sitting on the couch with her laptop and Lucy was in the kitchen making coffee.

"How's my boy?" she said as she squatted down to give Tramp a hug. Watson licked her face as she reached out to pat him as well. "Hey, buddy, good to see you again." She stood back up and smiled at Liz. "Summer school almost over?"

Liz nodded as she stopped typing and put her computer on the table. "One more week. I'm finishing my final paper and another class will be done."

"What class is this?"

"Horticultural diseases."

Maggie laughed as she waved at Lucy and plopped down in one of the armchairs. "Sounds deadly – no pun intended."

"That's funny. And it can be deadly – literally. Fascinating how many insects carry diseases that can sneak in and kill a plant. That's what my final paper is on."

"I am *so* glad to be done with school and papers, and ever so grateful that I was in social work and not greenhouse management."

Lucy came out with a tray with three mugs of coffee, all prepared as each preferred. "Bet you're glad you knew someone, though. Can you imagine how worried you'd be if Liz wasn't here to tend to Mr. Pritchard's roses?"

"I'd get down and prostrate myself on the floor if I wasn't so tired. Please tell me that there are no sneaky diseases over there."

Liz took a sip of coffee and smile. "Rest assured, they're all doing fine. They really are gorgeous roses. I've actually enjoyed stopping in to take care of them. How's the old guy doing, anyway?"

"I'll know more tomorrow, but it looks like he'll need a couple of weeks of rehab before he comes home. I'm actually trying to get him a bed the Manor if I can."

"That'd be awesome to be so close to home."

Lucy chuckled. "I don't know, you might find him showing up in his bathrobe while you're over there watering his flowers." She turned to Maggie. "How'd things go with Cassie today?"

"Great. Her folks had a welcome home banner strung up inside the front door, and even Philip seemed glad to have his sister home. I told her she could call anytime day or night if she needed to talk to someone."

"You're a good person, Maggie," Liz said. "She's lucky to have you helping her along."

She looked up at the clock and then added, "Hey, if we're gonna get the roses done before the mosquitos come out we should head over soon."

Maggie nodded. "If I wanted to cut a few roses to bring to the hospital tomorrow, would they still be okay by the time I got there? It wouldn't hurt the bushes or anything, would it?"

Liz chuckled. "Haven't you ever walked in and found roses on someone's kitchen table? Why don't we bring along a vase and you can put them right in water. They'll be fine for a week or so."

"Awesome. There's one under the sink I'll go and grab. If you guys don't mind, I thought I'd come along. I can keep these two guys happy while you're working."

Maggie grabbed a frisbee and a couple of dog toys and put them in a tote, which made both Tramp and Watson start to dance around the room as they tried to lead Maggie to the door. "Give us a little time, guys, and we'll be ready – I promise."

Within minutes, they were all heading off for the short walk to Carl's house. The dogs seemed disappointed when they head up the driveway, looking beyond to the park. Lucy laughed. "You brought their toys. They thought you were heading off to play in the park."

"Maybe I'll take them over for a walk while you guys are here. But first I want to see how the roses are looking."

As they walked around to the back, Maggie noticed the flower beds along the front and side of the house. "Liz, have you been weeding these as well? They all look so beautiful."

The tall brunette smiled as she got the hose off the hook. "Can't make the roses beautiful and then leave these to die. Remember, just as the vegetable garden is your happy place, the flowers are mine."

"I need to take some pictures to show Mr. Pritchard tomorrow."

"Get them on the way out. First, you have to see his pride and joy."

Maggie rounded the corner and the sweet smell of roses reached her almost immediately. As she got closer to the line of bushes she stopped to admire them. "Wow, Liz. These are stunning. I mean, you can see them from the community garden, but it's a whole different view when they're all right here in front of you. The colors and the scents are heavenly."

There was a small brick patio at the rear of the yard, and Maggie could picture a little bistro set up for seating and having a light meal outdoors. She wondered why the old man didn't have at least a chair to sit in and rest in while out working. "You know, this spot needs a little sprucing up. I might try to find a little table and a couple of chairs for Mr. Pritchard to have for when he gets home. He'll need a place to sit and rest when he gets back to his beauties."

"That's a great idea," said Lucy. "Although, knowing how stubborn the old guy is, would he object to the change?"

"I don't know," Maggie replied. "But if I got a set that he absolutely refused to keep, I could either sell it or maybe squeeze it on the front porch of the townhouse."

"Now you have me thinking it might be nice if he hates it," Lucy said with a wink.

Liz was walking around, surveying the various blooms. "Let's find a couple of each variety for your bouquet. I want to find some really beauties to make sure he approves."

"Trust me," Maggie said, "they all look incredible."

"Well, be sure to let the old guy know that I'll take care of them as long he needs me to. It's really good experience for me and I'm enjoying working with the different varieties. Some of these bushes are really old – maybe 25-30 years. It's impressive."

"Wow," Lucy said. "I didn't know roses could live that long."

"They've been well cared for to last that long."

"You're a gem, Liz. I know it'll be at least another two to three weeks, and who knows what he might need for help once he gets home."

"As long as he doesn't come out and yell at me for what I'm doing, I can handle that."

Maggie smiled. "You, I'm not worried about. But I can guarantee he'll come out and yell at Watson." The German Shepherd's ears perked up at the mention of his name. "And I guess I should go and give these guys a little playtime since I brought their toys. Would you guys mind if I took them over to the park? There's no one over there from what I can see, and we can play some frisbee for a while."

Lucy nodded. "Be sure to take a few photos of the side gardens on your way past. We'll bring your vase of roses back to the townhouse and get dinner ready for when you get back. You okay with something simple like Caesar wraps? We can leave the chicken out of yours."

Maggie nodded. "Sounds delicious. Feel free to cut up the cucumber and tomato that I picked this morning. But make sure to leave one."

"I know, I know. Someone needs his tomato sandwich tomorrow."

aggie headed over to Caldwell Manor in the morning. She had been out of work for part of the week and wanted to make up the time. She also had some research to do into how to make the short term respite for Carl a credible option. She'd be heading over to the hospital later in the day and wanted to run it by him while he was munching on her tomato sandwiches. Maybe he wouldn't be so against coming back to the Manor if she presented it right. She made a list of people she'd need to talk to that week, including Jason from physical therapy and the insurance company, but she was hopeful by the time she finished.

As she was leaving her office to head home some familiar voices greeted her.

"Maggie! What are you doing here on a Sunday?" She turned to smile at Teagan, who was working for a few hours. Beside her was Cassie.

"Catching up on paperwork," she answered Teagan, and then added to Cassie, "and I suspect that you're here to see one very happy grandmother."

Cassie nodded. "I'm looking forward to spending some *quality* time with her instead of all the past visits where I snuck off to dance or go for a run."

"She'll love that. I suspect Teagan won't mind any time you're around, either. How was your first night at home?"

"So far, so good. It felt good to sleep in my own bed again. Mom and dad surprised me by setting up a little art studio in the basement for me. I'm kind of excited about that."

"I'm glad you discovered other creative outlets at the Phoenix. It'll help your transition. Any old impulses to go out and run or dance? You know they're gonna be there at some point."

Cassie sighed. "I know. I'd like to say I'm ready for it, but I'm kind of scared to death. Even family dinners make me a little nervous – like, are they all gonna sit there and watch me eat like the nurses first did at the Phoenix?"

"I get it," Maggie replied. "Hell, my sister can *still* be a drill sergeant at times."

"They only do it because they love you," Teagan added.

"I know. I have to keep telling myself that. But if I get feeling a little crazy, can I call either of you?" asked Cassie.

Both of them nodded as they each hugged her from either side.

"Day or night," Maggie said.

"Ditto. That's what friends are for," added Teagan.

"Thanks. I know Teagan has to get to work, and I need to find my Gram. I have a little something to give her." Out of her pocket she pulled another rock. On it, she had painted a tiny replica of her house – the one Ida had first owned and lived in.

Teagan looked at the design and then her friend's face. "She's gonna love this, Cassie. I can't get over all the details. You even put a wreath on the door. How the heck do you do all that on a rock?"

Cassie smiled. "It's kind of like letting the paintbrush do the dancing until I can again."

Maggie took the rock, admired the image, and handed it back. "That's a great way of describing the process. I've never seen your house, but I'm assuming that's what this is; I'm sure Ida will love having a memory of it. Please give her my best. I'd go with you to say hello, but I have to stop back home and then head to the hospital for a bit."

"Going to visit the old man?" asked Teagan.

"Hmm – mm. Hoping he might be here in the next few days for rehab. We'll see."

"I really hope that works out," Teagan said. "Although didn't Charlotte say that he hated this place after his wife was here before she died?"

"Yeah, I know that's a challenge. I'm hoping I can help him to get past that."

Cassie smiled. "Don't worry. I'll tell my Gram to take care of him. From what Teagan tells me, she can be a pretty persuasive and positive lady in this place."

Maggie nodded. "That might not be a bad idea. If anyone can bring him around once he gets here, it would be Ida."

On her drive to Brentwood Maggie contemplated the challenges that still lie ahead for her neighbor. She knew adjusting to life after a heart attack would require him to be a little more involved with others. She was sure he'd hate any facility he had to go to for rehab, so why not Caldwell Manor? The memories might be tough, but he was a tenacious old man when he needed to be, and he'd at least be close to home.

Besides, that challenge was nothing compared to what awaited him when his memory totally returned. *Tim.* It all came back to him, and Maggie felt a strange connection to Mr. Pritchard as she struggled to make sense of how Tim fit into her own life. She kept trying to focus on the logic that indicated he hadn't meant to hurt her, but the heart was slow to catch up. Maggie suspected that the old curmudgeon might have the same reaction.

When she arrived at the hospital, she checked in with nurses' station to let them know about the tomato sandwich, which made the head nurse laugh. "Is that all it takes to make him less ornery? A tomato sandwich? Honey, bring him as many as he'll eat."

Maggie chuckled, knowing that the nurse spoke with a smile on her face. He'd never admit it, but the old curmudgeon had a way of making people like him – despite his grumpiness.

She found him sitting up doing the crossword puzzle in the newspaper. "Well, look at you, being all studious."

When Carl saw the vase that Maggie carried his whole face lit up. "My roses. You brought me some." He moved the newspaper to the side of the bed table and patted the spot in front of him. "Right here." She watched him as he fingered each bloom and leaned forward to slowly breathe in their fragrance. His eyes were a bit misty as he spoke to Maggie. "Whoever is taking care of them is doing a great job. They're beauties, aren't they?"

Maggie nodded, her heart filled with gratitude that such a small act could do so much for him. *"God, he loves these flowers."* As he continued to study them, she answered. "You have beautiful roses, Mr. Pritchard. My friend Liz, who's been taking care of them, said they were about the prettiest she's ever seen."

He sat back with an expression of both contentment and a bit of smugness at that comment. "I'll have to meet this friend someday to thank her properly."

"I didn't know you did crossword puzzles, Mr. Pritchard."

"Every day – first thing after getting my newspaper." He picked up the paper and pencil, tapping the end of the pencil under his chin as he shook his head. "Though I can't seem to get this one word, today."

"What's the clue? Maybe I can help."

He gave his usual scowl. "Ten letter word. Another word for grump. Begins with "c.""

Maggie laughed out loud. "Really, Mr. Pritchard? Look in the mirror." He gave her a confused look, and she returned a big smile. "It's *curmudgeon* – that should have been easy."

He counted the letters as he checked to see if it would fit, and turned the pencil around to add it in. "So it is," he said with a chuckle. Almost as if he didn't want the humor to last, he narrowed his eyes at her. "Where's that tomato sandwich you promised?"

"You think I'd forget?" She reached into her bag and pulled out a plastic container with two tomato sandwiches inside. "Hope you don't mind, I added a little lettuce and mayo."

He opened the container and took a bite. "Not bad, kid. Not as good as mine, but you make a pretty good damn sandwich." He took another bite. "You make good tomatoes, too."

"There's lots of vegetables coming in now. By the time you get back home you'll have all the fresh produce you can eat. Everyone's been asking about you – they all hope you get home soon."

"That makes all of us, then – except the doctor. Says I can't go right home. She don't know nothing."

"Now you're starting to sound like your old self, again," Maggie teased. "But she's right, Mr. Pritchard. You're gonna need a little more help before you can be safe on your own. We all want you to be okay when you're by yourself."

"Pfft. I've been on my own for years – I'll be fine."

"What's the longest distance you've walked since you've been here?" Maggie asked.

"Oh, now you sound like the damn therapist. Saying I can't walk that far without help yet." He sat there in silence, chewing his sandwich with a grim look on his face.

"You're such a stubborn old guy – but you'll get there. You gotta be a little more patient. Just like your roses. They're tenacious as hell, but it takes time for them to become as beautiful as they are now."

He scowled at her. "You calling me beautiful?"

She grinned at him. "See? That humor will get you through. Just take it a day at a time and do what you need to do to get back home."

"Since when did you get to be so smart?"

"A lot of practice – and a lot mistakes from letting my own pride get in the way."

He finished his sandwiches and sat back deep in thought. "Getting old is tough," he finally said. "I don't like the idea of having to rely on anyone."

"I'm sure it's a little scary, too, living alone. It's not necessarily a bad thing to consider that you might need some help." When he didn't answer, she continued gently. "So what if when you leave here you had the opportunity to hang out with me every day?"

He narrowed his eyes. "What do you mean?"

"If you have to do some cardiac rehab somewhere, why not do it right in Caldwell – and only a block away from your home?"

His expression got defiant and he crossed his arms over his chest. "Not there. No way."

He looked back at his roses and he had to wipe away a tear.

"That's where your wife died, isn't it?" He didn't answer. "I know that you used to visit her there every day. One of the nurses has been there a long time, and she remembers Ruth."

He sat quietly for a moment before speaking. "Shouldn't have to lose someone twice. I lost her long before she actually died."

"I know. Dementia's a horrible thing – especially for the families. Can you tell me about her? If you're up for it?"

His face softened. "She loved to laugh. I could never see why she was always so damn cheerful, but she just smiled and called me her old coot. Toward the end she didn't smile much anymore. She didn't even know me." His eyes were full of tears as he looked up at Maggie. "Sometimes I wish I could forget like she did. Having a sharp memory can be a curse."

"I imagine that's true."

"I never wanna go back to that place. It's more than I could handle."

"At least think about it. I know it has painful memories, but sometimes you gotta face the pain to get through it. Anywhere else you go you'll be totally alone – at least in Caldwell you'd see a familiar face every day. Don't let your stubbornness get the best of you."

He looked at her and shook his head. "Well, you sure have some sass, don't you?"

"Sometimes a good friend tells you what you need to hear, even if it's hard to hear."

"A friend? Heck, you're young enough to be my grand—" Carl suddenly got quiet, and had a confused look on his face. He muttered to himself. "Dang it."

"What it is, Mr. Pritchard?"

"I keep remembering this dream I had, and it's driving me crazy."

Maggie knew that her words might spark the missing memory, but she felt that he was so close. As gently as she could, she spoke. "Is it the same dream you told me about? The one about your grandson being here?"

His gaze met hers. "I told you about that?" She nodded. "About my grandson?"

"You were kind of in and out that first day here. But you did tell me about him. About Tim."

His eyes filled with tears as he looked at the roses. "I've never told anyone about him. All these years."

"It's okay, Mr. Pritchard," she said, reaching out to take his hand. "You told me. You told me all about him. And about the letters he sent you."

Carl nodded, as if remembering. "He sent me so many. I never should have sent them all back. What else did I tell you?"

Maggie spoke slowly, praying that the old man could handle the memories coming back. "You told me about Sharon, and how she left. I know that was really hard for you."

Carl wiped away a tear. "I lost her and the baby that day—I never should have let her leave. She told me she was pregnant and I was so scared that Steve was hurting her. Ruthie cried and we begged her to come home, but she left." He was obviously struggling to remember. "I swear he was right here – but he couldn't have been, could he?"

Maggie took a deep breath, and eyed the nurses' call button in case she needed to press it. "He *was* here, Mr. Pritchard," she said softly. "Tim stayed by your side that whole night."

As more memories became clearer, Carl seemed to get more confused. "He was? So I'm not crazy.......but why? And where is he now?"

"He's been waiting, Mr. Pritchard. For you to remember."

"Remember? Remember what?" He squeezed her hand as he looked at her. "Why was he here?" As his gaze returned to the roses in front of him, Maggie could see the final piece click into place. Carl's expression turned cold, and he let go of her hand. "He came back to take my roses away." He glared at her. "Didn't he? Him and that McClean kid."

She watched him, her hand finding the button and pressing it to call the nurse, who was there in a matter of seconds. As she caught the nurse's eye, she said quietly. "He's remembering."

He tried to push the nurse away. "He was at the town hall, wasn't he?" he said to Maggie, his voice getting louder. "He's working with him, isn't he?" The beeping on the machine beside his bed started to speed up.

The nurse put her hand firmly on his shoulder. "Mr. Pritchard, you look at me." He glanced at her, his body still full of tension. "Right in my eyes. You take a deep breath with me. C'mon." She breathed in deeply, watching him ignore her. "Look, Mr. Pritchard, I don't want you to have another heart attack, do you hear me?"

That seemed to get his attention, as he stopped a moment and met her gaze. "Now you take a deep breath with me and we'll face this memory together, okay?" This time he slowed his breathing a bit and closed his eyes. "That's it," the nurse continued, "slow that heart rate down for a minute or two and then we'll deal with it head on."

"You're a tough old man," Maggie said, grabbing his hand. "And you're strong enough now – I promise."

He laid back for a few moments, breathing in and out heavily. The beeping on the machine next to him started to slow back down, and as the nurse took his pulse and put the stethoscope to his heart, she nodded. "That's good, Mr. Pritchard." As he opened his eyes to look at her, she continued. "Sometimes we block the memory of a bad shock until the body is capable of facing it. That's why you couldn't remember. So the fact that you are now is a good sign – it means your heart is stable. But you gotta work with it and not push too hard, okay?"

He nodded, then turned to Maggie with a tired but resolved face. "Tell me everything you can about Sean McClean and that meeting. And why my grandson is working with him."

As the nurse nodded, Maggie took a deep breath and began. "First of all, nothing happened at the meeting. Sean's plans weren't even considered that night. He wasn't at all prepared and he didn't make a very good impression on the committee or the residents that were there."

Carl actually smiled a bit. "He doesn't make a good impression on anyone. But…..but why was Tim with him?"

"Tim can't stand working with him – he told me so."

"So then why did he come?"

"He came because of you. Because he thought it might be the only chance he'd get to be that close to his grandfather." Carl's eyes filled with tears as he searched her face for answers. "He wants so desperately to know you. And he was devastated when he heard about your heart attack. He felt that it was his fault."

"How do you know all this?" the old man whispered.

"Because Tim and I have been dating a little. I'm the one he told you about that night, when he talked about Caldwell and … the woman he thought he was falling in love with." Her eyes now matched his as she met his gaze. "I was as shocked as you were that night, finding out that he was both your grandson and Sean's partner. I had no idea before that."

The nurse handed them both the tissue box. "Before you get me started, I'm gonna leave you two alone to talk. You press that button if the beeps start back up, ya hear?"

Maggie nodded, and wiped away her tears. "I'll tell you whatever I can to help fill in the gaps. We're going to get through this together, okay?"

"I want to know all about Tim. Whatever you can tell me." As she began, way back on their first meeting in the garden, she found it somewhat healing to tell him the whole story of how they'd met and the time they'd spent together. She told him that he had talked about things being complicated, and continued with their conversations after the heart attack.

"Last year, your son-in-law died, and Tim inherited his half of the hardware store, along with a bunch of unpaid bills."

"Steve never should have bailed McClean out. He was just like him, though. Sharon hated me because I couldn't accept him into the family."

"Tim would agree with you about Sean. He had no idea that he'd have to deal with him."

"So you believe him then? About coming back here because of me? And not wanting to be a part of this whole messy business with McClean?"

Maggie nodded. "I do, Mr. Pritchard. I think he'd had done things differently if he could turn back time. But for now he's hoping that he hasn't ruined things forever."

"For you or me?"

"For both of us. He didn't want either of us to be hurt. He wants so much to know you."

"What makes you so sure that he's not just saying that until the next meeting is over?"

"Because he kept all those letters, Mr. Pritchard. He still has every single one."

"The ones I sent back?"

She nodded. "He showed them to me. Except the one that you kept."

He took a deep breath and closed his eyes. "I still have that photo in my desk." He sat a long time without speaking, and Maggie sat quietly, grateful that the beeping sound stayed steady. He finally opened his eyes and looked at her. "I wanna see him," he whispered. "I wanna see my grandson."

She nodded through her tears. "I'll call him. If the nurses are okay with it, I'm sure he'll get here right away."

She sat with him for the next hour waiting for Tim to arrive. His heart monitor occasionally sped up a bit, but she'd remind him to do the slow deep breathing that the nurse had done, and Maggie reassured him that all would be okay – even if she was petrified that Tim's arrival might cause another shock.

When he finally walked through the door, Carl was leaning back with his eyes closed and didn't hear him. Maggie's eyes met his and she could see the mixed emotions that he brought with him. She tried to give him a reassuring smile as she squeezed the old man's hand.

He opened his eyes and looked at Maggie, whose gaze led his eyes to the other side of his bed. His eyes got misty as he looked again at the one who had rushed in to cause his heart attack, but this time his grandson stood frozen, apprehensively waiting for him to respond.

"Tim," the old man whispered.

"Grandad." He took a tenuous step forward, and then as the old man reached out his hand, he closed the gap between them and grasped his hand. His own eyes fought back tears as he finally touched the grandfather he'd never known. "Are you….okay?"

The old man nodded silently, his wrinkled fingers caressing his grandson's hand. "Come….sit. Let me look at you."

Tim pulled up the chair across the bed from Maggie and sat down, taking Carl's hand in both hands. "I'm so sorry that I caused all…..this," he choked out, looking around at all the monitors.

Carl smiled weakly. "As long as that one keeps beeping we're good. You ….you look like your father."

Tim nodded, still blinking back tears. "Mom told me that a lot growing up."

Carl took a deep breath and sighed. "How…..how is she?"

"She's…..getting by. Still in Maine."

Carl nodded sadly, and then looked over at Maggie and back. "This one …..she told me about your dad. I'm sorry."

Tim shook his head. "Don't be. We didn't mourn because he died, but more that he never really lived. I wish that she'd consider coming back now that he's gone."

"She has no reason to come back here. I made her choose." He sat for a moment looking at his roses, and then looked at Tim again. "But you're here. In Caldwell."

Tim noticed his flowers, and nodded. "I love this town, Grandad, and I can assure you that nothing's going to happen to your roses. That's a promise."

As the old man squeezed his hand, the nurse returned to check in on the visitor's effect. "I see that you have another visitor, Carl. Maybe you're not as grumpy as we thought."

The old man smiled at her. "This is my grandson. Tim."

The nurse smiled at him warmly. "I'm glad you finally got to come back in." She turned her attention back to Carl and checked his vitals. "I'm only gonna let Tim stay a couple more minutes. You've had a lot to deal with today, and I think this old ticker could use a good rest period. I'll be back in a couple of minutes, and then Tim can come back tomorrow, okay?"

The old man nodded, squeezing Tim's hand as though he didn't want him to leave.

The nurse turned to Maggie. "Thanks for being here today. I'll leave some notes for Dr. Kovacs and I'm sure you'll catch her tomorrow."

"Absolutely. I'll be talking to her about Mr. Pritchard's release as well. I'm still trying to talk him into coming to Caldwell Manor so I can bug him every day."

Carl shook his head, but she could tell that maybe he was a little more open to the idea now that his grandson was sitting by his bedside. As soon as the nurse left, she quietly started to gather her things. "Why don't I give you two a couple of minutes alone," she whispered.

"No, stay," the old man whispered.

Tim nodded in agreement. "You belong here, Maggie. I'm so grateful that you've been here for him."

The old man chuckled, squeezing her hand as he spoke to Tim. "She's like your grandmother. Always smiling, but sure to speak her mind whether you wanna hear it or not. You'd better hold on to her."

Tim looked over at Maggie's blushing face. "I sure plan to do my best, Grandad."

Maggie sat, rather uncomfortably, watching the two of them gaze at each other, speaking volumes between them without uttering a single word. When the nurse came back a couple of minutes later they were still taking comfort in the presence of the other.

"Okay, Carl, I'm here to break up the party. You can pick it up again tomorrow after you've had your physical therapy session, okay?"

Maggie chuckled. "You get some rest, Mr. Pritchard. You've had quite a day."

"How about you? Will you bring me another tomato sandwich?"

"Unfortunately I have an appointment tomorrow after work. But I'll be back on Tuesday to talk more about getting you out of here for good."

Tim caught her gaze. "Can you wait for me?" She nodded and watched him say his goodbyes. "I'll be back tomorrow – right after your physical therapy, like the nurse said. I promise."

The old man smiled and nodded, leaning back and closing his eyes. "Won't be a dream this time. You're really here…."

They walked out together, and once the elevator door closed, Maggie turned to him. "You okay?" He instinctively wrapped his arms around her and hugged her. She rubbed his back, knowing how overcome with emotion he must be. When the elevator door opened on the main level, he slowly let go, but held on to her hand as they walked out into the lobby.

"Thank you," he whispered. "I'm not sure I could have seen him without you sitting there."

"I think both of you were pretty emotional up there. That must have been sort of surreal for you."

He nodded. "When you called, I hopped in the car and drove. But nothing really prepared me for walking into that room and finally seeing him there in front of me. I'm so glad that he wanted to meet me. It's been 28 years!"

Maggie squeezed his hand. "He's a tough old guy. I think you walked in and gave him every reason to fight hard to get better."

They headed out the door toward the parking garage as Tim took a deep breath. "I just met my grandfather. I still can't believe it. Hey, do you want to go to Gino's with me? I'm not sure I want to be alone right now – and I owe you *so* much for being there today."

Maggie gave him a smile. "Sure. But instead of Gino's, can I introduce you to the Caldwell Diner? It's another spot that you simply have to try at some point."

"The diner it is. I actually haven't eaten there yet, but drove past it one day."

"Are you sure you're up for being out? Or would you rather do takeout?"

"Actually, I really think I'd prefer eating there. I have a feeling that once I get home I'm gonna be one hot mess of emotions. But if you're not up for it, I totally understand."

"No, I'm enjoying seeing your face after finally connecting with him. You deserve to celebrate. You okay to drive?" When he nodded, she added, "Okay, I'll meet you back in Caldwell in twenty minutes."

Tim stopped and squeezed her hand. "Do you know how much I love thinking about being back in Caldwell? God, I've come to love that town, Maggie. It feels like the home I've never had but always wanted."

She looked back at the hospital and then at Tim again. "Something tells me that you have all the more reason to love it now – you have your grandfather."

CHAPTER 22

aggie noticed that Gino's parking lot was full as she drove by and was glad that she'd suggested the diner. They were generally busier earlier in the day with the breakfast and brunch crowd after the church services let out. Tim pulled in right behind her and parked beside her.

He got out and grinned.

"What's that for?" she asked.

"Just thinking about how perfect it is that a small town has a diner. Seems to fit."

"Well, if it's anything other than Italian that you might want, this is the place. They have Italian, and it's good, but it's not Gino's. They open at six in the morning and don't close until eleven during the week, and midnight on Fridays and Saturdays. Are you ready for another Caldwell initiation?" she said dramatically, trying to lighten the mood.

"Haven't had one yet that I didn't like – well, aside from that zoning meeting."

Maggie chuckled. "I guarantee this will be much easier."

They walked in and Maggie led him toward the back to a booth by the front window. A middle-aged waitress with gray hair and black rimmed eyeglasses headed over. She handed them each a menu and said hello to Maggie, then smiled at Tim. "What can I get ya' to drink, my dears?" asked the waitress warmly. "Coffee?"

"Make mine decaf," Maggie said.

Tim nodded and smiled back at the woman. "You can put her caffeine in my cup….Carol," reading the name tag on her pale yellow uniform.

The waitress looked at Maggie and gave her a look of approval with her eyebrows before heading back to the counter to get their drinks.

Tim smiled. "Not exactly the romantic routine you get from Gino, is it?" He flashed her that dimpled smile before burying his head behind the menu.

Maggie sat and watched him as she rarely needed to open a menu from any restaurant in town. He looked tired, but much more relaxed than he'd been. He also had a flick of excitement back in his eyes – surely from finally meeting his grandfather for the first time. She silently rejoiced for the reunion she had witnessed.

He noticed she hadn't opened the menu. "You mean to tell me that you have that whole thing memorized?"

She laughed. "Well, to be fair, I don't look at half of it since I don't eat meat. But the vegetarian options? Yeah, I think I could take a stab at knowing all of them."

"I'm almost tempted to take you up on that, but I don't think my brain could keep up with you. What are you going to order?"

"I'm actually in the mood for breakfast—it's one of those meals that you can enjoy any time of day. I'm considering a veggie omelet with home fries, but the Belgian waffle with strawberries and whipped cream might be calling my name as well."

"There's an easy solution to that. We can order the waffle as our dessert and split it."

"Okay, you sold me – maybe you should have gone in to advertising instead of architecture," she said with a smile.

Carol returned with coffee as well as two glasses of water. "You guys ready yet?"

They nodded, and Tim gestured for Maggie to go first.

"I'll have the veggie omelet with a little Swiss cheese – and onions in my home fries. I don't need any toast, thanks."

"You got it," she said as she turned to Tim.

"I'll have a western omelet with hash browns, and I'll take some rye toast. Oh, and we'd like a Belgian waffle with strawberries and whipped cream for dessert."

Carol smiled as she tucked her pencil behind her ear. "I'll put that in after I bring your eggs. Thanks, doll." She picked up the two menus and headed back to the kitchen.

"Gee, I might like this place," Tim said with a grin. "Gino might flirt with you, but I get called 'doll' here."

Maggie laughed. "Carol's been working here as long as I've been alive, and she calls every guy that walks through the door 'doll'. Sorry to burst your bubble." She took a sip of coffee and sighed, enjoying its rich and creamy warmth.

He took a sip of his coffee and clearly approved as well. "That's good. And hey, you can't burst my bubble. I think I'll remember this day for the rest of my life."

"I loved watching the two of you look at each other," Maggie said softly. "I'm sure he went to sleep with a smile on his face." She took another sip of coffee, and met Tim's gaze. "To think that none of us knew that his loneliness was far greater than losing his daughter and then his wife. I suspect you'll be the talk of the gossip chain in town for a bit."

"Yeah – the long lost grandson who partners up with the town's black sheep to come back and give his grandfather a heart attack. I'm surprised I haven't been kicked out by now."

"Don't forget, at the meeting you were only the mystery partner – I'm sure it'll take some time to filter down that you're also Carl's grandson. But yeah, they'll talk a bit, and I guarantee a full house at town hall for the next zoning meeting."

Tim winced a bit. "Not sure I'm looking forward to that. I'm hoping that some of the ideas I presented to Sean might make him reconsider. I'm determined to keep him from ripping out those roses to put in a driving range."

"I suspect that you'll end up looking like the good guy, no matter what -- if that helps."

"Considering I'm up against Sean, that's not a high bar to beat."

Maggie laughed. "This is true. How long did your dad work with him? And did you have to work with him on anything else?"

Just as Tim was about to answer, Carol returned with their plates of food. "Eat up – and enjoy. I'll keep an eye out and bring your waffle when you're almost done."

"Thanks, Carol," Tim said with a grin. "It looks great."

Tim took a bite of his omelet. "Man, I didn't realize how hungry I was." This is really good." He filled his fork with hash browns and swallowed those before answering Maggie. "Dad went into business with Sean right when they finished college, and they worked a lot of years together before Dad's drinking consumed him. Hell, they'd go day drinking together on the jobs in the early years, and then they started losing business since neither of them cared at all about doing quality work. There was at least one law suit filed against them because I found the records in his office. I think that's when my mom told him to move to the guest room in the basement. I don't think there was much of a marriage left at that point anyway."

"Did your dad ever get physical when he was drunk?"

Tim shook his head. "Thankfully, no. He sure got vocal when he came home some nights. My mom kept me in her room with her and the door locked sometimes. I was really scared of him back then, but as time passed I was more sad for my mom. She's been so unhappy for so many years."

"You don't have to talk about it if you don't want to. I know it has to hurt."

"No, Maggie – I want you to know. I want you to know everything about me; I don't ever want to hold something back again. I know how much you value honesty."

She nodded slightly. "It must have been hard growing up in a home like that."

"It got easier as I got older. As dad's drinking got worse my mom had to get a job to pay the bills, so I was home alone most of the time. He was hardly ever home during those years, and when he was he holed up in his office with a bottle. That's when I found some solace in the kitchen; besides, if I wanted to eat, I had to cook. Eventually I was making dinner every night. I'm not sure my mom would have even eaten some nights if there wasn't something waiting on the counter when she got home."

Maggie nodded. "I can relate to that. There were lots of nights when I had no desire to eat, but Lucy made sure that there was a meal on the table and I had to sit and eat with her. I'm surprised you didn't become a chef."

Tim shook his head. "I would have hated that. I think the pressure of having to create a special meal at a fast and furious speed would have killed my love for cooking. Besides, I was so into the History Channel and the Portland museums I was sure I'd end up as a History teacher or museum curator."

Maggie watched him as he shoveled a forkful of home-fries into his mouth. "Until that fateful day when Frank Lloyd Wright changed your mind."

Tim gazed at her and grinned as he swallowed. "You know, looking back, it might not be that surprising. I remember when my dad wasn't home I'd sneak into his office sometimes and look at his blueprints. I found them rather fascinating. I even stole one of his pads of graph paper and drew my own floor plans. I'd forgotten about that – thanks for bringing back some of the memories that weren't as painful."

Maggie smiled. "I'm glad that your childhood wasn't all bad." She paused a moment to take a sip of coffee. "Changing the subject entirely, what I can't figure out is why did Sean hold on to the old hardware store all this time? He clearly didn't want it, so why not sell it and make some money?"

"Honestly? I think it was to spite my grandfather. I think Sean has this sick sense of satisfaction that he somehow came out ahead. He turned down his dad's initial offer to take over the store, introduced my mom to my dad, and left my grandparents sitting there alone, wondering what might become of the old property. He's such a self-centered ass – pardon my language."

"So what makes you think that he'll listen to you now?"

"He's getting older, and I'm not sure that he cares as much anymore. As long as my options make him look better I think he'll consider them. It's kind of ironic that he wanted revenge at the old man for trying to get my folks to move back to town and leave him in the dust. In the end he's gonna be the old grumpy one sitting all alone – it won't be my grandad."

"Some would call that some sweet karma," Maggie said. Her eyes looked past Tim and she smiled as she saw a golden brown waffle piled high with fresh strawberries and cream. "Get ready for dessert – I hope you're still hungry. I know I'll find room for a few more bites."

They ate the waffle in silence aside from comments about how good it was. Maggie only managed one of the quartered sections of the waffle before putting her fork down. "I think the rest is on you – or a doggie bag if you like it cold. I'm full."

He grinned and pulled the plate from the center of the table over in front of him. "I think I'm up for the challenge; I haven't eaten that much the past few days. You can change your mind any time if you want another bite, though. So tell me, what are the chances of getting my grandad to Caldwell Manor?"

"I think they're good. I need to talk to the physical therapist tomorrow as he's an outside contract worker, but if he can take your grandfather on then I'm sure I can fight with the insurance companies. It's not my favorite part of the job for sure, but I'm pretty good at it."

Tim stopped between bites. "If it's only insurance that's in the way, let me know. I could help with the expenses."

"To be honest, I think the biggest obstacle is going to be your grandad. He's been pretty adamant about not wanting to be there, and I can understand why. He has nothing but sad memories from the Manor. It's hard enough when a person realizes that they can't handle the needs of a spouse with dementia. But to then watch them slip away behind this curtain that only opens every now and then for a few moments – that's gotta be hell. I always tell my families that dementia results in a long drawn out grief period – and that's before the body finally takes its last breath."

"Sounds like death would almost be a relief at that point."

Maggie nodded. "For many it is. But there's also some guilt for feeling that way, or wondering if they could have done more to keep them alert longer. Add that to the guilt that your grandfather was already feeling for pushing his daughter away and I'm sure he had more than his fill. It's gonna be a hard transition if he ends up back in Caldwell."

"Won't it still be easier being here at home than at some place over in Brentwood where he doesn't know anyone?"

"I think so. That's what I'm hoping for, but Carl has to see that for himself."

"Any chance he could go straight home if he had the nursing and therapy he needs?"

"For a lot of heart patients, that might work. But even if we could manage to have someone there with him around the clock, I think he'd push himself too fast and too soon—and maybe end up right back in the hospital. I think he needs a couple of weeks with cardiac rehab before he's back in an environment that he's in charge of."

Tim nodded. "You're right. I wouldn't be able to commit to being there the whole time anyway." He saw Maggie's face grow concerned, and he reached out to take her hand. "Look, I do need to tell you something. Once he's settled in at rehab – wherever it is – I'm gonna have to be gone for a few days. There are a few things I need to tackle up north that I can't do here. I wish I could, but some things you can't do remotely."

Maggie looked him in the eye. "You're not planning to skip town once this whole zoning thing is over, are you?" Even though she said it sarcastically, her heart raced a bit at the thought of never seeing him again.

He shook his head incredulously. "I'm sorry I put that kind of doubt into your mind. I have no intention of skipping town. You can even ask Barb – I asked if I could extend the apartment lease for another month."

Maggie sighed a bit of relief. "Okay, so you'll be here for at least another month?"

"Maggie, I'm planning on being here a lot longer than that. I can't stay at the B&B after next month because she has another rental lined up, but it gives me time to find another option in town. After that visit with my grandad today there's no way I'm leaving, but I do have to go up and explore whether I need to maybe give my notice at the firm in Danvers. That's one of the reasons I need to head back up there."

"One of the reasons?"

Tim leaned back and put his napkin on the table. "I need to go up to Maine as well. There's some things I need to take care of with my dad's files, and I need to see my mom."

"I'm sure you want her to know how wonderful it was for you to see him, but don't expect her to feel the same," Maggie said with concern.

"Look, I know there's a whole lifetime of hurt between them. I may be dreaming too big, but I'm still hoping that I can talk her into coming back to Caldwell to see him. I think they both need it badly but are too stubborn to compromise."

"Oh, Tim," Maggie whispered. "Do you think he could handle it right now? That's a way bigger shock than you showing up."

"Well, I won't even bring it up unless she agrees. I'm hoping by the time he's back home she might consider coming down to see him. What can I say, I still have dreams of the small town 'happily ever after' ending."

"Then count me in to help," said Maggie shyly. The idea of happily ever after pulled on her own heart strings as he flashed that dimple from across the table.

CHAPTER 23

Monday morning Maggie was the first to arrive at the garden. She could see Barb starting her walk from the other end of the park, and she knew the other two would be arriving at any time. She was always amazed at how fast vegetables grew this time of year. She picked some extra cucumbers, tomatoes, and zucchini to bring to work – the chef at the Manor always loved the fresh produce that various staff members brought in.

"Morning, Barb. Gonna be another warm one, I think."

The older woman wiped her brow and rearranged her sweat band. "It's that time of year. The gardens are all exploding from the heat. I think I could sit and literally watch my tomatoes grow."

Maggie laughed as she saw Colleen and Brooke both pulling in. "They must have had breakfast at the diner first – they do that once a week, I think."

"How come you never join them?"

"I'd have to get up even earlier. Besides, I was there yesterday."

"Now isn't that funny. A certain tenant I have wasn't all that hungry for dinner last night. Said he'd been to the diner for the first time."

Colleen and Brooke had heard Barb's comment and looked at Maggie expectantly.

"Yes, I was with him. It was a huge day for him yesterday – he finally got to meet his grandfather for the first time."

"Wow," Colleen said. "That must have been pretty amazing for both of them."

Brooke nodded. "How's Mr. Pritchard doing?"

"Better. Actually, way better now. It was incredible to sit and watch them finally connect with each other. I think there's a lot of time to make up for."

"Well, I know that Tim's in town for at least another month – he lined up the extended rental on Saturday," Barb replied.

Maggie nodded. "He's hoping to get here long term as soon as he can. Although he did say that he'd be away for a bit once Carl is settled in rehab. He needs to deal with some stuff up in Gloucester, and then head up to Maine after that."

"Isn't that where his mother is?" Colleen asked as she dug up some carrots.

"Yeah. He's actually hoping to convince her to come down and see her father."

Barb leaned back on her calves and straightened up. "That would be huge. Can the old guy even take it? I mean, Tim showing up almost killed him."

"It'll be a slow process. But I think he's right – a reconciliation would be good for both of them. They've both been hurting for so long; Tim wants to bridge that gap and help them both to start healing."

Brooke smiled. "Sounds like somebody else's hurt is starting to fade. Are you guys okay again?"

Maggie smiled. "It's getting easier. I think my own stubborn heart is healing, too."

"Good," Brooke said. "Cause we don't want to have to find you another guy – we get a good vibe from this one, even after the bombshell meeting."

Colleen stretched. "Aw, Maggie, I still wish you could have been there to see Sean in action. You absolutely can't miss the next one!"

"Trust me, I'll be there. Tim said he's met with Sean and given him some other ideas. He's making it his mission to make sure the driving range doesn't go through."

Barb laughed. "Hey, I don't think Sean's chances were all that good with the zoning committee or the residents anyway– but add in his partner and I'd say he's kinda screwed. I think he deserves that."

The others all laughed, and then Brooke asked, "So how long will Mr. Pritchard be in the hospital?"

"Probably another day or two. I've got a ton of calls to make today to try and get that bed for him here in Caldwell." Maggie stood up and stretched. "I should probably get moving on that."

"Listen," Brooke said, "I know you're busy with the old guy and Tim, but if you should talk to Cassie in the next couple of days, could you ask her to drop by the shop? I really wanna get someone hired soon and I think she might be the best candidate."

"I'll put it on my list as soon as I get to work. Have a great day, ladies, and I'll see you all tomorrow."

Maggie took Tramp home and got the vegetables sorted, packing some for work in a bag. After a quick shower she gave the beagle a bowl of food and water and bid him farewell for the day. "See you tonight, boy….enjoy watching the world go by." He licked her hand and trotted off to the bay window to watch her leave and to keep an eye out for squirrels.

Maggie spent the next few hours on the phone or meeting with folks on the medical team at Caldwell Manor. By lunch she was pretty confident that the bed would work for Carl's rehab as long as *he* was willing to take it. She decided she needed a breath of fresh air after sitting in her office all morning, so after grabbing a bottle of water she headed out to the back porch and garden area. Quite a few residents were out enjoying the summer sunshine.

"Maggie!" a familiar voice called from the other end of the garden. She looked down to see Ida Vasilikas gesturing for her to join her. On her other side was Cassie, who had called out to her. She walked down and Ida grabbed her hand to greet her. "How's my favorite social worker this morning?"

"I'm doing well, Ida. And it's obvious you are, too, with your granddaughter here." She looked beyond the older woman and smiled at Cassie. "Glad to see you. You look happy – and *healthy.*"

Cassie nodded. "It's nice being home, and I'm enjoying my visits here a lot."

Ida reached out her other hand and patted Cassie's hand as Maggie sat down with them. "I have my Cassandra back – and I'm so grateful to you and Teagan and all the others who helped to make that happen."

"Well, in fairness, Ida, it was Cassie who did all the hard work. We were just helpers."

Cassie smiled. "You were way more than helpers -- I'm not sure I would've even gotten to the Phoenix without you – and I might not have stayed once I got there."

"How are you doing?"

"Okay – a little restless at times, but I'm hanging in there. I went bowling with Teagan and some of the theater gang on Sunday. I did terribly, but it was still fun to be with friends. I even got a small order of cheesy fries that were delicious. I nearly had to fight Teagan for the last one."

"Now that's progress!" Maggie said with a chuckle, "I think I'm hungry myself now. Listen, I saw Brooke over at the gardens this morning, and she wanted me to ask you to stop by the store soon to talk about the job offer."

Ida smiled at her granddaughter. "Maybe your mom can stop there after she picks you up today."

Cassie shrugged. "I don't know. I got the feeling she was dropping me right off at home and then heading back out for a couple of deliveries. She ran a few parties this month and a lot handbags were delivered over the weekend."

Ida shook her head. "I'll never understand why women need so many different kinds of bags and organizers, but it sure keeps Eliana busy, so there must be a demand."

Maggie laughed. "Listen, if your mom wouldn't mind me driving you home, I could bring you down to Brooke's when Ida goes in for lunch and then drop you at home afterwards."

"Really? It would be nice to have you there as support when I talk to her."

"Okay. Give your mom a call and check in with her. In the meantime, I'll be in my office – come and find me when you bring Ida down to the dining room. And you," she said to the older woman, "I might need to ask for your help in the next day or two. We might have a new resident here for a couple of weeks that doesn't really want to be here."

"I'll do whatever I can to help, my dear."

Maggie squeezed her shoulder. "You're quite a leader here, Ida. The residents all love and respect you, and the staff adores you."

The older woman smiled. "It's become my home. And I'm blessed to have two families-- both here, and down the road," she said as she winked at Cassie.

"I'll talk to you later, for sure. Enjoy your lunch – I brought in fresh cucumbers and tomatoes today and they said they'd be serving it as the lunch salad."

"Gee, maybe I should stay to eat – that sounds good," Cassie said.

Maggie headed back inside and worked until Cassie appeared in her doorway. "Ready whenever you are – if you're sure you can take the time."

"Hey, we all get lunch breaks," Maggie said, checking her watch. When she saw Cassie's expression she added, "Don't worry, I always eat lunch. I hope you do, too."

Cassie nodded. "There's leftover Chinese in the fridge when I get home. I'm kind of looking forward to it. I don't' know how I ever convinced myself that lo mein noodles were terrible."

"Well then," Maggie replied. "Let's get out of here so I can get you to it as soon as possible."

Within minutes they entered Brooke's Treasures and were greeted with the subtle scent of fresh apple pie. Maggie grinned. "She knows that lighting her candles make people more likely to buy one. At

Christmas time she'll light the one that smells like sugar cookies and place it right next to a display of homemade baked goods – she's an expert at marketing."

The owner was just finishing up with a customer and turned to greet both of them as they approached. "Hey, Maggie, nice to see you. You must be Cassie; it's nice to officially meet you. I think you've been in a few times over the years."

She nodded. "I've always liked the vibe here. Peaceful, and it smells heavenly. I know I'm not the first person to say this, but I love your candles. I don't what you do, but the balance is always perfect."

"Maybe I'll share some of my secrets with you before long," Brooke replied. "But for now, I really need someone to help put things out, arrange displays, occasionally help with the register, and hopefully create a fair amount of new stuff to sell. I've seen some of your work, and I'd love to have you on board, if you're interested."

Cassie nodded shyly. "I think I might really like that."

"Great. I know Maggie said you still had therapy over at the Phoenix, but if you give me your schedule, I'll work around it. I'd like you here a couple of days during the week and then maybe some time either Saturday or Sunday if that works for you."

"Sounds perfect. Thanks so much for the opportunity," Cassie said humbly.

"I'm glad I could offer it. I know where you're coming from, and I think I can be supportive of your recovery. I've been friends with Maggie for a while now and she speaks highly of you."

Cassie blushed, not used to the attention. "She's said the same about you."

Maggie grinned. "Sounds like you two will hit it off tremendously. For now, let me get this one home so I can get back to work. I'll see you tomorrow in the garden."

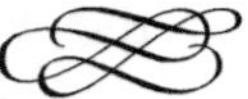

CHAPTER 24

A couple of days later, Maggie stood with Tim and Charlotte outside of Caldwell Manor, impatiently waiting for the ambulance crew that was transferring Carl over from Brentwood Hospital. She remembered how hard he fought her about coming here, but finally listened to Tim explain that without a bed at the Brentwood facility he'd be heading either in toward Boston or out toward Worcester – where he'd be totally alone. She chuckled to herself and Tim heard it.

"What's that for?"

"I was just remembering yesterday when he called you a black-mailer. I can't believe you told him he'd have no visitors from anyone unless he was here."

Tim grinned. "It worked, didn't it?"

As the ambulance pulled in and backed up, the three of them walked down the ramp to greet their newest resident.

"Good morning, Mr. Pritchard," Maggie said in her cheerful voice. "Welcome back to Caldwell."

The old man scowled as they started the wheelchair lift to lower him to ground level. "You want it to be a good morning? Then push me down the street another block and get me home. They wouldn't listen to me."

One of the EMTs chuckled. "He tried, believe me. I think there might have even been some bribery thrown in at one point."

"Hey, Grandad," Tim said as he reached the ground.

"And you! You're the worst of the lot!" Despite his arguing, Maggie could see the smile he was trying to to hide. He was happy to have his grandson in front of him.

"Mr. Pritchard, this is Charlotte Hurd," Maggie said. "She's the director of nursing here and she'll be in charge of your medical care while you're here."

Charlotte extended her hand. "I've heard lots about you, Mr. Pritchard. Good and bad."

Carl squinted as he looked at her. "You look familiar."

Charlotte nodded. "I've worked here a long time, Carl. I was here when you'd come in to visit Ruth."

The old man crossed his arms across his chest and looked down at the ground. "I knew this was going to be a bad idea."

Tim patted his shoulder and got behind him. "You're close to home, Grandad, and you'll be there in no time. Do you see that garage over there behind the Bed & Breakfast? That's where I'm staying – so I'm close by if you need me."

"Whatever. Let's get this over with."

Luckily Carl's room was on the ground floor, so he'd never have to pass by the second floor room that had been his wife's home for the last three years of her life. Maggie had brought in fresh roses that morning and that's what he saw first when they wheeled him into his room.

"I'm sure that was your doing," he said to Maggie.

"I wanted you to have a reminder of where you really want to be – hopefully within another week or two."

Charlotte went over his basic schedule, including therapy sessions with the physical and occupational therapists every day. "I also don't want to hear that you're sitting in your room passing time by yourself. It's important to build up your strength, and the best way to do that is to be out doing things. I have to go and get your meds sorted and go over things with a couple of the other nurses. I thought Maggie or Tim could take you down to the activity room and introduce you to other residents."

"Too noisy. Let me sit outside till lunch."

Tim nodded slightly to Charlotte. "Tell you what, Grandad. I'll sit outside with you until lunch and you can tell me more about the house and the neighborhood. Once lunch starts Maggie can take you down and find someone interesting to sit with. How's that sound?"

"Whatever will pass the time here the fastest. That's what I want."

"Sounds like a plan," Maggie said politely. "I'll come and get you in a little while. In the meantime, if you try to escape Tim has permission to drag you back in by your feet. Now behave – both of you." The old man crossed him arms and tried to hide a smirk as Tim flashed that dimple.

She and Charlotte headed down the hall toward their offices, chuckling as they heard the old man complain all the way back to the door. "Tim wanted quality time with his grandfather. Boy, is he gonna get some," Charlotte said with a chuckle..

When Maggie went out to fetch her newest resident for lunch, she found them seated at one of the tables by the garden. Tim was scribbling something down on the back of an envelope. "So is that the great escape plan?"

Tim smiled as the old man rolled his eyes. "There are a few things that Grandad would like from his house. If they're approved, I volunteered to stop by later and pick them up and bring them here."

"Unless they're weapons, medications, or sharp objects, I think anything will be fine. It's always nice to have a little something that reminds you of home while you're here. I think your keys are in the main office for safe keeping but I'll get them for you. Right now, however, it's time to go down for lunch. And I put in a special request just for you, Mr. Pritchard."

"Better not be liver and onions. Or beets. I hate beets."

Maggie laughed. "None of the above." She looked at Tim and

added, "Why don't you come down as well so you can see the layout and maybe meet a couple of your grandad's neighbors."

"I'm not here to make friends; I'm the old curmudgeon, remember?" the old man scowled. "I'm not gonna be here long enough to make it worthwhile."

"And that's why I didn't say friends – I said neighbors."

Tim laughed. "She's got you, grandad, and it's always nice to be at least civil with our neighbors, isn't it?"

Maggie had made arrangements for Carl to sit between Ida and Melvin, with Kitty and Gladys finishing out the table. "Carl, I want to introduce you to a few of the residents. This is Kitty, Gladys, Ida, and Melvin."

"Hello, handsome," Kitty said with a wink.

"Jeez, he just got here. Keep your britches on," Gladys said to her, shaking her head. "I'm Gladys, and don't get excited. She says that to every man who walks through the door."

Melvin stuck out his hand. "She's right. I'm Melvin. Nice to have another guy here to help me fend them off when they get frisky."

Ida turned to Carl and studied him carefully for a moment. "I'd say welcome to the Manor but I'm sensing that maybe you don't want to hear that. So instead I'll say welcome to lunch – you picked a good place to eat."

Carl looked down at his plate, which had a small bowl of corn and potato chowder. Next to it was a sandwich brimming with bacon, lettuce, and fresh tomatoes, and his face lit up.

Maggie patted his shoulder and whispered in his ear. "Those are straight from my garden. I picked them this morning for you. Enjoy your meal, Carl, and I'll be back in a few minutes to check up on you." She looked over at Ida and winked. "I know I'm leaving you in good hands."

She walked back toward the door with Tim. "Ida will watch out for him, and Melvin will keep him laughing. He'll be okay. What's on his list from the house?"

"Mostly some clothes, and socks. Oh, and he wants his slippers and bathrobe for night time. Then a few books, and a stack of crossword puzzles that he said he cut out of the newspaper but hadn't gotten to yet."

Maggie smiled. "I know he did them in the hospital, so that will be good – although Teagan always has some in the activity room. He and Ida might hit it off – she enjoys them as well." Getting more serious, she stopped before he got to the door. "Are you gonna be okay going into his house to get his stuff?"

Tim sighed. "God, you know me so well. Excited as I am to see the inside, I'm also petrified. Any chance you might come with me? I could swing back later today to get you and then we could bring the stuff back here together."

"I'd like that. I'm here until four – I hope that works okay."

He nodded. "I have some calls to make on a certain piece of property across the way. Four is perfect."

"Okay," she said. "I'll get his key from the office. If I'm not out on the porch, my office is the third one on the right just down that hallway. My name's on the door."

As Tim left, Maggie grabbed the attention of Jason Johnson, the physical therapist, as he was passing by. "Jason, are you ready for your new patient today?"

He flashed a smile and nodded. "You betcha. You can either bring him to me or I can fetch him from his room, whatever's easiest."

"If I can't bring him myself I'll be sure that someone else does. I'll pop in to see how things are going before I leave today."

"I'll take good care of him, don't you worry, Miss Maggie May."

Only Jason had permission to call her that. When he first started working at Caldwell Manor he was quite taken with her and would sing the lyrics from an old Rod Stewart song about a girl named Maggie May. While she was somewhat interested in him early on, it never clicked for them. Despite some of their coworkers trying to set them up, they agreed early on that a friendship was all that was every going to emerge. She watched him walk down the hall, wondering why certain people could come along and not create any spark, while others could do so almost instantaneously. As she headed toward her office, her thoughts immediately went to Tim, and she could feel that spark jump to life as soon as he came to mind.

Maggie was on the phone when Tim showed up at her office door. She gestured him in to sit and looked at the clock. It was close enough to four to take off once she got the information she was waiting for. "I'm on hold," she whispered, "but I'll only be a minute."

He sat down and looked around the office and watched her as she scribbled information down. "Thanks so much for your help," she said to the person on the line, "and you have a good day yourself." As she hung up, she smiled at him and stuck the post it note inside the open file on her desk and closed it. "I feel like my ear's been glued to this phone all day. Thanks for the rescue."

She picked up a set of keys off her desk that had a tag with Carl's name on them and they exited her office. Before they could head for the exit the sounds of yelling came down the hallway. The voice was familiar to both of them. "Looks like we're not leaving quite yet," she said. "Come on."

They strode down the hallway toward the physical therapy room and could hear Carl complaining loudly. "I'm not walking up no stairway to nowhere!"

As they entered, his back was to the door. He was sitting in his wheelchair next to a therapy staircase that had five steps and a platform at the top. Jason was kneeling down in front of the wheelchair. He had quietly gestured with his hand to Maggie not to interrupt, and she pulled Tim's arm to stop him and put her finger up to her mouth to signal silence. Tim silently nodded and they both stood quietly watching the session before them.

Jason stood up and folded his arms in front of him, mirroring the stance of the man seated before him. "Okay, here's the deal. I want you to do the steps, and you want to go home. So let's do it. If you can get out of that chair, walk down the hall and out the door, then walk down the street and up the steps of your front porch, all without being tired or falling on the ground with another heart attack, I'll walk right alongside of you so you can slam the door in my face at the other end. Steps here or down the street – you pick. Either's fine with me."

The old man put both hands on the arms of his wheelchair and looked up at Jason. "I don't think I like you very much. Now wheel me closer and help me out of this damn chair."

Maggie and Tim watched him reach out for the railing of the stairway, and they quietly slipped back outside. Tim chuckled. "I think Grandad's met his match."

"Yup. I knew Jason would be the perfect fit for him. Come on, let's go fetch some things."

CHAPTER 25

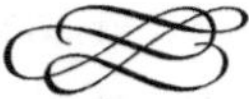

hey took Tim's car the short distance down the street and pulled into the driveway behind the old man's car.

"He still drives?" Tim asked.

"Not often. He walks almost everywhere here in town. But he'll still drive to the market or up to the diner."

Tim didn't get out of the car right away. "I can't believe I'm sitting in his driveway, and that I'll be going in that door. I've walked by this house a hundred times since I've been here, but didn't think I'd ever be welcome in it."

"We'll take whatever time you need in there."

As they got out of the car Tim eyed the garage. "So that's where he had his office. I wonder if it's still intact."

"Only one way to find out," Maggie said. She used the key to open the door on the side of the building, and they were faced with a door directly in front of them and a stairway leading up on their right. A sign reading "Carl S. Pritchard, Structural Engineer" hung off a string in the window on the other side of the door. Tim peered inside. "Looks like a decent office."

"I always assumed his office was upstairs, but I guess he converted the whole garage. Should we take a quick look up there?" Tim nodded, and they went up the stairs to the loft. There was an old couch, a formica table with chairs, and a counter with a sink in the corner, an old hot plate, and piles of boxes. A small bathroom was in the corner by the sink.

"Looks like they started to make this a living space," Tim said, "but I guess it ended up as storage."

"Let's go see the house," Maggie replied. As they came back out of the garage, she stopped and smelled the air. "God, you can smell the roses from here. Such an inviting smell. Come on, you have to see his roses."

She led him out to the back yard. A small deck was just outside the back door of the house, and a stone walkway led down to a small patio next to the roses. Tim looked them over with admiration, stopping to breathe in their sweet scent as he lightly touched the petals. "These are so much more beautiful up close than how they look from the gardens" he said softly, gesturing across the side property line toward the park. "He must spend a lot of time caring for them."

Maggie nodded. "Now you can see why he's so headstrong about Sean's plan to get rid of them. Did I tell you that Lucy, Liz, and I are getting a little bistro set to leave here for when he gets home? Liz thinks he should have a nice place to sit and rest when he's working on the roses."

"That's really thoughtful of you. I wonder how long before he's able to get back to it?"

"Dr. Kovacs seems to think that he can get back to his gardening pretty quickly once he's stable on his feet again."

They slowly walked back around to the front porch where two rocking chairs sat with a small table between them. Tim sighed. "I bet those rockers go back to before my grandmother died. They probably sat out here together."

Maggie took the key out of her pocket and looked at Tim reassuringly. "Are you ready?"

Tim nodded, and after she unlocked the door he followed her inside. It was a simple house, with a living room on one side and a dining room on the other. In the back was the kitchen and a small bedroom, with a full bath between them. Tim walked slowly around the living room, fingering the furniture as he took in every detail of the home. "I wonder how many hours I might have spent here during my childhood if things had been different."

His gaze fell on two photographs on the mantle – one of Carl and Ruth's wedding, and another taken when they were much older. Maggie studied the latter photo. "This was taken at Caldwell Manor, I think. I'm pretty sure that's the dining room area."

"Probably one of the last photos they ever took together," Tim said softly.

They found several of the items that were on Carl's list in the living room, and more in the back bedroom. The stack of crossword puzzles was on the dining room table, along with a fair amount of clutter.

"It looks like he was living primarily downstairs," Tim said. "Maybe that's something to keep in mind for when he comes home."

Maggie nodded in agreement. "I think this house could use a good cleaning before he gets home, too," she said, wiping a bit of dust off of one of the shelves. "We also might have Jason and Katie come through to make suggestion on how to make the space easier to move around in."

"Katie? Is she another physical therapist?"

"Occupational. She'll come in to look over his items of daily living and make suggestions on any adaptions that might make it easier for him. Look, we have all the items that Carl requested, but I'd like to check upstairs to see the layout. It'll help to give as much information to the team in getting him home as soon as we can."

Tim followed her up the stairs. On one side, over the kitchen and dining room was a big master bedroom with a small half bath. Maggie could tell that Carl hadn't stayed up here for a while as there were boxes on the bed full of his old files. A small sitting area was beyond the bed near the front of the house with two chairs and a bookshelf.

"It's a little musty up here – could probably use a good airing out," suggested Tim.

Maggie nodded. "I suspect it hasn't been used since she died."

At the top of the stairs next to the master bedroom was another full bath, and then off to the right was a small office/den and another room with the door closed. When Maggie opened it to another bedroom she stopped short in the doorway. "Oh my, God. Tim, come see this."

They walked slowly into the room that had clearly been Sharon's. An old pink bedspread and frilly curtains accented a white dresser, desk, and bookshelf. Old photos of Sharon's high school and college days were scattered around the room as well as memorabilia tacked to a bulletin board over the desk. It was like stepping back in time, and Tim stood frozen with tears in his eyes as he slowly took it all in. "They haven't touched it since she left," he whispered.

Maggie reached out for his hand, but instead Tim embraced her tightly, overcome with emotion at the thought of how his grandparents must have grieved when their daughter left. Maggie held him, all the while studying the various items and photos that she could see. When he finally released her, he sat on the trunk at the foot of her bed. "My mom has no idea that it's all still here."

"You okay?"

He nodded as she stepped closer to look at the photos on the book shelf. There was one in a prom dress that caught her eye. "Oh my, God, Tim – is that Sean? Would they have gone to prom together?"

"Probably. I know Barb said that they dated briefly in high school." He picked up the photo and wiped the dust away. "She's aged a little better than he has, that's for sure. But she sure doesn't smile like that anymore."

"Tim, look at these!" Maggie was wiping off another photo that had a blue ribbon attached to it. In the photo was Sharon and her mother, standing in front of rosebushes. Sharon held a certificate of some kind, and the mom the ribbon. She looked out the back window as she spoke. "My God, those aren't his roses – they were *hers.* Does your mom garden?"

Tim nodded. "She does. Not like she used to, but she still has a few things. And, Maggie, she has roses."

Maggie shook her head, incredulously. "That's why he so adamant about not having them pulled out. My God, I remember Liz saying that some of them were really old. He's been taking care of your mom's roses all these years……or maybe your mom's and grandmother's, I don't know."

"I think I need to get out of here," Tim said. "It's a little too much to take in right now."

Maggie nodded, and they slowly walked out and quietly closed the door behind them. She followed him back down the stairs to where they had left the box that Tim had brought along on the dining room table. Tim leaned back against the table and ran his hands through his hair.

"All this time she's been thinking that her father wrote her off when she chose to leave, and that she'd never be welcome again. So why is there is there a museum up there with all her stuff?"

Maggie took both of his hands and met his gaze. "That's not the action of a man who didn't want her back. That's the action of a man who's felt guilty for pushing her away."

"I really have to go and see her. She needs to know what's going on here."

"I agree," Maggie answered gently. "But you also have to consider the timing. I'm not sure your grandad would understand you leaving right after he ends up at the Manor."

"Should I tell him that I went upstairs, and that I'm going to see her?" He grabbed her hands, looking desperately into her eyes. Her went out to him and she spoke gently.

"What if it doesn't make a difference? You can't get his hopes up that she might come home and then go and find out that she's not interested. I'm not sure his heart could take that."

Tim released her hands and turned to pick up the box. "You're right. His heart needs to heal, not be broken again. I sure have a whole lot to do to help with that healing, and not a lot of time to work with —I know I have to be back by next week for the meeting.

"How can I help?"

"I'll spend the day with him tomorrow, and then take off for Gloucester tomorrow night. I think I can deal with stuff there relatively quickly – or go back to it later. That'll give me a few days in Maine to look over what needs to be dealt with in terms of the business, and then I'll have some time with my mom. I can do a lot of the prep work for the meeting up there, I think."

"If there's anything you need at this end, call me. Even Lucy can help with anything at town hall. Just make sure you spend time with him tomorrow, and explain that it's the business that needs the time. He might be more supportive of you leaving him temporarily if he thinks you're working on a plan to save his roses from Sean McClean."

"That's a good approach," Tim said, as they walked back out on to the front porch. Maggie locked the door behind them, and he stood looking at the rocking chairs. "I'll have to tell him that there's no place I'd rather be than right here on his porch, sitting with him in these chairs."

"I think he'll believe that, but he needs to hear it from you. Of course, he'll still complain about it the whole time that you're gone." Tim chuckled as he put the box in the back seat of the car.

"Maybe. But he has the next best thing."

"Oh, yeah? And what would that be?"

Tim looked over the roof of the car just before they opened their doors. "He has you."

* * *

MAGGIE WAS full of news when she arrived at the garden the next morning. She described her incident inside Carl's house and the discovery of Sharon's bedroom left intact.

"Wow," Brooke said. "That's a long time. I'll have to ask my brother if Sharon was into gardening at all. I know there were scout troops that met at the church down by the diner at one time, so maybe that's where the award came from."

"Poor Carl," Colleen added. "He must have carried so much guilt with him all these years. No wonder Tim's arrival caused a heart attack."

Maggie nodded. "Tim's heading out of town tonight and will head up to Maine within a day or so to see his mom. He wants her to know about the room and all that Carl has done to preserve her things."

Barb shook her head, trying to take it all in. "Do you think it will make a difference? I mean, that would be huge if she were to come back to see him."

"She didn't come when he had a heart attack," Colleen replied. "Why would she care now?"

"I don't know," Brooke said. "Knowing that he's saved every piece of her life since she left? If it were me, I might start to think differently. Actions speak louder than words sometimes."

"That's what Tim is hoping for," Maggie added. "I can't think of anything better than Mr. Pritchard and his daughter reconciling after all these years."

Brooke nodded. "Nothing would heal that heart of his faster. Or hers, for that matter."

"What about you and Tim?" Barb asked. "Has that reconciliation finally happened?"

"Not officially," Maggie said with a blush, "Maybe when he gets back."

Colleen chuckled. "Not officially? Just what does that mean?"

Brooke laughed. "It means she hasn't kissed him yet, silly."

Maggie rolled her eyes and turned her attention to her tomatoes, all the while wondering when that kiss might finally occur and if she was ready for it.

* * *

LATER THAT DAY, when Tim was finally leaving Caldwell Manor to head north, she thought about kissing him then, but could tell that his mind was already focussed on his trip.

He hugged her tightly, and then softly stroked her cheek with his thumb. His caress wiped away every bit of remaining doubt still in her heart. "Take care of him for me," he whispered softly. "He might be a little more ornery tomorrow."

She slowly pulled back as the hug ended, but she reached out to take hold of the hand that had touched her so softly. "A little?" she joked. "How did things go with him today? Is he okay with your trip?"

Tim nodded. "He chewed me out a bit and said my timing was horrendous – but he knows that I'll be back as soon as I can be."

"I'm glad he's at least confident that you two will have time to catch up."

"Oh, it's not that. He told me that he knows I'll be back because of a certain social worker in my life." Maggie blushed as Tim went on. "And then he told I'd better fix the damn rosebush dilemma."

"That's sounds more like him," she said with a chuckle, releasing his hand as he opened the car door. "Look, I hope everything you're going to deal with works out. Just don't get your hopes up with your mom. I don't want you get hurt."

He leaned his arms on the top of the car door and smiled at her standing on the other side. "Thanks, Maggie. I know you'll take care of him."

"Stay in touch, and text or call if you need anything – or if you need to vent."

He nodded. "I will. I guess I'll see you at the meeting next week."

"I guess. Safe travels."

He hesitated for a second but then leaned forward to kiss her cheek. "You have no idea how much I'm going to miss you. Good bye, Maggie."

She watched him drive away, her heart already missing him. *"Time's too short,"* she thought, *"and I don't want to lose another minute that I might have with him."*

CHAPTER 26

*L*ater in the day Maggie received a text. *"Wish you were here in Gloucester. The beach is empty without you."* She sent back a heart emoji with a simple thought: *"Miss you, too. Hope all goes well."* She smiled when her phone signaled a reply right away, but felt a little sad by the message. *"I'll be swamped for a day or two. Will let you know when I arrive in Maine. Have a nice weekend, and give my love to Grandad."*

* * *

MAGGIE WOKE up early Friday morning and got to the garden before the others arrived. She got to work and let Carl know that Time had texted her the previous evening. Her day was equally swamped with meetings and phone calls, and she was glad to arrive home Friday evening to an empty townhouse. After a long walk with Tramp, she made a couple of cheese and tomato sandwiches and settled down on the couch to watch a movie by herself. Halfway through, she got a phone call from her mom in Florida, and it felt good to fill her in on everything.

"Sounds like you're ready to jump back in," her mom said reassuringly. "Romance will always have its ups and downs, but true love will weather any storm, honey."

"Thanks, mom," she said before hanging up. *"True love,"* she thought to herself, feeling the butterflies and the yearning. She looked down at Tramp and scratched him behind the ears. "I think I really do love him, Tramp, and I'm not scared anymore." Tramp wagged his tail approvingly.

* * *

Monday morning Maggie got a simple text at work. *"Arrived in Maine. Give him my love. Miss you."* Her heart sang as she typed a reply back. *"Miss you, too. Good luck with your mom and hurry home. I'll be waiting."* She added a heart emoji and hit the send button before heading off to find Carl.

She looked in his room which was empty, and headed down to see if he might be in the activity room. Teagan was in the middle of a bingo game and smiled at Maggie as she stopped in the doorway. "He's out by the garden," she offered, before raising her voice and yelling out "B-3!"

As Maggie opened the back door she stopped short. *"Is that him laughing?"* Not thinking it was possible, she looked over toward the garden and found the old curmudgeon seated at one of the tables without a wheelchair, and he was indeed laughing. Next to him, seated in her wheelchair, Ida was responding with animated chatter. When she saw Maggie approaching, she waved her closer.

"Tell this old coot that he shouldn't be calling people names," said the old lady lovingly.

Carl had a scowl on his face, but his eyes were twinkling. "Hey, if it's good enough for a crossword puzzle clue then it's legit."

Maggie laughed as she pulled up a chair and joined them. "Okay, now I'm intrigued."

Ida picked up the pencil and pointed it down at the puzzle, which was about half done. "There," she said. "The word is fulcrum. And he had the nerve to say that I was the fulcrum of Caldwell Manor."

"It fits. She seems to run the place," Carl insisted.

Ida poked him in the arm, then laughed as she added, "I told him that technically Teagan was the fulcrum, because all the *activity* really revolved around her."

The old man was still chuckling as he turned to Maggie. "This one's okay. Heck, she even gets engineering puns."

"Well, hats off to you, Ida – there aren't many that can keep this old guy in line. It looks like you guys have really hit it off with the crossword puzzles."

"Turns out she knew me," Carl said with a smile.

Maggie looked perplexed, but Ida jumped in. "When I first moved here to Caldwell with my family –that was back when Eliana was a teen – my husband had hired Carl a few times for some engineering work. I'd actually gone over a couple of times and visited with Ruthie while the men gabbed in the garage."

"You knew Ruthie?" Maggie asked curiously.

"I only met her those few times – but she was so friendly and vivacious."

Maggie watched Carl and was amazed at the transformation a few days at Caldwell Manor had brought about. She had expected him to keep to himself and grumble throughout the rehab period, but instead he was bantering with Ida and Jason, and even now with Tim gone he seemed relatively happy.

"Well, I'm glad you're keeping him on his toes." Maggie turned to Carl and added, "At the rate you're going, you'll be back down the street in no time at all. I wanted you to know that I got another text from Tim. He's really busy, but he wanted me to be sure to let you know he's thinking of you."

"When's he coming back?"

"He didn't say, but I know he'll be back no later than Wednesday for the meeting."

"He better be. Someone has to keep that McClean kid in line. I should be there."

Ida patted his arm. "And where would that get you? Back in the hospital?"

The old man scowled.

"She's right, and you know it," Maggie said with a smile. "Even though you'd love to see Sean taken down at the meeting, you're going to have to settle for hearing about it the next day. So promise me you won't go anywhere until then."

He shook his head with a smirk. "Nope, can't make that promise." Before Maggie could protest, he added, "This one's dragging me out this afternoon on some van ride."

"Ida, you signed up to go!" Maggie beamed. "Good for you!"

Ida chuckled. "Teagan got Cassandra to nag me. She knows that I wouldn't say no to her. I figured if I had to get out I wasn't going alone, and poor Carl here was an easy mark."

"Easy? I'm the old curmudgeon and don't you forget it.," he said with a smirk. "I'm only going because Jason threatened to keep me here an extra week if I didn't start getting out of my room more." He turned to Maggie. "You make sure you find me first thing Thursday morning to give me the dirt on Sean, ya hear?"

"That's a promise I'm happy to make. Although Tim might get here first. I think he's anxious to get back to his grandfather. You two have a great day—especially on that van ride."

She was still smiling as she headed back inside. Charlotte was in at the front desk checking messages when she passed by. "What's up? You look a little dazed."

Maggie laughed. "I think I am. Did you know that Mr. Pritchard is not only smiling, but laughing? I think we need to put Ida on staff – she has the magic touch."

"Must be just her. Jason said he complained all the way through therapy – but he did everything he was asked to do, so that's something."

"Oh, I think Jason and Ida make a great team. Carl's actually going on a van ride today. I guess Ida insisted on it."

"Leave it to a strong woman to get things done. So any word from Tim?"

Maggie nodded. "That's why I tracked Carl down. He's made it up to Maine – he didn't say much, but at least I know he's okay."

"He's got a lot on his plate from what you told me – but I'm glad you heard from him." She walked back down the hall with Maggie as they headed to their offices. "And how are you holding up?"

Maggie smiled. "I'm good. I realized this weekend that I didn't like him being away. My heart's ready for him to come home."

Charlotte gave her a hug and whispered in her ear. "I can't tell you how happy I am to hear that. He's a good man, and you deserve to be happy."

* * *

BEFORE LEAVING work Maggie called in an order at Gino's, and decided to first stop by Brooke's shop to see how Cassie was doing at work. Brooke was with a customer but smiled as Maggie entered. "She's in the workroom," Brooke called out. "Go on back."

Maggie walked down the hallway toward the back entrance and heard singing. She stopped outside the door before Cassie could see her. She was singing the song "Hercules" by Sara Bareilles and sounded wonderful. When Maggie finally stepped into the doorway, Cassie stopped just before the end. "Hey…..how long were you standing there?"

"Long enough to hear a whole lot of good stuff coming out of your mouth. Damn, girl."

Cassie smiled as she turned off the blue tooth speaker in her ear. "I can't believe she lets me sing as I work. It's not quite as wonderful as dancing, but pretty close."

Maggie got closer to take a look at Cassie's latest creations. On the table before her were wooden plaques with autumn scenes and black cats painted on them, little pumpkins adorned with silly faces, and small brooms decorated with dried flowers.

"Brooke asked me if I wanted to do a whole display of autumn stuff. It's been fun to do."

"Fun and profitable I'm sure! I suspect these things will sell like crazy with fall not that far off."

"That's the idea," Brooke said as she entered. "Great stuff, right?"

"That's what I was just telling her."

"Cassie," Brooke continued, "I just got another custom project for you – someone saw one of the welcome slates out front and asked if it could be personalized – I think you'll have a whole slew of custom requests coming in once a few get out there."

"Bring it – I'm up for a challenge and it keeps me busy – *and* getting paid!"

Brooked headed back out to the front, and Maggie got more serious.

"Are you doing okay? I've been thinking about you and wondering how you're settling back into some sense of routine."

Cassie got quiet for a minute. "I had a rough day yesterday, but I'm trying really hard to see it as a positive thing….I hit the fifteen pound mark of weight that I've regained since going to the Phoenix." She sighed as she gazed down at the floor.

Maggie crossed to her and hugged her. "I'll never forget when I reached that same goal – you hear the praise from the doctors and therapists telling you that your body is healing and everything is good, but your brain tries to scream at you and call you a fat failure – am I close?"

Cassie smiled weakly and nodded. "I knew that you'd get it. It's another five pounds, you know? A part of me wanted to die."

"Or sneak out and go running for an hour?"

Cassie nodded. "Natalie called last night and again today to check in on me. She has me doing some art journaling every time I have to eat, and then she told me to write a letter to my eating disorder about the milestone. Even with the extra support it's tough."

"Just wait until you get to normal body weight and they tell you that you can resume some of the exercises you've had to give up. If you're anything like me, that day will be even tougher. You can call me anytime – day or night. I mean that."

"I know, and I might – it's only another five pounds."

Maggie smiled. "It sounds like you might be ready for adding in an activity when school starts again. I imagine that will a hard decision."

Cassie sighed. "Not really. Much as I love dance, I think recovery has shown me that I'm not ready for the studio – I think it would trigger my exercise obsession. I might be able to do the musical, though. We'll see."

"Recognizing your boundaries is huge. I'm proud of you."

"Thanks. It really helps knowing that someone else understands exactly how it feels."

Maggie looked at the clock. "Hey, I better get going. I came in to buy a few candles but my order at Gino's is probably ready. It was good to see you – and I'm glad the job is working out for you."

"Me, too – and thanks for stopping by."

Maggie picked out four of Brooke's candles, thinking that the Pritchard house might need some subtle fragrances after sitting empty for weeks. She didn't know how Carl would react to an offer to help do some cleaning, but she thought she could at least introduce the candles. Even he couldn't complain about their simple aromas.

She sent Lucy a quick text to let her know that she was bringing home dinner. She knew Liz had a class tonight so it would be the two of them.

She got a text back immediately suggesting a movie night as well, and Maggie smiled. Pizza and a movie – best way to forget about the rest of the world, even if only for a few hours.

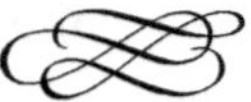

The days leading up to the town hall meeting were long and full of chatter throughout the community. After hearing about Sean's performance, along with the mystery partner and Carl's subsequent heart attack, there was more curiosity than ever about how the zoning meeting would go. Lucy had promised to save five seats for Maggie, the gardening gang, and Liz.

Maggie planned on heading over right after work to get in line, as they expected a full house. Tim had texted that morning that he was on his way – whether that was from Maine or Gloucester she didn't know, but at least he'd make it back on time. How his presence would change Sean's behavior was still a mystery.

At the moment, however, she was watching Carl Pritchard in his physical therapy session. He had already been out for a walk around the building and now he was back to his stairs. This time he didn't complain, though. He and Jason had found a bond in sarcasm.

"You think someday this damn staircase might actually *go* somewhere?" the old man joked.

"Where would you like it to go, Mr. Pritchard?"

"Hmm….how 'bout town hall? I think I'd like to walk over there this evening – I hear they're gonna have some kind of entertainment."

Maggie laughed as she approached them. "Mr. Pritchard, you know darn well that your doctor would never okay that – but I promise you a full run down in the morning."

"She should tape it for you," Jason offered.

"Hey, yeah – that's a good idea, tomato girl!"

"Yes, a fantastic idea …..will you come with the bail money when I'm arrested for illegally taping it?"

"Yeah, I probably would. I don't think my grandson would approve if he came home to find you in jail because of me. So when the heck is he getting back here?"

"He'll be back in time for the meeting – but it might be tomorrow before he gets here to see you."

"As long as he takes care of Sean McClean I can wait if I have to."

Jason laughed. "Sure, you can…..you were just telling me when you got here that you wanted to be back home tomorrow, remember?"

Carl thought about it a moment and nodded. "Yeah, I think I do. But I might actually walk up here and visit from time to time. There's a few decent folks here."

Maggie chuckled. "I'm sure Ida will be thrilled to know that." She approached the old man and patted his shoulder. "Now I have to get going, but I promise I'll be here first thing tomorrow to fill you in. Don't worry about your roses, Mr. Pritchard – we'll protect them no matter what."

She had packed a sandwich and grabbed a banana for dinner, and she ate them quickly in her office before heading out. She decided to leave her car in the lot at Caldwell Manor and walk to town hall. On her way over she kept an eye out for Tim's silver sedan, but only recognized Lucy's car outside.

She texted her sister to let her know she was there early, and got a reply to head in. Lucy opened the door of the meeting room and pulled her inside. "I figured you can sit with Liz and save seats for the others between you. She's already in place."

Liz waved as Maggie came down to the first row of seats behind the table where Sean and Tim would stand. "You sit down on the aisle – you'll get a better view. I don't mind sitting on this end."

"Hey, thanks again for taking care of the roses all this time. Carl may be home in the next week, and then we'll have to find out how much he can do from there."

"If he still needs help, let me know. I've loved getting to know his roses, and it's given me a ton of experience working with older bushes. I hope he approves of the patio set you ordered. It was delivered today."

"I can't wait to see it."

They chatted as other committee members wandered in and out, and a few other folks who were allowed in early to get seats. Lucy handed out pads of paper, pens, and files to each spot. Rich O'Sullivan waved at her as he wandered in and took his seat. By 6:15 they opened the doors early as there were already quite a few folks waiting. Brooke and Colleen came in together and made their way to the front.

Colleen filed in first and sat next to Liz, and then Brooke sat next to Maggie. "Barb texted. She's getting dinner on the table now and then she'll head right over. She even has Scott managing the guests and cleaning up after the meal so she can be here. Any glimpses of the good guy or the jerk yet?"

Maggie shook her head. "I'm praying that Tim is here soon. I don't think any of us want to see Sean in action at this point. Besides, I'm sitting too close – I might have to hurt him."

"Don't worry, I'll hold you back if I have to," Brooke said with a smile.

Colleen leaned over with a twinkle in her eye. "I may disagree with you on this one, Maggie. I think a whole lot of people are here because they *want* to see the jerk in action. It might be fun to hear the comments and hopefully a verdict tonight."

"I guess Mr. Pritchard won't be here tonight?" Brooke asked.

"He wanted to be, but he was smart enough to know it might not be the healthiest choice for him. I'll tell ya, the past week he's been almost cheerful at times – I think he's enjoyed his time at the Manor way more than he'll ever admit."

Barb slid into place about five minutes before the meeting was about to start and sat between Maggie and Brooke. "Guess who I saw getting out of his car across the street? Give you a hint – he has the best dimple I've ever seen on a man."

Maggie breathed a sigh of relief. *"Thank God he made it back."* There was still no sign of Sean, but at least there would be a voice of reason. She watched as various committee members sat down and began looking through their files. Many spoke softly between themselves, smiling and nodding. Were they laughing at Sean's ideas, or had he listened to Tim's suggested improvements?

She was suddenly aware of Tim passing by as he made his way to the table in front of her. He placed his computer and files on the table, catching her eye and giving her that dimpled smile that made her heart sing. She returned the smile and held up crossed fingers on both hands. She watched as he went over to Lucy and handed her a flash drive. Lucy nodded and handed it to a clerk who brought it over to a computer hooked up to a smart board.

"He's already way ahead of his partner – organized, polite, and ever so handsome in that suit.."

Right at 7:00 Rich O'Sullivan called the meeting to order. Maggie looked down at the ladies and saw Colleen mouth "Where's the jerk?" Maybe he'd be making a big entrance.

"I want to welcome all of you to this continuation of the zoning proposal made two weeks ago by Sean McClean regarding the old building over beyond the Caldwell Bed & Breakfast. Most of you will recognize Tim Collins, who is Sean's partner. I can tell you that there have been some changes made since last meeting, but I'll let Mr. Collins give you the updated information." At that point, Rich gestured for Tim to take the floor.

Maggie hadn't been in the meeting when Tim arrived last time, but she loved watching him speak to the crowded room. He seemed comfortable in front of a microphone, and after introducing himself he actually pulled the microphone out of the stand and held it so that he could move around and look at people in the eye as he spoke.

"I want to thank the committee members for giving me this opportunity to speak tonight, and I appreciate the turnout of so many Caldwell residents who I hope will leave tonight feeling much more positive about the property in question. To begin, I want to make it known that Mr. McClean is no longer a partner in this proposal."

Immediately murmurs were heard throughout the room. Rich O'Sullivan used his gavel to quiet folks down. "Look, everyone, I know some of you might have returned only for the drama, but I assure you that tonight's meeting will be different. Mr. Collins has been in close contact with me throughout the week and has provided me daily updates. As it stands, he has made an offer to buy out his partner's shares and that offer was accepted. I'll let the new sole owner of the property fill you on changes to the proposal. Tim, if you please?"

Maggie tried to catch his eye, but he continued on addressing the room as a whole.

"First, I want you all to know that there won't be any golf balls flying around behind the park – nor will there be a golf shop. If any of you were coming to express your concerns about that option, you can rest easy." Maggie looked over her shoulder and saw numerous heads nodding. Tim no doubt had their complete attention.

"I want to share something that a wise woman told me recently." As he began to speak again, he passed by and gave her a quick wink. "She told me that all we really have in life are the choices that we make – and that every choice has a consequence that can effect not only the person making the choice, but others around them." Tim began walking to the other side of the room, and every eye followed him.

"After the last meeting, I realized that I had to make a choice myself on whether I would continue working on a project that I didn't support, or do so with a partner that I didn't respect. When I thought about the consequences that would affect various members of this community, I knew I had to make a different choice. One thing that I truly believe is that a driving range is not the best choice for the town or the residents who live here."

Several residents applauded at this point, and Maggie's heart was full to think that he had quoted something she had said to him. She listened attentively along with every other person in the room.

"I've only been in this town for a short while, but I can tell you that I've come to love it here – and the people that I've met so far. This is the kind of town that people read about in books or see in a Hallmark movie – a small town where people still care about each other."

He continued, turning at times to address the committee members, who were all highly engaged and smiling as he spoke, and then pivoting back to talk to the residents."In talking to a few of you, I also realized that while Caldwell is an ideal town, there's still one thing lacking here." The murmurs began again, but Maggie could tell that he was just giving them a moment to build the suspense.

"What this town really needs, and what I'm proposing, is that the old hardware store be converted into a space that the entire community can utilize, like a community center or a center for the arts."

Maggie's eyes teared up as she heard him speak, not only because he shared her idea for the space, but because he truly believed in it himself. She also knew that he was as committed to the town of Caldwell as he was to the family roots that had led him back here. She could hardly wait to wrap her arms around him and welcome him home after the meeting.

There was more applause, but he held his one hand up to quiet them down as he spoke a little louder to regain their focus. "I have some basic designs of what the property might look like once converted, and I'll ask the clerk to turn down the lights so you can see them while I talk – but know that the final design is contingent on the needs of the community. One of the first proponents of this new proposal is a task force of community members to help determine how to best utilize the space. The entire process may take months to complete, but I think it's worth the time. Meanwhile, the work can at least begin on cleaning up the property and doing some basic renovations."

"As you can see from the images, the space would have one big open room for community events – with a stage at one end for possible theater productions or award ceremonies." He signaled for the next slide. "Here you can see a fully updated kitchen to allow for community events with food – because one thing I've learned in

Caldwell is that you guys know how to cook and love to eat." There was significant laughter as Tim continued. "The kitchen might also be used for local cooking or baking classes. The smaller rooms in this slide could be used for various community groups, other types of classes, meetings, or possible camps. I'd also like to have one room, shown on this slide, with a technology center so that kids could take classes in coding or gaming while older residents might enjoy learning how to use social media to keep in touch with family."

The last slide popped up showing the overall outside design included landscaping and walking paths that led out to where the driving range had been proposed. "You'll see one side of the building has a large open space. I'd love to propose a mural of some kind to reflect the town somehow. Finally, I hope that the outside space can be utilized for nature study, exercise groups, or a place to enjoy the outdoors in addition to the great park and community garden next door."

As he signaled for the lights to come back up, the room broke into applause. Tim smiled, and added a couple of closing thoughts. "Now I know that almost every one of you probably has a great idea for how this space could be used, and I encourage you to jot those ideas down and mail them in. The clerk will hand out cards with a post office box that I've already set up for receiving your ideas. If there any of you who own small businesses in town that might want to be involved on the planning committee, please include that information or call town hall during business hours. Lucy, can you stand up?" Maggie watched her sister stand up and wave and then sit back down.

"Lucy will take your calls and relay the information on to me, and once the committee is formed we'll get busy figuring out the optimal design for what this town needs. Much as I'd love to sit and listen to every single one of you tonight, I thought this method might give all of you a chance to share your thoughts instead just a few of you getting time with the microphone."

Barb poked Maggie in the side. "You better be ready to grab this guy for keeps as soon as this meeting ends, or every single girl in town is gonna be your competition."

Maggie chuckled and smiled at the man in front of her as their eyes met. He flashed her that dimpled grin before turning back to the room. "Don't worry," she whispered. "It's at the top of my agenda."

* * *

AFTER THE MEETING she waited outside by his car until he finally walked out of the building. He was looking satisfied but a little disappointed until he saw her leaning against the trunk, and then his entire face lit up as he crossed the street. "I was afraid that you'd left already."

She shook her head, her eyes locked on his. "Not on your life, mister. I didn't want to share my time with anyone else."

He unlocked the car and put his computer and briefcase in the back seat and then turned to find her stepping in close. "God, I missed you, Maggie. I have so much to tell—"

"Shut up and kiss me," she whispered, as she closed her eyes and felt his lips on hers.

They stood blissfully in each other's arms, oblivious to the traffic passing by as the last of the town hall folks headed home. Maggie looked up at him, still holding him close.

"You were amazing in there. And your ideas? They're perfect for this town – everything you did tonight was perfect."

"Even the kiss just now?" he asked quietly.

"Especially the kiss," she said, feeling the flush in her cheeks.

He gently cupped her face in his hands. "That's too bad, 'cause I really wanted to practice a little more…"

After several minutes of delicate kisses he led her around to the passenger door. "Come on, I'll drive you home. We'll get your car tomorrow."

She got in to the car, and as soon as he was got in he reached for her hand and kissed the back of it. "I wanted to tell you all of this, but there were so many little things that could have gone wrong, and I didn't want to disappoint you if any of it fell through."

"I can only imagine how busy you've been dealing with it all – but first, I'm dying to know how things went with your mom. Did you see her?"

He smiled. "I did. We had some real quality time together, short as it was. I'll fill you in, but first tell me how my grandad's been since I've been gone."

For the short ride home back to her apartment she filled him in Carl's progress, as well as his budding friendship with Ida. "I'm sure he'll complain to you for days since you left him, but know that he's been laughing – I've heard him with my own ears."

Tim grinned. "I look forward to hearing more of that. And leave it to a woman to finally get him laughing again."

He pulled up in front of Maggie's apartment and she turned toward him. "Do you wanna come in for coffee, or are you beat?"

He sighed and kissed her hand again. "I'm afraid that if I come in I might not wanna leave tonight, and we're not gonna rush that. I will, however, walk you to the door so that I can kiss you goodnight."

He took her hand as she got out of the car, and she met his gaze. "Okay, so what happened with your mom? And what about Sean? How the hell did you get him to walk away?"

"He was easy – it was all about money. I told him I'd fight him on the driving range because I knew he was doing it to spite my grandfather. Then I offered to buy him out if he wanted to finally be free of Caldwell forever. As expected, he opted to take the money and run."

"I know a lot of people were hoping to see him humiliated tonight."

"I hope they weren't too disappointed, but I wanted to resolve it before the meeting."

"I didn't see a bit of disappointment on those faces tonight. I hope that Sean didn't cost you a ton of money."

"Once he realized that he wasn't going to win, he accepted a pretty modest offer to walk away. Between my savings and putting the townhouse on the market I knew I'd have the money."

"You're selling your townhouse?" Maggie asked as they reached her front porch.

He wrapped his arms around her and gazed into her eyes. "I don't need the townhouse, Maggie. My family is here in Caldwell – and so is my heart."

She felt her heart spill over as she looked into his eyes. "That's good to hear, because I've fallen in love with you."

"Maggie," he whispered softly, pulling her tight and kissing her, slowly at first and then more passionately. Maggie responded eagerly, feeling his lips on her cheeks, her eyes, and back to her lips. She wrapped her arms tightly around him, wanting the moment to last forever.

He pulled back and held her gently as he met her loving gaze. "You have no idea how long I've waited to hear those words," he whispered. "I love you so much." His eyes were misty as he kissed her again, and they stood quietly together feeling the healing peace of their embrace.

Maggie finally pulled back a bit and softly put her finger on his lips. "What about your mom? Were you able to tell her? About the house?"

He nodded. "She wants to see him – she's coming to visit as soon as he's back home."

"Oh Tim, I'm so happy to—"

"Everything else can wait until tomorrow. Now *you* shut up and kiss me goodnight one more time."

She smiled warmly. "As you wish."

CHAPTER 28

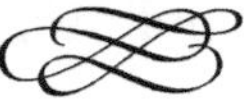

The next morning Maggie found Carl as he was finishing breakfast. "Morning, Mr. Pritchard. I heard you gabbing as I walked into the room. I think this has been a great table for you." She greeted the residents and then noticed that Carl didn't have a wheelchair. "No wheelchair today? Carl, that's awesome!"

He smirked as he looked up at her. "Never mind that. What happened last night?"

"I thought we could go out to the garden and I can fill you in. Do you need help?"

He shook his head as he grabbed a cane he had beside him. "Nope. Jason said I have to use this dang thing for balance if I wanna go home, so I better get used to it." He looked back at the other residents. "See you all at lunch. I'll have a story to tell."

Kitty squirmed in her chair, wiggling her fingers in front of her. "Court room melodrama! Can't wait!"

They all laughed as Maggie and Carl slowly walked down the hall. As they reached the door, Maggie opened it for him and smiled. "I thought you might like to sit out here. You have a guest waiting for you."

Carl looked over to see Tim approaching from one of the tables.

"Hey, grandad. I missed you. And look at you getting around on your feet." He gave Carl a hug and the old man held on tightly.

"I was afraid you might not have gotten back."

Tim shook his head as the three of them walked over and sat down. "I wouldn't have missed that meeting for anything in the world."

Carl leaned forward in his chair. "So what happened? And start with Sean."

Tim chuckled. "You'll be happy to know that Sean is no longer involved. I doubt he'll ever step foot in Caldwell again." As he saw the old man relax, he added, "And no one is ever going to try and remove your rosebushes, and there's not going to be any golf shop or driving range, either."

The old man sighed with relief. "Thank you," he whispered.

Maggie reached out to pat his arm. "You should have seen your grandson in that meeting, Mr. Pritchard. He was amazing. I imagine the whole town will be talking about him for weeks to come."

Carl looked over at Tim and smiled. "So you gonna tell me about it?"

They proceeded to fill him in on the proposal and the various options for the property. He listened intently, nodding at the possibilities offered. "Won't be too loud over there, will it?"

Tim and Maggie both laughed. "Mr. Pritchard, you must be feeling better – it's nice to hear you complaining again."

Tim's expression grew more serious as he looked to Maggie for reassurance. "There's something else I need to tell you about, Grandad. Much more important."

"What the heck could be more important that getting rid of that McClean kid? Wait, you're not leaving town again, are you?"

Tim shook his head. "I can assure you that I'm not going anywhere. In fact, I'll be looking for a permanent place to live, right here in Caldwell."

"Never thought I'd hear that," Carl whispered.

"Well, there's more," Tim said quietly. "Grandad, this past week I went up to Maine to see mom."

Carl's body stiffened up. "You saw Sharon? Why?"

"Well, I needed to fill her in on all the loose ends from dad's business and estate."

"That makes sense," Carl replied. "How….is she?"

"We had a long talk," Tim replied. "And before I tell you about it, I have a little confession." He looked at Maggie for some reassurance and she nodded.

"A confession?" Carl asked, noting the looks between them. "What's going on with you two?"

"It's my fault," Maggie started. "Tim asked me to go with him to your house last week to get the things you asked for."

"What's that got to do with anything?"

"Grandad, Maggie wanted to see the upstairs so that she'd be able to coordinate your care better when you get back home."

Carl's eyes narrowed. "You went upstairs?" As he realized what they had done, he sat back in his chair and crossed his arms. "No one was supposed to go in there. Ever."

Maggie spoke first as all eyes at the table grew misty. "Mr. Pritchard, I'm sorry, but I had no idea that it was Sharon's room. You must have missed her so much to leave everything as it was."

Carl's eyes filled with tears. "It was all my fault. Ruthie would go in some days and sit for hours, sometimes crying. I couldn't bring myself to….."

"Clean it out?" Carl nodded quietly as Tim spoke for him. "I'm glad that you left it. It was pretty special to walk in and see what life had been like for my mom back then – when she was happy."

"I'm sorry for taking all that away from her – and for robbing you of a different life. I can't blame her for being angry at me all these years."

Tim reached out and took his hand. "Grandad, she hasn't been angry at you – she's been angry at herself because she knew that you were right."

Carl looked up at him as he continued. "She knew early on that she'd made a huge mistake staying with my dad. And she knew how much she had hurt you and her mom when she left. She didn't think she'd ever be welcome back here in Caldwell."

"She what?" he whispered. "But that's not true. It was my fault, not hers."

"Mr. Pritchard," Maggie said, knowing that neither of the men could speak through their emotions, "If anyone was to blame, it was Sean McClean. You and your daughter had a huge fight years ago because of his influence on Steve, and because of misconceptions and probably some pride, you've both spent all this time thinking that the other person didn't care anymore. Going into Sharon's room showed us that wasn't the case at all."

The old man shook his head. "It's too late now. Too much time has gone by."

"That's not true, Grandad," Tim said through his tears. "Mom wants to see you."

"She what?" As Tim nodded, Carl's body shook with sobs. Maggie rubbed his back and Tim grasped his hands. Maggie looked across at Tim and saw the love in his eyes and smiled through her own tears. Finally, the old man was beginning let go of years of guilt and sadness.

He eventually reached into his pocket and pulled out a handkerchief to wipe his eyes and nose, and Maggie was the first to speak. "Are you okay, Mr. Pritchard? I didn't know if you needed me to get Charlotte to check your vitals and your heart."

Carl smiled as he put his handkerchief back into his pocket. "My heart," he said, "is feeling better than it has in years." He turned to Tim, who was drying his own eyes. "When-- when is she coming?"

"As soon as you're ready to see her, Grandad."

The old man thought for a moment. "I don't want her coming here. I want to be home when she arrives."

Tim nodded. "I think she'd like that, too. Besides, from what I hear, you're making incredible progress in your rehab. You'll be back home in another week or two at most."

"Knowing that Sharon is coming to see you will keep you motivated," Maggie added.

"I'll need to clean up the house a bit," Carl said.

Maggie laughed. "You'll do no such thing – at least not right away. But if you're willing, I think Tim and I could manage getting the house spruced up a bit for when you get home."

"We could absolutely do that. I'm assuming that you're gonna want to stay in that downstairs bedroom for a while when you get home?"

"I've been in there for years. Don't go upstairs anymore."

"That'll make it even easier for you to get home," Maggie said. "But we'll clean both upstairs and down and make sure it's all aired out before you get home." She looked at her watch, and then added, "And I'm gonna have to leave the two of you at this point as I have a meeting in a few minutes. I think you'll have plenty to talk about without me, anyway."

Tim smiled at her. "Can we plan on Gino's tonight? I can pick you up."

"I'd love that. Does 6:30 work?"

"Perfectly."

"Okay, okay," Carl chimed in. "Get to your meeting and give me some time with your boyfriend."

Maggie laughed as she stood up to go back inside. "You take all the time you need, Mr. Pritchard. He's not going anywhere."

"And that," Carl replied. "That 'Mr. Pritchard' nonsense has gotta stop. I'm not just your neighbor anymore. If you're gonna be hanging out with my grandson then you better start calling me Carl, ya hear?"

"Carl it is, then. You have a great day, you old curmudgeon." She winked at Tim, and headed back inside, smiling all the way to her office.

Later that afternoon she changed into a pale yellow sundress for her dinner at Gino's. As she came out of her room Lucy looked up from where she sat on the couch. "Looking good, sis. Try not to spill any tomato sauce on that thing."

"I'll be careful," Maggie replied with a smirk. "Should I ask Gino for a bib?"

Lucy laughed. "It's so nice to see that smile back on your face. I take it things are back to normal?"

Maggie nodded. "Last night I told him that I loved him."

Lucy jumped up to hug her. "What?! You should have woke me up last night with that news! I'm assuming that he shared equal sentiments?"

Maggie laughed. "You assume correctly. I feel so amazing, sis – like my heart can't love him any more than I do right now."

"Honey, you'll be amazed at much love the heart is capable of feeling, trust me." She sat back down on the couch and smiled back at Maggie. "He's a great guy. Everyone at town hall was raving about him today. I even had a couple of single coworkers asking if he was available."

"I hope you told them no."

"Don't worry, sis," Lucy replied. "It's clear to me that he's only interested in one person right now, and after dinner tonight I suspect everyone at Gino's will know as well."

Tramp's bark and wagging tail at the window announced Tim's arrival, and Maggie opened the door to see him dressed in dark blue trousers, a light blue shirt, and a blue paisley patterned tie. He held one red rose in his hand. "Mr. Lincoln and I would love to escort you to dinner," he said, gently kissing her as he entered. "You look beautiful, Maggie." He waved a greeting to Lucy, and then bent down to pat Tramp. "How's my favorite dog?"

Maggie took the single bloom and sniffed it. "Hmmm…so nice. I hope you got permission from the owner to take this from his rosebush or we'll both be in trouble."

"He told me to tell you that it was from *both* of us."

Maggie laughed. "Let me put this in a little vase and we can go." She grabbed one from under the sink and left the rose on the kitchen counter. "That one bloom will make the place smell wonderful when I get home. See you later, Lucy." She gave Tramp a good head scratch. "And you be a good boy while I'm gone."

They drove the short distance to Gino's, and as they entered the restaurant the owner looked up and smiled. "You came back! I have your table all ready!" He grabbed two menus and gestured grandly for them to follow. Maggie looked at Tim, who flashed his dimpled smile. "I called and made a reservation for our special table."

Once they were seated, Tim reached over and gently took her hands. "I can't tell you how many times I looked at the clock today. God, I've missed you."

Maggie smiled shyly. "Me, too. I haven't been able to stop smiling since last night. I think you might have something to do with that."

"That's funny, I've had the same grin on my face," Tim said as he caressed the backs of her hands. "I wonder if it has to do with the fact that I'm madly in love?" He flashed that dimpled smiled and Maggie squeezed his hands.

"Have I ever told you how much I love that dimple?" she said, gently reaching up to touch the side of his face. He covered her hand with his and brought it to his lips, gently kissing her hand as he gazed into her eyes.

She sat for a moment and relished the warm feeling inside before bringing them both back to reality. "How long did you stay at the Manor today?"

Tim picked up a menu and handed it to her as he opened the other. "Right up until lunch, actually. He got more animated as the morning went on. I think he'll be the most motivated patient that cardio rehab has ever seen."

"I was smiling all day thinking about the two of you and your mom. Did you get a chance to talk to her?"

Tim nodded. "I called her when I got back and filled her in. She sounded pretty excited about coming back to see him. I offered to go up and drive her down when the time comes; I think she'll be too nervous to be driving all the way herself. I'm hoping you'll be here to keep my grandad calm when the time comes."

"You know I will. So--what are you having tonight?"

Tim perused the menu for a minute and then closed it. "I think I'll try the chicken marsala tonight. I believe it was one you'd recommended that I haven't tried yet. How about you?"

"I had thought about eggplant parm, but since Lucy pointed out earlier that tomato sauce probably wouldn't look good on yellow if I spill, I think I'm going with the fettucine alfredo with some broccoli instead. Did you fill your grandad in on the details of your trip and the meeting?"

Tim paused to give the waiter their orders before he answered. "We talked about everything. I found out that you were right about the roses. Sharon had planted them for Mother's Day shortly before she got pregnant. She had come alone since my dad wasn't welcome in the house, and grandad said that it was the last day they all got along. Later that fall she came to tell them about being pregnant, and that was when he begged her to come home. He's been taking care of those roses ever since-- it was all he had left of her."

"I'm so glad that Liz has kept them alive and well through all this. She said she'll be happy to continue on even after he's home if he needs help."

"That's good to know. I wonder what my mom will think of them when she comes."

"Let's concentrate on getting your grandfather back home first."

As their bread and salads arrived, Tim held off eating. "So something else came up while we were talking today. I was telling him about putting my townhouse on the market."

"I imagine that confirmed for him that you weren't going to take off any time soon."

"Actually, he asked me to consider moving in with him when he gets home."

Maggie put her fork back down. "Wow. That's a pretty big gesture knowing him."

"I agree. He said there was no pressure. He didn't want me to feel obligated, but also talked about how much time we've missed out on. He also offered his old office to me if I wanted it – even if I chose not to move in."

They had hardly touched their salads when their meals arrived, but they slid them over on the table and told the waiter they planned on a relaxed dinner. Maggie twirled some pasta around her fork and took a bite before speaking. "Sorry, the cheese was calling me. That's a huge offer to consider. I hope you make the choice for you and not him."

Tim nodded as he swallowed his first bite and smiled. "Another win for Gino – this is delicious. I told him I'd think about it. Quite honestly, I was so excited at the idea of finally having a real home and family that I really can't imagine turning it down. I know he's set in his ways, but with two floors and an outside office, I think we could stay out of each other's way when we needed to, or if I needed some privacy." Maggie's face blushed as he continued. "Let's face it, I think he'll be way happier knowing that someone is around, just in case."

"I agree – and not only because of his health. I think being at the Manor helped him to see how lonely he's been. He's been a lot less of a curmudgeon the past couple of weeks, that's for sure."

"Well, he made me swear to think about it for a few days, so I will – but I'm leaning toward saying yes. For one thing, I might be able to hold on to the townhouse and still manage to pay Sean off. I could rent it out for part of the year and then have it for some weekend getaways for myself -- and maybe someone else." He winked at her as he took another bite.

"Sounds like you still have a lot of things to think about, Mr. Collins. That's a lot of decisions to make."

"Well, at least there's one area of my life that's stable again. I haven't been able to get you off my mind all day."

She reached over and squeezed his hand. "You weren't alone."

"Have I told you today just how much I love you?"

She nodded and smiled. "I'll never get tired of hearing it. I hope it's okay if I return that love from here on in."

His dimpled smile was the only answer her heart needed.

EPILOGUE

Two weeks later Maggie arrived at Carl's house right after breakfast. He had been home for a week, and was now able to do simple gardening and cleaning, but minimal stairs at this point. Jason was coming to work with him three times a week and a visiting nurse stopped in the other two days. He had tried to refuse the home health aide who helped with meals and laundry, but both Tim and Maggie had been adamant about him using all the resources he had to get better. In the end, he agreed, and his scowl wasn't nearly as big as normal.

Just before he'd moved back home, Tim and Maggie took a few days to give the house a good cleaning, and to pack up the items in the main upstairs bedroom so that Tim could move his things over from the bed & breakfast. He and Carl had agreed to a "trial" run for a month, but Maggie couldn't imagine either would want a different arrangement after seeing them together.

Today, however, was another huge milestone. Tim had driven up to Maine the night before and was now on his way back with his mother. Maggie knew that Carl would be nervous all day, so she agreed to spend the day and make him lunch, and then have dinner ready for when his daughter arrived.

During the day she made some muffins, a pot of soup to go with his tomato sandwich at lunch, and was now making a cheese sauce for her macaroni and cheese. She had picked up a rotisserie chicken to make meal time easier, and had a salad ready along with a package of peas to cook last minute.

"The house smells good, Maggie. Reminds me of when Ruthie would spend the day in the kitchen."

"Happy to be here, Carl. I just hope you're not too nervous to eat."

He paced back and forth in the kitchen. "What'll I say? It's been so long; I feel like I don't even know her anymore."

She came over and patted his on the shoulder. "Just be yourself. She's going to be just as nervous as you are. Now how about we walk out to the garden together and pick some of her roses to welcome her home?"

He nodded with a smile, and they headed out the back door where the flowery scents wafted across the lawn.

"That Liz has done one heck of a job out here," he said.

"She's enjoyed every bit of it, Carl. Said she'd be happy to keep it up if you want help."

"Might be nice to not have to be out here every single day. Maybe I'll talk to her."

They chose a couple of blooms from each variety and brought them in for the dining room table. Maggie took a long whiff as she put them gently in place. "That'll be the first thing she smells when she walks in."

They spent some time working on crossword puzzles until Maggie heard the car door outside. She looked over at the man who had become family and smiled. "You ready?"

He nodded as Maggie extended her hand to help him up.

"Ready as I'll ever be, I guess. Stay here next to me, and grab me if I start to faint."

Maggie grinned. "You'll be fine. And I'm so happy for you right now."

The door opened, and Tim walked in smiling. He left the door open behind him. "Grandad, I believe there's someone here that you've been waiting to see." He turned as they all watched the older woman appear in the doorway.

Maggie wasn't sure if her eyes filled with tears before the old man next to her, but he heard him whisper her name.

"Sharon."

The woman stepped inside, looking nervous as she gazed across the room with misty eyes. "Hello, Dad. I'm home."

COMING IN BOOK THREE...

Return to Caldwell and find out more about the renovations for the old hardware store, and enjoy Maggie & Tim's growing romance. Cassie, Teagan, and Brian celebrate their senior year with one more musical together, but will Cassie's recovery from anorexia be threatened in the process?

————————————————————————————————

If you or anyone you know is struggling with anorexia or other eating disorders, know that there is lots of support available. Please contact the National Eating Disorders for help in your recovery.

National Eating Disorders: (800)-931-2237
   https://www.nationaleatingdisorders.org/help-support/contact-helpline

SPECIAL THANKS TO…

Noel Sellon, for my beautiful cover design

Sarah Neville, for the gorgeous map design of Caldwell

Cheryl Conlan, Michele Connelly, Sarah Neville, and my fellow authors in our writers' cafe, for their valuable critiques and keen eyes during the revision process

For my fellow writers in the Greater Lehigh Valley Writers Group — your camaraderie and support will forever be appreciated

For Cheryl, Maria, Patti, Randi, and Jackie — your love and friendship keep me laughing and believing in myself

Most of all, for my family — Bob, Beth, and Rebecca. You continue to be my reason for living

ABOUT THE AUTHOR

Laurel Wenson's love of reading and writing began in her childhood home of Concord, Massachusetts, a place rich with the literary history of Thoreau, Emerson, Alcott, and Hawthorne. After 15 years of teaching English and theater in the homeschool community, she retired in 2016 to rekindle that love of writing. Her first book, *Sets on a Shoestring:How to Build Sets and Props on a Limited Budget,* was published in July of 2019.

Her love of small town life has served as an inspiration for the Caldwell series, which began with *A Promise to Keep*, published in July of 2020. The final two books of the series will be out in 2021.

Laurel lives in Bethlehem, PA with her husband, two daughters, and a frisky feline. She is a member of the Greater Lehigh Valley Writers Group and an avid participant in National Novel Writing Month.

Follow her on social media or visit her website at: laurelwenson.com

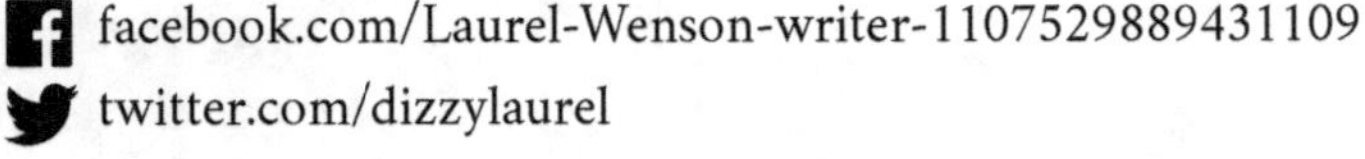

facebook.com/Laurel-Wenson-writer-1107529889431109
twitter.com/dizzylaurel

9 781735 047010